NINE NUNS

by Stephen Wheeler

Text © Stephen Wheeler

Cover photograph of Castle Acre Priory © Philip Moore

By the same author

THE SILENT AND THE DEAD

Brother Walter Mysteries:
UNHOLY INNOCENCE
ABBOT'S PASSION
WALTER'S GHOST
MONK'S CURSE
BLOOD MOON
DEVIL'S ACRE

Prologue
Spring 1219

You must forgive my untidy scrawl but my hand is still shaking. I have just received the most marvellous news. A fellow student from my college days who I haven't seen in four decades has arrived unexpectedly in Bury. I had no forewarning of his arrival, none at all. It has come as a complete shock. I can hardly believe it. As soon as I've finished writing this I shall be rushing off to greet him.

So what, you say, an old friend has come to visit? Nothing particularly noteworthy in that. Except that Lucatz and I were more than just friends, more like brothers. Not a blood brother, you understand, or even adopted like my brother Joseph, but a brother nonetheless and more brother than monk, although he is that too.

Oh dear, I'm babbling aren't I? But that is how the news has left me in a complete maelstrom. How can I explain? You know how with some people there is an instant rapport that is as inexplicable as it is real? You recognize that you have met a soul-mate who will remain so for the rest of your life. That is how it was with me and Lucatz. We were drawn to each other from the first day we met as undergraduates in the hallowed halls of the Montpellier school which is curious considering how different our lives had been up till then.

I am as English as Dover mud, born and nurtured in the ancient Saxon town of Ixworth in Suffolk. Lucatz by contrast is a native of Languedoc which is the most southerly region of France. The name "Langue-d'oc" literally means "folk of the oc tongue", "oc" being their word for "yes". It is quite different to the French spoken in Paris or even Normandy where the word for yes is "oui". As a student I was constantly exposed to the dialect. In fact until I returned to England it was the only form of French I knew.

But it is more than just the language that distinguishes *Languedociens* from the rest of the French nation. Indeed, they barely think of themselves as being French at all. I put that down to the geography of the place. Backed by the slopes of the great Massif Central it encourages them to look south towards the warm Mediterranean rather than north towards the cold German Sea. Lengadocians, as they prefer to call themselves, are a ferociously independent people which was one of the things that first attracted me to them, and Lucatz is typical. They do not take kindly to being dictated to by outsiders.

We met, as I say, when we were students. Like me, he attended the world-famous medical school at Montpellier which sits at the heart of the Languedoc region, and like me he later joined the Benedictine Order. Unlike me, however, he took his vow of stability, which keeps a man confined to his community, more seriously than I ever did. Indeed, I believe he never ventured outside his abbey from the day he entered it which makes it all the more astonishing that he is here now. I had truly given up hope of ever seeing my old friend here in Bury. But here he is and in a few minutes I will be able to greet him for the first time since we graduated forty years ago. Clap your hands all you nations! Shout to God with cries of joy!

PART ONE

Chapter One
A DECENT PROPOSAL

Forty years is an unconscionably long period of time. Would Lucatz have changed? Had I? Would we even recognize each other? These thoughts crossed my mind as I hurried out through the cellarer's gate. But I needn't have worried. Despite the passage of years, the greying of his beard and the thinning of his hair, there was no mistaking him waiting outside the guest hall. He was still the same Lucatz, as tall as a tree and as lean as Lent. My stomach lurched with delight to see him.

My joy, however, was somewhat tempered by the presence of the other two people who were with him. One was Prior Herbert who was looking mighty pleased with himself. This is always a worrying sign. It usually means someone has been thwarted in their ambitions – me more often than not. On this occasion, however, his smile seemed genuine enough without leaving me feeling I needed to look over my shoulder to see what disaster was following me. But one can never be sure with Herbert.

More worrying was the third member of the trio. This was Bruno, the husband of the daughter of my father's half-sister and therefore my cousin by marriage. What he was doing with the other two I couldn't imagine. He wasn't a monk or had any connection with the abbey as far as I knew other than me. The only time I ever saw him was when he wanted something – money usually. Like a fool I had always given in to him for the sake of his wife with the inevitable result that he kept coming back for more. Was that his intention this time? It wasn't a social visit of that I was certain. And why was Herbert here with them? Normally anyone below an abbot Herbert would leave to one of his underlings to deal with. Lucatz, as far as I knew, was just an ordinary monk of no special standing. More cause for concern perhaps?

'Dear Brother Walter,' beamed Herbert as I approached. 'Look who is here. Brother Lucatz come all the way from the abbey of Saint Gilles in France to see us. You two are old friends, I believe. Marvellous! It is good to greet old friends is it not?'

'Yes, isn't it?' I agreed warily.

'Walter,' smiled Lucatz. 'How are you my friend? You are looking well.'

'As are you,' I smiled back.

You'd have thought from that brief exchange that we'd last seen each other a week or so earlier instead of four decades. But personal relationships are frowned upon in a monastery. Our calling is for the benefit of the entire human race – in theory at least. And besides, I was determined not to display too much enthusiasm in front of the prior.

Herbert was watching us carefully and continued to smile like a benevolent uncle. 'And this person I believe you know also,' he said, indicating Bruno.

'Cousin Walter,' Bruno mumbled.

'Bruno,' I nodded back.

Oh yes, I knew that look well enough. If I had any doubts before I had none now. The shifty eye, the shuffling feet. He had something on his mind other than cousinly good wishes all right and it didn't take a genius to work out what especially given the circumstances.

I should perhaps just explain that this was the summer of 1219. In January I had received the distressing news that my mother had finally succumbed to the inevitability of her own mortality and joined my father in the churchyard of Saint Mary-the-Virgin, Ixworth. According to Oswald, her faithful retainer, she died of apoplexy one winter's morning while seated on her daily offices – a not uncommon event.

The loss of one's mother is supposed to be one of the most traumatic events a child can experience. For me with my mother I have to say it was not especially so and not just because as monks we are supposed to have cut our ties with our natural families. Lady Isabel de Ixworth was, after all, in her eighty-sixth year of life and her demise had been expected for some time. As mother and son we had never been particularly close as anyone who has read any of my earlier jottings in these pages will know, and even less so in her final years. Nonetheless when the moment finally arrived I did find that it affected me more than I had anticipated. This surprised me. I must have liked the old harridan better than I thought.

1219 was a distressing year for other reasons too. The country had just come through what was probably its most turbulent period since the Anarchy of Stephen and Matilda. The causes are too many to go into here but suffice to say King John had never been the most popular of monarchs. The loss of Normandy, his financial demands to recover it, and his increasingly tyrannical governance all combined to incite rebellion among his barons. On top of that there was the Interdict during which the religious life of the country had practically come to a halt. That was finally lifted in the summer of 1214, and with the sealing of the barons' Great Charter on the field of Runnymede the following year it had been hoped that all dissension might have come to an end. Alas the barons did not think so and continued to press for more liberties. The king refused and the result had been civil war.

That was four years ago. Since then King John has died and his eldest son crowned King Henry III of England. Of course a nine year old child cannot rule in his own name and the greatest baron of them all, earl William Marshal, was declared regent. His immediate action was to confirm the barons' Great Charter thus removing the chief cause of the rebellion. A fragile peace had at last broken out. Alas in May of this year the old earl died throwing the country back into political uncertainty once again.

So much for the woes of the nation. The abbey too had had its share of difficulties. For four years since the death of Abbot Samson we had had no abbot at all and King John had been in no hurry to fill the vacancy. Finally, however, in that same field of Runnymede immediately following the sealing of the Great Charter John confirmed Hugh Northwold as our new abbot. Although another Norfolk man, Hugh was of quite a different stamp to his predecessor who despite being a baron of the realm, judge delegate and member of the king's high council, was always a father to his flock and ever ready to listen to our concerns. Of Hugh, by contrast, we have seen very little since his inauguration preferring as he does to spend so much of his time in the heady atmosphere of high politics and leaving the running of the abbey to his prior - hence Herbert's presence today. Or so I assumed. After all, what other reason could he have for being here?

'Well now,' said Herbert still wearing his host's hat. 'I will leave you now to renew old acquaintances. I am sure you have lots to talk about. And when you are done, Walter, perhaps you could join me in my office.'

With one last brimming smile all round he spun on his heel and bounced merrily off leaving Lucatz, Bruno and me alone together.

In retrospect I suppose I should have picked up on that final comment of Herbert's. But I was so keen for him to leave that I let all else pass me by. Besides, there was still Bruno hovering about when really all I wanted to do was to greet my old friend properly and preferably in private. After forty years we had lots of catching up to do. But I supposed I'd better find out what Bruno wanted first.

'Well, cousin,' I said to him pointedly. 'It's very nice to see you again - unannounced as ever. To what do I owe the pleasure this time?'

Bruno looked from me to Lucatz and back again. 'It's a personal matter, cousin,' he mumbled. 'Do you think perhaps we might…?'

'Brother Lucatz and I are old friends,' I interrupted. 'Anything you wish to say to me can be said in front of him.'

It was mean of me to involve Lucatz in personal family matters in that way, I know. I was sure he wasn't in the least interested. I was hoping, in fact, that Bruno would be the one to take the hint and disappear for a while. Possibly for a very long while. But I was underestimating my cousin's tenacity.

'It's about cousin Isabel.'

'My mother? She's dead.'

'I know. That's what I've come to speak to you about.'

Hm, I was right then. It was about money. Sensing the delicacy of the matter, Lucatz now offered to be the one to withdraw.

'No no,' I said to him firmly. 'This won't take long. Bruno merely wishes to know what is going to happen to the family estate now that my mother is no longer in control. Isn't that right, cousin?'

Bruno scowled. 'Do we have to discuss this in public?'

'We don't have to discuss it at all.'

'We do,' he insisted. 'You are your mother's only child, Walter. And given your situation…'

And on it went, the usual argument. He was referring to the fact that I was a monk and that when a man enters the cloister he renounces all worldly possessions, including any future inheritances. However, my mother would have ignored all that and left me, as the sole product of her loins, heir to her not inconsiderable possessions in Ixworth and the surrounding countryside - roughly speaking, six hundred acres of prime Suffolk farmland, half the manor of Ixworth, the advowson of its church, two water mills, four fish-ponds, a dozen acres of woodland and lordship over the lives of nearly two hundred souls. I know this because before she died she'd shown me her will and had been goading me with its contents in the vain hope that I might give up the religious life and manage the estate instead. Not that she particularly valued my skills in that regard. It was more that she wished to keep intact all that she had built up during her long widowhood and I was her least worst means of achieving it.

Her next nearest living relative after me was my cousin Rowena, Bruno's long-suffering wife. If Rowena inherited the estate it would mean Bruno would have effective control. But Bruno was even less suited to the role than I was. He had already frittered away a small inheritance of his own through his own incompetence and would likely do the same with my mother's. That would have been enough to make the old Medusa turn in her grave and haunt us all for the rest of our lives. I was almost tempted to do it, too, but I knew it wasn't what she or father would have wanted.

Ideally she would have liked to leave it all to my adopted brother, Joseph, whose business acumen she did value. But Joseph was not a blood relative and, more pertinently, he was a Jew. In law, a Jew could not inherit the property of a Christian - or if they did it would go to the king when they died and that would have been the worst outcome of all as far as my mother was concerned. In any case such an arrangement would be open to all sorts of legal challenges that could hold up any satisfactory conclusion for years by which time all would be in ruins. No, like it or not, I was her best hope. But I was still a monk with that bothersome vow of poverty.

'As far as I'm concerned the matter is already sorted,' I told Bruno now. 'It shall go to the abbey.'

If I had punched Bruno full in the belly he could not have looked more winded. His face went deathly white.

'But you can't!'

'I don't see why not. It's the obvious solution. I have no need of it. Possessions are a cumbersome inconvenience to someone who has given his life to God. What better solution than it should go to where it can do some good?'

'I should have thought God was rich enough already.'

'Now now cousin, remember where you are.' I turned to Lucatz. 'What do you think, brother? As a fellow monk who has also abandoned the material world? Should I leave it to the abbey? I don't know if I want to be shackled with the tiresome business of possessions.'

'I'm really not the one to ask,' said Lucatz. 'I gave up all earthly possessions years ago.'

'Quite right,' I agreed. 'Anyway, I haven't finally decided yet. I'm still in mourning over the grievous loss of my belovèd mother so I won't be giving the matter much thought for some time. Come back then cousin and you will have my decision.'

'Grievous loss!' Bruno snorted. 'Everyone knows you couldn't stand your mother. Meanwhile fields remain un-tended, fences go un-repaired, rents don't get collected.'

'Oh, the Lady Isabel will have delegated all that to her officers years ago,' I dismissed. 'The place practically runs itself. I have every confidence the steward and his bailiff will continue to manage Lady Isabel's affairs without supervision from me.'

'And line their own purses in the process.'

I feigned shock at his words. 'Why Cousin Bruno. Are you questioning the honesty and integrity of my mother's devoted servants?'

He snorted again. But even he could see he wasn't going to get anywhere today. He was about to march off but not before he had one last blast:

'Rowena is next in line after you.'

'Is she? Yes, I suppose she is. But only when I'm dead. Don't get your hopes up. I have no intention of dying just yet.'

'We never know what may be waiting for us round the next corner, cousin.'

'Is that a threat, cousin?'

He pouted. 'I only want what is my due.'

'Your due is what I say it is.'

'I am as capable as the next man.'

'Bruno, the next man to you is a baboon.'

His face went purple. Stumped for a suitable reply he stomped off.

'I'm sorry you had to witness that, my friend,' I sighed watching him go. 'Not at all the welcome I would have wanted for you.'

'Family matters are always difficult. I'm sorry to hear about your mother. But weren't you a little harsh on your cousin.'

'Oh, don't worry about Bruno. It's all bluster with him. I'll give him something, but not until I'm certain he thinks I won't.'

'Possibly. But your mother has never died before.'

I suppose the stakes were a little higher than usual, and Bruno a little angrier. But I dismissed the thought that he might wish to harm me.

'Well now my friend, to more pleasant matters. We have much to talk about.'

I took Lucatz back to my laboratorium where for the next hour we reminisced over the past. We spoke a lot in the Lengadocian dialect. I was delighted at how much of it I could remember. The sound of its heavy guttural tones brought back memories I'd thought lost for ever. We talked about former teachers, their different idiosyncrasies, the beatings we got – there were plenty of those. I'd forgotten just what a couple of young tearaways we were in those days. I blame Lucatz entirely for that. He was always getting into trouble and dragging me with him. But we were boys then, free of our parents for the first time in our lives and eager to sample what delights the world had to offer before submitting the remainder of our days to the service to God. And it didn't stop us reliving the memories now:

'Do you remember that ale-house wife who took a fancy to you?'

'I don't recall any ale-house wife.'

'Yes you do,' I chided him. 'The pair of you disappeared for a couple of hours leaving me to pay for the ale. The inn-keeper was very suspicious. When you eventually came back you had your hose on back to front.'

He frowned. 'I don't remember any of that. Are you sure it was me?'

'You know perfectly well it was. You were always the more worldly of the two of us. I was the shy one. Not that I would have swapped places with you on that occasion. Dear Lord, the woman must have been forty if she was a day - and ugly. My God!'

'Her husband might have wished her uglier. Looks can be better than a chastity belt.'

'You see, you do remember!'

'I deny it all,' he put up his hands laughing.

'You can't fool me. This is Walter you're talking to.' We both laughed. 'God, it is good to see you my friend. You've hardly changed at all.'

'Neither have you.'

'Older, fatter,' I smiled patting my belly. 'But seriously, how are things in the south really? We have heard disturbing reports.'

I was referring as he knew to the struggle against the Cathar heresy that had been raging in Languedoc for more than a decade. A religious war of a particularly vicious kind the like of which hadn't been seen in Europe before, certainly not in my lifetime. A struggle for no less than the souls of men.

Catharism is a perverted version of Christianity that has infected the south of France particularly around the town of Toulouse whose count, Raymond, is thought to be a sympathizer. It has existed as a minority religion for as long as anyone can remember. I knew of it when I was a student there although it was rarely mentioned. Most of the time it was tolerated in the expectation that it would eventually burn itself out. So far that had not happened. Indeed it has continued to grow and spread to the point where it can no longer be ignored. At least, that was the opinion of the church fathers. Not that I took much notice. I had more pressing matters to worry about – my exams for one.

There is nothing new about such delusions. Since the beginning of the Christian era there have been religious disputations - some deluded theologian or other who thinks he has exclusive access to the mind of God. Since his inauguration Pope Innocent III had taken a particular interest in this one trying to dissuade the adherents from their error. He would have preferred to do this by argument but with little success. The Cathars remained stubbornly loyal to their beliefs. In recent years, therefore, Innocent resorted to more direct means calling on all true

Catholics to take up arms against the heretics. The response was more than he could have anticipated. Nothing like it, in fact, had been seen since Pope Urban a century earlier exhorted all Christendom to recover the Holy Land from the infidel. I'm sure that wasn't Innocent's original purpose but once he let the cat out of the bag he could no longer control events. He had unwittingly unleashed the most appalling suffering on the people of Languedoc including rape, murder and torture. It cannot help but have affected everyone living in the Occitan, even monks like Lucatz secluded in their abbey fastnesses.

'Things have not been easy for my countrymen,' he agreed sadly. 'But what about you? England too has had its troubles recently.'

'Nothing like yours, my friend. And ours was a political rather than doctrinal dispute, hopefully now at an end.'

'Ours too has subsided with the death of Pope Innocent and of my Lord Montfort, his chief lieutenant.'

'Let us pray it will continue to be so.'

The bell sounded for sext. So engrossed had we had been in our conversation that I hadn't noticed how late it was getting. I stood up.

'Will you join us in the church, brother, to sing the holy office?'

He grimaced. 'Would you mind very much if I didn't? It has been a long journey and I am very tired.'

'My dear fellow of course, you must be exhausted. How unthinking of me. Rest, recuperate. We can pray together later. Have you sorted out your accommodation yet? Would you like me to have a word with the guest-master? Brother Jocelin is a good friend of mine. I will ask him to make you comfortable in his best room.'

'Please, don't go to any special trouble on my behalf.'

'No trouble at all. How long will you be staying, by the way? I'm forgetting myself. You haven't even told me why you're here yet.'

'I'm on a sort of pilgrimage,' he hedged.

'Just at the abbey or further afield?'

'The abbey - and elsewhere. Perhaps "pilgrimage" isn't quite the word for it. More a sort of mission.'

'A mission to do what?'

'Your prior will tell you.'

'Can't you tell me?'

He grimaced. 'Better it comes from the prior. But it has to do with the new nunnery the abbey are proposing to establish. For the moment that is all I can tell you.'

'Intriguing. Very well. Herbert said he wanted to see me. I dare say he'll explain all when he does. But we will meet again later?'

'Indeed. I'm sure over the coming days we will be seeing much more of each other.'

Prophetic words indeed.

Chapter Two
OUR LADY OF IPSWICH

Over the years I had many laboratory assistants, some good some bad. For various reasons they never seemed to last very long. My latest was a novice called Nahum, a young man with more curiosity than was good for him and more cheek than a butcher's slab. As Lucatz went out, he came in. Seeing my excitement about my old friend's visit he was keen to know more about him:

'You say you were students together, master?'

'We were indeed, Nahum. Students and young lions ready to take on the world,' I growled.

'Take on the world, master, or just Montpellier?'

I looked at him. 'At the time, my young friend, Montpellier was the world to us. It was Europe's finest school of medicine - at least we liked to think so. They turned out some of the best physicians equipped with the very latest theories taught by some of the greatest medical minds in the world.'

He nodded. 'I see.'

'Do you? You look confused to me. What's troubling you, I wonder? Come along, speak up. Ask me whatever you wish.'

'Well master, if you both wanted to be doctors, how is it you both ended up in holy orders?'

'Quite simple. As well as medicine we also shared a common calling to serve God. You see? Even then we thought alike. It was probably Lucatz, in fact, who finally convinced me to take the tonsure - he was always keener on his church than I was. The arguments we used to have staying up late into the night, my God!' I chuckled shaking my head at the memory. 'So we made a pact. We both agreed that after graduating we would each join our respective abbeys as novitiates, Lucatz to the abbey of Saint Gilles – that's near Arles in the south of France in case you didn't know - and me here at Saint Edmund's. You could say our careers have been mirror images of each other's ever since.'

'And all this began forty years ago?'

'Indeed it did.'

'Gosh.'

I smiled benignly at my youthful assistant. 'You are impressed that we have remained friends despite never having seen each other in all that time?'

'No master. I'm amazed you can still remember.'

'How old are you Nahum?'

'Nineteen master.'

'Do you wish to be twenty?'

Lucatz was right about the abbey wishing to found a new daughter house for the care and honour of women. Chapter business had been taken up with little else over the past few months. I mentioned earlier that England had recently gone through a vicious civil war. It is often the case that at times of political unrest such as this the foundation of a new religious house is seen as a way of restoring peace and harmony in the land. To many, including a good few of my brother monks, the real cause of our troubles was not a bad king or recalcitrant barons but mankind's sinfulness. All the pain we had suffered from civil war and lawlessness was God's way of chastising us for deviating from the path of righteousness. Surely, it was argued, the best way to placate an angry God was through the work of the religious orders – monks and nuns. To this end the more who could be persuaded to fight the good fight the better. And as it happened there was a clutch of newly-invested nuns ready to devote their lives to the cause. All that was needed was to find somewhere to put them. But there was a problem.

As you can imagine, the founding of a new religious house is an expensive business and money, as ever, was in short supply especially in these difficult times. We had therefore to choose our site carefully – hence the months of wrangling in the chapterhouse. However, a consensus was eventually reached. The nunnery was to go to Ipswich some 25 miles south-east of Bury. There was already a shrine there to Our Lady of Ipswich at the little church of Saint Mary Elms just outside the west gate of the town and the new nunnery was to be attached to it. It seemed a pragmatic, not to say prudent, choice. But therein lay our difficulty for the port of Ipswich lies not within the Liberty of Bury but that of Ely whose bishops have never been great friends of the abbey. Abbot Samson had several rows with Bishop Eustace in particular which had soured the atmosphere between our two houses. Our new abbot, Hugh Northwold, has done much to repair the damage and, conveniently, Ely has no bishop at the moment thus placing us at a unique advantage. After some gentle arm-twisting the monks of Ely have at last agreed to allow us to found our nunnery in their town – at our expense, naturally.

But our problems didn't end there. Those of you who have read any of my earlier jottings will know that Saint Edmunds already had a house for women: the convent of Saint George and Saint Gregory located a dozen miles north of Bury in the town of Thetford. Splendid though the sisters of St George are and wonderful the work they do healing the sick and teaching the children, there are but very few of them - seven at last count including novices, hardly enough to do all the work required of them. Compare this with the nearly eighty monks we have here at the abbey. Also, having no income of their own Saint George's is reliant on supplies we send them from the abbey each month to maintain themselves – food, ale, clothing. So small and ill-endowed is Saint George's in fact that they simply don't have the resources to support themselves. Any new convent of similar size would be in the same perilous position.

Now, call me nit-picking but it seemed to me crazy to even contemplate going to all the trouble and expense of establishing a new nunnery when an existing one was already available and underutilized. Surely it would make more sense to send any new recruits to Saint George's first. If at a later date St George's became over-crowded - hardly likely given the numbers involved – that would be the time to consider branching out, or so I argued in chapter along with a good many of my brother monks. But we were overruled. It seemed the women in question - nine in all - insisted on having their own separate house. From this point they would not budge. A new separate house for them alone or none at all. Their prioress, one Dame Flora de Ros, in particular was adamant. I supposed she did not care to relinquish her position. There can, after all, be only one prioress per nunnery. In the end we had no option but to agree or lose the nuns entirely. A new house in Ipswich for the exclusive use of these nine nuns it was. But this was an internal matter for the monks of Bury alone. I couldn't imagine what it had to do with Lucatz.

Still, I supposed I was about to find out as I made my way to Prior Herbert's study later that day. Herbert's clerk, the estimable Jephthet, was also there, quill poised as ever ready to take notes. He was looking mighty chipper so I knew something serious was afoot and that I needed to be on my guard. The news when it came quite stunned me...

'You are saying the new nunnery in Ipswich is not now going ahead after all, Brother Prior?'

'It is, but not in Ipswich.'

'Then where?'

'Beside the abbey of Saint Gilles.'

I frowned. 'Saint Gilles? You mean Saint Gilles in the Occitan? Brother Lucatz's Saint Gilles? *That* Saint Gilles?'

'Is there another? It is why Brother Lucatz is here: to escort the nuns to their new home.' He gave a wry smile. 'You didn't really think he came all this way just to see you, did you?'

Beside me Jephthet sniggered as he dipped his quill into the ink and started to scratch away.

I flushed red. 'No no, of course not. But I thought all that had been settled. The nuns got their wish, didn't they? A new house for their exclusive use beside the church of Saint Mary Elms.'

'That was the original idea, yes,' Herbert agreed airily. 'However, this new proposal not only satisfies the requirements of the nuns but meets the objections of some of our brother monks – you among them as I seem to remember.'

Now I was beginning to see why Herbert had been looking so pleased with himself earlier.

'What precisely is being proposed?' I asked.

'It would appear the monks of Saint Gilles wish to increase their influence in their part of the world to the Glory of God and the comfort of His people. Now, they could do this in the normal way, of course, by attracting new recruits from the surrounding populous, but that would take time and there is some urgency in the matter. As you know, the Church is currently engaged in a titanic struggle with the Devil in that country. The cry has gone out from Rome for new blood and the Sisters of Our Lady of Ipswich have answered it.'

I nodded. 'Yes, Brother Lucatz and I were discussing this earlier. Some terrible atrocities have been perpetrated against the local people.'

'Atrocities committed on both sides, brother. You have to fight fire with fire. I am sure only the very minimum force necessary was used.'

'Minimum force? Like rape? Murder? Torture?'

'You shouldn't believe everything you hear,' Herbert said waving a dismissive hand. 'Be that as it may, since Pope Innocent's untimely death three years ago the impetus has gone out of the struggle somewhat. Matters have been allowed to drift. This new pope, Honorius, is too old, too lax, too...'

'Compassionate?'

'I was going to say "indulgent". It does no good to be easy with heretics. The Cathar delinquency persists despite the Church's best efforts to stamp it out. Ordinary folk are being coerced against their will.'

'My understanding is that it is highly popular among ordinary folk.'

'Who are easily led, brother. The commonality will follow their lord wherever he leads them. This count Raymond is a notorious heretic who does not scruple to have his perverted way.'

I didn't know much about the Cathari but the few of them I had met while a student seemed good, honest, hard-working people. However, it was not my job to argue their cause for them.

'What has any of this to do with us or our nunnery?'

Herbert held up a finger for patience. 'Some time ago the abbey of Saint Gilles contacted us explaining their need and asking for our help.'

'They wrote to us?'

'Not just us, they approached a dozen other abbeys and priories right across Europe asking for recruits. But I gather we were their preferred source. I dare say your connection with Brother Lucatz had something to do with that. It was a timely request, you might even say divinely inspired. As soon as I received it I saw immediately a way to kill two birds with one stone.'

'I hope you don't mean that literally, Brother Prior.'

He glowered at me. 'I meant fulfilling Saint Gilles's and our needs at one and the same time. And it will do no harm to show that we at Saint Edmund's are fully behind the pope's efforts.'

Oh yes, I'd forgotten that side of it. No doubt letters of commendation were winging their way to

Rome even now - with Prior Herbert's personal seal on them, naturally.

'What do the nuns say about it? Being uprooted from their native home to go to a foreign land hundreds of miles away cannot be easy.'

'The nuns will go where they are sent,' he sniffed. 'But as it happens their prioress offered no objection. In fact I'd go so far as to say she embraced my suggestion with enthusiasm. We have therefore agreed that the nuns will travel as a single group to the south of France under the auspices of Brother Lucatz.'

'I see.'

'I'm glad you do, because I want you to go with them.'

He paused to see my reaction which was one of total surprise. 'Me? Why me?'

Herbert gave a knowing smile. 'Don't you want to? I should have thought you'd jump at the chance. An opportunity to renew your acquaintance with your friend. But remember, this is an important mission for the church, not a jolly jaunt for old pals.'

'Well yes, I can see that. But I still don't see why I have to go, or anybody from the abbey for that matter.'

'Neither does Brother Lucatz. He'd rather do it alone. But I overruled him. A single monk with with a bevy of females travelling half way across Europe.' Herbert shook his head. 'It's asking for trouble. And we need a representative from the abbey. These are our nuns remember. We owe them a duty of care. You know Brother Lucatz, you know the country and you speak the language. You're the ideal candidate.'

So that's why he was with Lucatz when we met earlier. It was beginning to make sense now. He wanted to test the water, to gauge for himself just how friendly we were. But I wasn't going to disagree with him. The thought of a trip to the south of France in the company of my old friend and the chance to see the haunts of my youth was immensely appealing. Of course it wouldn't do to let Herbert know that. If he thought I liked the idea too much he might just change his mind and send someone else instead out of spite. I had to put up a token resistance.

'What about my medical practice?' I pouted. 'My patients. I can't just leave them. I could be away for months.'

'You have an assistant don't you?'

'Nahum is a boy of nineteen.' And an idiot to boot, I could have added.

'I have already spoken to Brother Nicholas in the infirmary. He is confident he can deputize for you. You've no cause for concern.'

He had it all worked out. Not that I was complaining. But why was he being so accommodating? Best not to look a gift horse in the mouth.

I sighed with resignation. 'How exactly are we to get to Saint Gilles?'

'I should have thought that was obvious. Mule to Ipswich to collect the nuns; ship to Bordeaux; then overland to the abbey where you will deposit your cargo hopefully intact.'

'You make them sound like chattel, brother prior.'

'On the contrary. These nine nuns are a delicate commodity who I wish – the abbey wishes – to deliver in good order to our brother monks at Saint Gilles.'

'Is this an order or a request?'

'A request. But you would do well to consider it.'

'I'll think about it.'

'You do that. But don't take too long. Brother Lucatz will be returning to France in three days' time. I want you packed and ready to leave by then.'

I got up to leave.

'Oh, by the way,' he added as though an afterthought. 'I was sorry to hear about your mother. You have my deepest sympathy. Lady Isabel and I did not always see eye to eye, but she was a grand lady who will be sadly missed,' he smiled.

Didn't see eye to eye? They loathed each other. I wasn't surprised he knew of her death but I was surprised he bothered to mention it. His next statement answered that question:

'No doubt you and your cousin will wish to sort out the lady's affairs before you leave.'

So that answered my other question of why Bruno had been with him earlier. Herbert wanted my inheritance to go to the abbey and he expected me to tell Bruno so. I should have guessed something of the sort. Call me cynical but that wouldn't be one of the reasons he was sending me on this trip, would it, partly as inducement, but also part-surety that should anything happen to me whilst abroad the abbey, as my beneficiary, would inherit? No, not even Herbert could be that opaque – could he?

'The matter of my mother's estate is in hand, Brother Prior,' I told him firmly.

'I'm sure it is and I'm sure you will come to the right decision.'

'I'll bear it in mind.'

'And this: Decisions are never final, brother. They can always be reversed. Think on that when you make your calculations.'

29

As I turned to leave Jephthet got up and held the door open for me with a broad smirk on his skull-like features. It was a pity he was facing me. I should have liked to kick him up the arse.

I caught up with Lucatz again as he was coming out of the guest dormitory.

'You're a dark horse.'

He frowned. 'A dark horse?'

'It's an English expression. It means someone who likes to keep things to himself.'

He shook his head. 'I fear I am never going to understand this strange tongue of yours. So tell me my friend, in what way am I a "dark horse"?'

'By not telling me why you are here.'

'Did your prior not explain?'

'He did, but I'd like to hear it from you.'

He frowned looking about him. 'It is too cold to stand around draughty corners discussing such matters. Can we go somewhere a little more sheltered?'

I led him into the cloister where many of my brother monks were already busy at their daily tasks of writing and copying. We found a quiet corner in the late spring sunshine and sat down on the wall bench.

'Your prior has already told you the reason for my visit – yes?'

I nodded. 'To escort the Sisters of Grace to the Occitan. A rather extreme measure, wouldn't you say? Have you no nuns of your own?'

'Yes of course, but it takes years to fully profess a nun. We need to increase numbers now.'

'Why the urgency?'

He sighed. 'We talked earlier of the Cathar heresy and the Church's struggle to convert them. In recent years the Cathars have grown disproportionately in number and threaten to overwhelm the Catholic majority.'

'Regrettable but hardly threatening, surely. Don't forget I lived among these people when I was a student at Montpellier. I made some good friends among them. They always seemed perfectly ordinary decent folk to me. Exceptionally so in fact.'

'They attack the sacraments of the Church.'

'Plenty of others do that.'

'They maintain that the bread of the Eucharist is nothing but that, bread. They deny transubstantiation. You cannot agree with that?'

'But they are still Christians. They believe in the revelations of the Gospels.'

'They reject the Trinity. How can a man call himself a Christian if he rejects the fundamental tenets of the church?'

'Our tenets maybe. But they have tenets of their own.'

'Which do not coincide with orthodoxy.'

'None of which justifies murder and rape.' I shook my head. 'I'm surprised at you, Lucatz. I took you to be more understanding than this. Live and let live used to be your motto. What's happened to you?'

'You have not lived in the Occitan for forty years, my friend. You do not know what has been going on there.'

'Well it looks as though now I might.'

'Yes, Prior Herbert told me he wishes you to accompany me back to Saint Gilles.'

'Which you objected to. Why? Because you knew I would not agree with you?'

'Because I did not wish to fall out with you – and it appears I was right to be concerned. We seem to be doing so already. I would prefer that we reflected on the past and parted as friends.'

'Well it looks as though we are going to get plenty of opportunity to reflect on a lot of things over the coming weeks. Our friendship included.'

Chapter Three
JOSEPH AND HIS HAT OF MANY COLOURS

So ended Lucatz's first day with us. Not the overwhelming success I had hoped it would be. I don't know what I was expecting – that he would be the same as I remembered all those years before? I suppose that was unrealistic after four decades, but I was surprised at just how hardened he seemed to have become. I was particularly disappointed in his attitude towards the Cathari, so different from how he was when we were students together. I suppose it gave the truth to the old adage that when young we are narrow-waisted and broad-minded while as we get older the reverse is true. But I was determined that it wasn't going to affect our relationship. It would be a tragedy if we were to fall out after forty years. However it did make me slightly nervous about what I planned to do next.

We had just a couple of days left in Bury and I wanted to take him to see my brother Joseph. I was very keen that these two people whom I loved more than any other should meet and this might be their one and only opportunity to do so. The only problem was that Joseph was a Jew and given Lucatz's attitude toward the Cathari I wondered what his reaction would be. Not that Joseph wore his

Jewishness upon his sleeve. On the contrary, I often chastised him for not being Jewish enough. On balance I thought it worth taking the risk. Lucatz would at least see what a truly liberated mind was like, one unencumbered by the prejudices of others but which thinks for itself, even if on occasion the conclusions it comes to are misguided, misinformed and downright wrong.

I am immensely proud of the man I call my brother even though he is nothing of the kind. Those who have read my earlier jottings in these pages will know his story already but I will repeat it again briefly. Though not related in any way by blood Joseph and I call ourselves brothers for the simple reason that we grew up together. Both our fathers were medics during one of the religious wars in the Holy Land though on opposite sides of the conflict. They each admired the other's work and became firm friends despite the war. Once the fighting was over Joseph's parents came to live in my father's house in Ixworth to work and study with him and that was where Joseph and I were born.

As children we were inseparable even though our later lives diverged, I to my studies in Montpellier and him to start an apothecary business in Bury. Having an Arabic father and Jewish mother he was never going to be allowed to practice medicine which had been his fondest hope, but pothecking was the next best thing. And he made a great success of it. But then Joseph would make a success of anything he undertook.

'He's a charming fellow,' I told Lucatz as we climbed the hill to Heathenmans Street where Joseph's shop was located. 'Exceptionally bright and a superb apothecary, probably the best in England which is why I use him of course.'

'Not because he's your brother?'

'No no, good lord no. Well yes, that too. But he is the best in the business. People come from all over the country to his shop – from all over Europe I shouldn't wonder. Nobody knows the apothecary business better than he does. Well now, here we are,' I said pausing outside the entrance. 'Ah, I see his wand is not lying across the entrance - his *Caduceus* as he likes to call it. That's a good sign. It means he's in. Caduceus is the rod of Hermes, by the way – that's the Greek god of medicine.'

'Asclepius,' said Lucatz.

'Beg pardon?'

'Asclepius was the Greek god of medicine. It's his rod that symbolizes our profession. I grant you it's often confused with Caduceus. Hermes was the god of thieves and travellers. Nothing to do with medicine.'

'Was he really?' I said vaguely. 'Fancy that.'

Lucatz smiled. 'You say Joseph is a Jew.'

'Jewish mother. Arabic father. Though you'd never know from the look of him.'

'Does he practise his faith?'

'No, not at all. Actually,' I said lowering my voice, 'it is something of a bone of contention between us. If there's one thing worse than bad religion it's having no religion at all, I always think. I'm afraid Joseph is one of those. Claims he doesn't believe in anything. Can you credit that? Ridiculous idea! Everyone has to believe in something,' I laughed nervously.

'Only the reason I ask is that I couldn't help noticing the mezuzah in the doorway.'

'Hm? The what, sorry?'

I looked to where he was pointing. Sure enough there was the little decorative device attached to the door-frame about shoulder-height. I'd seen these miniature caskets before on the door-frames of Jewish houses and knew they contained scrolls with religious writings on them and were always touched reverentially by the home-owners whenever they went in through the door. But never on Joseph's door.

'Funny,' I smiled. 'I never noticed that before. Er, shall we go in?'

Joseph's shop like most others in Bury is divided into two parts with the business end at the front nearest the street and the living quarters at the back. The front half is where he mixes his potions and serves customers. It is filled with every kind of exotic spice and herb all in multi-coloured bottles and jars with various weighing apparatuses and grinding implements. The heady aromas instantly conjure images of the Kasbah and the mysterious East, which is the point of the exercise of course. It's also where I would usually find Onethumb, Joseph's assistant and an old friend of mine. Today however there were no customers and no Onethumb. The shop was empty.

'God bless all in this house,' I intoned in a loud voice as I entered, partly in greeting, partly to announce our presence. Immediately the curtains parted and Joseph emerged with his arms held out before him in greeting.

'Ah-haha, my dear brother,' he beamed striding towards us. 'How good it is to see you,' whereupon he took me by the shoulders and hugged me warmly to his breast - rather too warmly actually. He's not usually this overtly affectionate, at least in public.

And that wasn't my only surprise. I hadn't been to Joseph's shop for a while and frankly I was shocked to see him now. I know pothecking is something of a mystical art and Joseph's usual garb of a cloak covered in stars and moons is designed to make the point. But with Joseph it's just flimflamery nonsense to enhance his image as a mystic and magician - good for business, as he never ceases to remind me. Today, however, he was dressed not in his cloak but in a flowing robe, one I knew to be called a *jubba* that only Jews wear. Also instead of his multi-coloured conical *pilos* he had on his head a plain black *kippah*, the skullcap worn by Jewish men. With that, his gown and his long-flowing beard he resembled nothing so much as an Old Testament prophet. This wasn't the Joseph I was used to seeing at all.

'Er yes – good to see you too, my brother,' I said slightly confused.

'And who is this you have you brought to my humble abode?' he beamed at Lucatz. 'I wasn't expecting guests.'

Now I knew he was lying. Joseph is never surprised by visitors. He prides himself on being one step ahead at all times. But for now I went along with the charade introducing Lucatz to him, explaining who he was and where he was from – all of which I was sure he already knew. It was only when I'd finished that the second figure emerged through the curtains.

'Bruno,' I said with surprise. 'Well, we meet again. Not following me by any chance are you?'

'Pure coincidence, cousin. I didn't know you were going to be here. I came to visit cousin Joseph. He is my relative too, you know?'

That too annoyed me. 'You, Bruno, are my cousin by marriage and Joseph is my brother by adoption. That makes you two about as related as… as...' I fumbled for an appropriate simile. 'Pigeons and peacocks.'

At that Bruno snorted.

'You know what I mean,' I frowned.

'Whatever we are, we are all one family before God, are we not?' smiled Joseph affably. 'But come, welcome to my house one and all! Let us go in together.'

He ushered us through the curtains into the back room where I was to have yet another shock. Prominently placed in the middle of the room on an enormous pedestal was a copy of the Jewish Bible. The display was so big there was hardly any room for anyone to stand. It stood open no doubt at some uplifting passage. I wouldn't know where since I don't read Hebrew script, but from its position I guessed we were somewhere among the Psalms. How about Psalm number 10? I thought: "His mouth is full of lies and threats; trouble and evil are under his tongue." I resisted the temptation to quote it.

'Well now, can I offer you some refreshment?'

He clapped his hands and a servant entered carrying a tray of delicacies and offered them round.

'Ooh, yummy!' exclaimed Bruno and immediately began grabbing handfuls of canapés balancing one on top of another. 'I missed breakfast,' he explained as I glowered at him.

The servant then offered the tray to Lucatz who politely declined. I too declined while Bruno continued stuffing his face practically demolishing the display single-handed.

'You don't know what you're missing with this,' he said, still with his mouth full.

This wasn't going at all well. I had envisaged a polite *mélange* between the three of us with a bit of light social chit-chat sprinkled with amusing anecdotes. Instead, Joseph's over-effusiveness and Bruno's boorish manners had reduced it to an ale-house revelry.

'Where's Onethumb?' I asked eyeing the servant suspiciously.

'In the west country buying spices from the Bristol merchants,' said Joseph, adding for Lucatz's sake: 'I find they are the best.'

'Well when he returns, can you ask him to deliver my usual order for the next three months.'

'Are you going somewhere?'

'Don't you know? Lucatz and I are leaving for the Occitan the day after tomorrow.'

'How delightful,' Joseph beamed. 'The south of France at this time of the year is wonderful. How are you getting there? Boat or horseback?'

'What would you recommend?'

'Oh, boat,' he nodded firmly. 'Definitely. A month at sea with nothing to do but eat and dream. I do envy you both.'

'I doubt it,' I said. 'Wizards don't do well crossing water.'

'That's running water,' he smiled. 'Not oceans.'

I glowered at him in silence.

'You, erm, source most of your spices in England?' Lucatz asked politely.

'It gets shipped here from the orient,' said Joseph. 'Nobody's quite sure from where. India possibly, or further afield.'

'Did I smell nutmeg when I came in?'

'How clever - you did indeed.'

'Also coriander? Turmeric? Cloves?'

'All of those – and more,' said Joseph, impressed.

'Better than the smell of hypocrisy,' I growled.

'We have the port of Marseilles,' Lucatz explained. 'Many of these spices come along the middle passage. A dangerous and tortuous journey.'

'The spice trail,' smiled Joseph, then laughed together pleasantly.

There was a lot more of this sort of pointless nonsense until it was time to leave. I didn't contribute much. I was too annoyed. This wasn't at all how I had planned our visit to be.

Once outside and a little way down the road away from the shop, I stopped and slapped my forehead.

'I've just remembered something. Lucatz, would you mind if I just pop back and have a quick word with Joseph? An order I'd forgotten. I shan't be a moment. You and Bruno carry on. I'll catch you up.'

Back in the shop the servant was clearing up the detritus of food.

I dragged Joseph to one side. 'All right. What's going on?'

'Going on, my brother?' he smiled.

'Don't play the innocent with me, Joseph. You know perfectly well what I mean, acting as though you didn't know who Lucatz was. Bruno would have told you that much at least. And what was all that other nonsense - the food, the clothes, dressing up like some latter-day Zephania?'

'Tsfanya.'

'What?'

'You Christians call him Zephania. We Jews call him Tsfanya, not to be confused with that other Zephania who was put to death by the king of Babylon "at Riblah in the land of Hamath",' he quoted.

'Since when were you ever interested in Jewish prophets? And why is the Old Testament open in the middle of the room?'

'You mean the Tanakh. Christians call it the Old Testament to differentiate it from the New Testament. To us it is the only Testament. The Bible – the *real* Bible.'

'I know what it's called, I'm asking why you've put it on such prominent display. You never have before.'

He shrugged. 'I'm merely celebrating my heritage.'

I snorted. 'Your heritage! You change your heritage like a snake changes its skin.'

'That's very good,' he smiled. 'I'll have to remember that.'

'And in any case,' I went on undeterred, 'you're only half Jewish. Your father was a Muslim.'

'Ah, but my mother was a Jewess and in Jewish law it is through our mothers that we Jews are defined. I keep being told I'm Jewish so I may as well behave like it. And why shouldn't I? I'm proud of my heritage.'

'I'm sure you are. I just question why you're doing it now - and so conspicuously.'

'Old age, Walter my friend,' he sighed. 'I am no longer a young man. There comes a time in life when one sees the end rapidly approaching and one feels one must return to one's roots.'

'You're three years older than me.'

'Precisely.'

'I don't believe a word of this. I know you, Joseph. You're up to something.'

He put on a look of hurt innocence which only convinced me all the more that I was right. He was plotting something. But whatever it was I knew better than to try to wheedle it out of him if he didn't want to tell me.

'All right then tell me this. What was Bruno doing here? You hardly know him.'

'Bruno came to commiserate over the loss of your dear mother.'

I snorted. 'Over the loss of her estate more like. He wants you to use your influence to get me to transfer the rights to him.'

'Do I have such influence?'

'After today, no.' I started to leave.

'Erm…?' he said as I was about to go out the door. 'Pigeons and peacocks?'

I looked shamefaced. 'I was angry. It was the best I could come up with at the time. Anyway, it was appropriate. The two faces of Joseph - one dull and commonplace and the other flamboyant and preposterous.'

He smiled and nodded. 'Then pigeons and peacocks it is.'

'I hope your brother wasn't offended,' said Lucatz once I'd caught up with him again.

'*Him* offended? How was he offended?'

'By my refusing his offer of food. Only I am still a little queasy from the boat trip.' He patted his stomach.

'No,' I frowned distractedly. 'He won't have been offended by that. I didn't have any either.'

'I did,' said Bruno.

'So I noticed.'

'It was delicious. All that chicken and lamb and beef. The liver and bean-curd pasty was particularly tasty.'

'Never one to refuse a free meal, eh Bruno?'

'What do you mean by that?'

'You know perfectly well what I mean.'

He pouted. 'You're so suspicious, Walter. I told you, I didn't know you were visiting cousin Joseph today.'

Maybe not. But Joseph certainly did.

Chapter Four
TO IPSWICH

For the rest of that day and most of the next I didn't see much of Lucatz. He was in conference with the prior making final arrangements for the transfer of the nuns from Saint Mary's to Saint Gilles and I was busy organising my own affairs. It was probably for the best we didn't meet. I wouldn't have been very good company. Our visit to Joseph had put me in a bad mood. I had so much wanted it to go well and it had been an utter disaster. In fact nothing about Lucatz's visit so far had gone well. I could only hope that the journey south would prove more gratifying.

The morning of our departure arrived all too quickly. I admit I was nervous about going away for so long and even more nervous about leaving my assistant, Nahum, in sole charge of my laboratorium. He was new to my department, young and like all youth over-confident and far too enthusiastic. And clumsy. But I don't think my fears showed.

'Make sure your stocks don't get too low. I've re-ordered everything in triplicate so you shouldn't run out. If you do, have a word with Onethumb. He'll be able to get you what you want. You know how to get in touch with him?'

'Yes master.'

'He's at my brother Joseph's apothecary shop in Heathenmans Street. You know where that is?'

'Yes master.'

'It's at the top of Cooks Row, second turning on the left. Now, what else?' I frowned tapping a nervous finger on my chin. 'Ah yes, I've left a list of all outstanding patients and their medications. Look to their needs first but resist any attempt by them to increase their dosage – they will, you know.'

'I do, master.'

'Don't whatever you do agree to take on any new patients. And no surgery. Definitely no surgery. I don't want to be sued for mutilation. Their boils can wait till I return. Speak to Master Nicholas in the infirmary if you get stuck. He'll be able to advise. And most important of all, make sure you put out any fires before you leave at night. It's taken me years to build my laboratorium I don't want it burning down in a month. Best thing to do is listen for the curfew bell. Take that as your signal to douse any naked flames.'

'I will master, and I'll swamp the room with river water just to make sure.'

'Good – you'll do what?'

He smiled. 'Master, I'm quite capable of running things on my own.'

'Of course you are, my boy, of course you are, I never doubted it for a moment,' I said patting him lightly on the shoulder. 'Forgive me, it's been a few years since I left the confines of the abbey for any length of time.'

'You mean, since you handed over to a child with a memory like a sieve and the competence of a two-year-old.'

'I didn't say that. Did I say that?'

'No master, not in so many words.'

My bag was packed, I was ready to leave. I was sure I had everything. I could be away for anything up to a month so I thought I'd better take a change of underwear just in case. Also a spare robe made of a lighter wool – I know how hot it can get in the Occitan at this time of year. Outside I could hear the sound of mules being brought round.

'Well I'd best be off,' I said to Nahum.

'Don't let me keep you, master.'

I took one last look round. There was so much more I wanted to tell him but there simply wasn't time.

'I think I've covered everything. If anybody wants me I'll be in Ipswich for the next few days. After that the high seas – into God's good hands,' I chuckled nervously.

'I'll see that he is kept informed of your progress.'

I looked at him warily. I'm never quite sure when Nahum's being serious. Lucatz was already mounted on his mule and waiting while I strapped my bag to the back of the baggage mule before climbing up onto my own. The prior and Jephthet were there to see us off. Herbert made the sign of the Cross and gave us a perfunctory blessing. We didn't move.

'Well? What are you waiting for?'

'Our escort.'

'Escort? You won't be getting an escort.'

'But Brother Prior, you surely don't expect us to ride twenty-five miles in these trying times defenceless? The roads are infested with cut-throats and robbers.'

It was a genuine concern. Since the civil war there had been a massive breakdown of law and order and not just because there was no-one around to catch the offenders. In order to swell the ranks of his armies King John had handed out pardons to all who were willing to fight for him. In the process he emptied the prisons of felons and murderers none of whom were returned once the fighting ended. They were now out of the army but still free and roaming the countryside in gangs attacking unwary travellers at will. Everyone knew the identities of the culprits but there was little chance of their being caught. No-one of any age, sex or condition was safe. Anyone contemplating braving the king's highway was well-advised to travel in groups and preferably with two or three armed guards.

But Herbert was having none of it. He was shaking his head dismissively. 'Nobody is going to take any notice of a couple of monks. And you do God's work, remember. You will have his divine protection.'

'I'm greatly reassured by your words, Brother Prior.'

'So you should be.'

'Do not worry my friend,' said Lucatz. 'We will travel only in daylight. We are both strong and fit and able to defend ourselves. All will be well.'

'I'll send you a report on our progress,' I said to Herbert. 'Assuming we are still alive to do so.'

'Do that,' he said and then came a little closer and held my mule's head. 'Did you, erm, manage to sort out that business with your cousin?'

'That business, Brother Prior?'

'Don't be coy, Walter. You know exactly what I'm talking about. Your mother's estate. I wouldn't want you to leave with matters outstanding.'

'In case of mishaps along the way, you mean?'

'I told you, there will be no mishaps. But just to be on the safe side…'

'It is in the hands of my lawyers,' I hedged. 'But I don't think you need worry about it.'

Herbert gave a hesitant smile. 'Good. Well, God speed. And give my regards to Dame Flora when you see her. It has been a delight, Brother Lucatz.'

So saying, he nodded to the stable boy who smacked our mules' rumps and ready or no, we were off.

'Dame Flora,' I said to Lucatz once we were clear of the abbey gate. 'Isn't that the name of the prioress in charge of these nuns?'

He nodded. 'It is.'

'What do we know of her?'

'I confess I have never met the lady but we have corresponded. In many ways she has been the driving force behind this whole enterprise.'

'So it wasn't your abbot who originated the request for recruits as Prior Herbert suggested?'

'Possibly. I can't remember the exact sequence of events. In any case the matter was dealt with quickly.'

'I'm surprised Herbert accepted so readily. He usually doesn't like to take decisions. Makes it difficult to blame someone else when they go wrong.'

Lucatz smiled. 'Dame Flora can be very persuasive. She believes that she is divinely inspired to establish a new house for women. Her efforts to achieve it have been tireless. Without her I doubt it would have happened. She seems to have overcome all obstacles and won over all doubters.'

'Impressive. What about the other eight nuns?'

'All were recruited by Dame Flora. Most are very young.'

'And yet they are fully professed?'

'The pope permitted a special dispensation of the normal three year novitiate in view of their mission. He is as keen as any to bolster the presence of the Church in the Occitan. For this reason we needed to sure. Each nun was required to state in writing that she was doing this willingly and that her family agreed. We did not wish coercion. I also wanted to be convinced that they knew what they were doing.'

'And are you convinced?'

'I wouldn't be here were I not.'

We were soon out of the town and headed south on the Stowmarket Road. It was a dry day. There had been no rain for several weeks so the ground was hard and good going so it shouldn't take more than a few hours to cover the twenty-five miles. But shortly after we left the precincts of the town I became aware of some movement in the bushes behind us. I was still worried about robber gangs. I'd had experience of such gangs before on the open road and knew what they were capable of. And unlike Prior Herbert, I didn't think our our tonsures would protect us.

'Don't turn round,' I said quietly to Lucatz, 'but I think we're being followed.'

Lucatz continued to look straight ahead. 'Yes I know. He's been there for some time.'

'Are we to be murdered, do you think? Should we make a run for it?'

'On these mules?'

'What should we do then?'

'You see that copse up ahead? I will dismount as though answering a call of nature. You wait on the road. Do nothing to alert him. I will double back and surprise him from behind.'

'Are you sure? These men are wise to such deceptions.'

'Have you a better suggestion?'

When we got to the little group of trees we halted. Lucatz dismounted and casually wandered off into the bushes while I waited with the mules. A minute later there was a scuffle behind, a yelp and a figure fell out of the bushes with Lucatz behind pushing him. Whoever it was wore a riding-cloak and wide-rimmed hat so that at first I couldn't see his face. But then Lucatz snatched his hat away.

'Bruno!' I exclaimed part in anger and part in relief. 'God in Heaven, am I never to be free of you?'

'Aow!' he scowled at Lucatz rubbing his arm. 'You needn't be so rough.'

'You needn't be so deceitful,' said Lucatz throwing his hat after him.

'Bruno, why are you here?' I asked him.

'You know why.'

'I've already told you, I can't help you. Go home to your wife and children. They need you.' As a rat needs fleas, I could have added.

'I can't go home. I'll be murdered if I go home.'

'Nonsense! Who'd want to murder you? Apart from me, that is.'

He grimaced. 'Creditors.'

'What are you talking about now?'

'That's what I've been trying to tell you. I bought some land.'

'You did what?'

'Thirty acres. And twenty head of cattle.'

My jaw dropped open. 'On what surety? No, don't tell me. My mother's inheritance.'

Of course it had to be. He didn't have money to buy a sack of grain let alone thirty acres of farmland. No wonder he kept pursuing me so assiduously.

He frowned. 'You don't know what it's like. A new baby. Another mouth to feed. It's all right for you. You have all your needs taken care of by the abbey.'

I looked with incredulity at Lucatz who was standing quietly holding his mule's head and saying nothing.

'I'm sorry Bruno, but this time you're on your own. Brother Lucatz and I are on important business for the abbey and I don't have time for this. Go home. Face your creditors.'

'They'll kill me.'

'They won't. Not if they want their money.'

'They'll chop my fingers off. Or worse.'

'Well that certainly won't get them their money back. Delay them. Tell them I'll deal with them when I return.'

'By then I might be dead.'

'Don't worry. I won't let Rowena suffer.'

He pouted. 'Can't I come with you?'

'After all I've just said? What do I have to do to get the message into that thick skull of yours? Get back on your mule and go home!' I looked around. 'Where is your mule?'

'I don't have one. I sold it.'

'Bruno you - !'

'I had to eat.'

I shook my head in disbelief. 'Bruno, you are a complete wastrel. Why cousin Rowena ever married you I'll never know.'

51

But of course I did know. The usual reason. The irony is that first child was still-born so she needn't have married Bruno after all. But by then it was too late. We had all been putting up with his idle fecklessness ever since.

'You go back and sort your cousin's business,' said Lucatz. 'I will continue on alone.'

'You can't go on alone,' I frowned. 'Besides, if I go back the prior will simply order me out again.' I turned back to Bruno. 'No, I'm sorry but there is no help for it. You dug yourself into this hole, you must find your own way out.'

With that I turned my mule's head resolutely and started to trot away leaving Bruno to stare after me. A few moments later Lucatz caught me up. And thus we continued our journey alone.

At Stowmarket we stopped for lunch. A pie-seller in the market sold me a meat and onion pasty and Lucatz a cup of broth and a hunk of bread. We squatted by the roadside to eat. The town was busy, at least as busy as Bury with people coming and going doing what business I could only imagine. We sat watching them for a few minutes in silence.

'He's still there,' said Lucatz finally nodding to where Bruno had squatted twenty yards behind us. He'd followed us at that distance on foot all the way never coming any closer but never out of view.

'He's free to do as he likes,' I said and carried on eating my pie.

Eventually I could stand it no longer. I got up and went over to him.

'Have you eaten?'

'Not since this morning.'

I handed him half my pie which he gorged as though he'd starved for a month.

'Bruno, do you know what we're about?'

'You go to Ipswich,' he said wiping his mouth on the back of his hand.

'Yes, but do you know what we do when we get there?'

'Something to do with nuns.'

I looked despairingly at Lucatz.

'We find a barque to carry us to Bordeaux. You know where that is?'

He shrugged.

'It's in France. *France*, Bruno. Have you got it yet? We can't take you with us. You will be left alone in Ipswich. Is that what you want?'

'I'll take my chances.'

The story of his life. Whatever my feelings about my cousin's husband he was still family and I couldn't just leave him. Besides, he'd probably continue to follow us whatever I said.

'Here,' I said handing him the reins of our baggage mule. 'I suppose one more silly ass won't make any difference.'

Chapter Five
GIPESWIC

Ipswich, or *Gippes-market* as our Saxon forefathers would have known it, is not a town with which I'm very familiar. It lies beyond the boundary of our Liberty of Bury so there is little reason for anyone from the abbey to ever go there. The only religious foundations of any note are the two priories of Holy Trinity and Saints Peter and Paul and both are Augustinian. The new nunnery was to have been the Benedictines' first major presence there. Now even that tenuous connection was about to be severed.

Having said all that the town is still important to us. As Bury's nearest major port it is through here that much of our cloth trade passes on its way to and from the continent. Ipswich is also famous for its pottery, a plentiful supply of which we have at the abbey. As such Ipswich is quite unlike Bury with sounds and smells unfamiliar to me. Even at a distance it was possible to see the tall masts of the sailing vessels riding at anchor in the river estuary, to hear the strange sounds of a busy dockyard and to smell the sea beyond. I have to admit I was quite excited by the prospect of doing a little exploring before we departed. However, that would have to wait. For the present we had more pressing matters to attend to.

The shrine of Our Lady of Ipswich stands just outside the west gate of the town, conveniently for us as this was the direction from which we approached. Nearby is the church of Saint Mary Elms which was where we were due to meet up with the Sisters of Grace. We reached the church late in the after-noon. Apart from our momentary fright with Bruno there were no further incidents on the road so maybe Prior Herbert was right and we were under God's special protection after all. Bruno, however, was still under ours though not for much longer if I could help it. I was determined once we arrived at our destination to see the back of him once and for all.

'I'm afraid this really is where we will have to part company,' I told him as we stopped outside the church gate. 'I'm sorry you've had a wasted journey, but you were warned.'

'Never mind cousin,' he said sliding down from the baggage mule. 'I've enjoyed the trip.'

He seemed to have perked up a bit from his earlier sourness, I was pleased to see. I would hate to have parted on bad terms.

'What will you do?' I asked him. 'Go back to Bury?'

'No, I think I might just wander down to the docks for a bit, see what I can find.'

I was afraid of that. 'Well, try not to get into trouble. Ports are rough places where a man can lose more than just his purse. Remember, I won't be around to help you this time.'

'Don't worry about me, cousin,' he grinned. 'I can take care of myself.'

'I was thinking more of your wife and child. They are relying on your safe return.'

'They'd be relying a whole lot less if I returned with money in my purse.'

'Now don't start all that again. You know my answer. I'm sorry about your problems with your creditors but you'll have to sort them out yourself.'

'And I will cousin, never fear,' he said cheerfully. 'I have good feelings about this place. I think a man could do well here.'

I could only pray he was right. 'Here.' I dipped into my purse and gave him a few pennies. 'It's the best I can do. Try to use it wisely.'

With that he skipped off in the direction of the town. I watched him go with an anxious feeling in my belly. For all that he was a fool and a wastrel he was still my cousin's husband and I would not wish him harm. I supposed the least worst thing that could happen to him would be to lose what little money he had to some quayside trickster and have to beg his way back to his home village.

By now Lucatz had finished hobbling the mules and came over. 'Will he be all right do you think?'

'So long as he keeps his head. Bruno's a bit of a phoenix. When all around is fire and destruction and he somehow manages to emerge unscathed.'

I only hoped this time he would do so again.

Lucatz nodded towards the church. 'We'd better go in and meet our new charges.'

I was first through the door and so first to greet whoever was there. As soon as I did so a middle-aged nun came bustling over with an anxious look on her face:

'Brother Lucatz?'

'Er, no,' I said pulling back a little. 'This is Brother Lucatz.' I indicated the man behind me.

'Oh thank God!' She instantly fell to her knees before him and taking hold of the hem of his robe, kissed it repeatedly. 'We were so worried. We were beginning to think you would never arrive.'

Now, I know some nuns can be, shall we say, a little demonstrative when it comes to male members of the clergy. I well remember the sisters of Saint George greeting Abbot Samson like he was the pope when we visited once. But even they didn't go down on their knees and kiss his hem. But then again, they weren't about to undertake a journey to a far corner of a foreign country. Even so, this did seem a little excessive. From Lucatz's reaction he seemed to think so too.

'Please, Dame Flora,' he said placing a hand under her elbow to raise her from her knees. 'There is no need. We are here now. This is Brother Walter - from the abbey.'

She looked at me in surprise. 'From the abbey? But I thought -' she frowned but said no more.

'Thought what?' I asked in innocence, but the lady merely glowered.

'Brother Walter will be accompanying us to Bordeaux.'

'I'm very pleased to make your acquaintance Dame Flora,' I said as affably as I could.

She didn't reply but continued to glower. I must say I was taken a little aback by her behaviour. I don't expect everybody to take to me instantly but at least give me a chance to prove myself before making up your mind. I deduced she had no idea I was coming and didn't seem to like the idea very

57

much. Well, it was early days. Plenty of time for the famous Walter charm to works its magic.

My impression of her was a little more, shall we say, neutral. How can I best describe the lady? A Scot, self-evidently. She had one of those accents that to my southern English ears sounded like smoked herring smouldering slowly over a bed of charcoal. The wind whistled through her every aspirate – who, which, where, why and when. Such an accent always sends shivers down my spine. I could happily have listened to her voice for hours. It was beautiful.

Her looks, however, were a different matter. Not to put too fine a point on it, she had a face like a punched cabbage. It was mainly her nose, all deformed and off to one side. Frankly I've seen pigs look less porcine. That's not her fault, of course, she can't help her looks. She was also a big woman with big bones. I'd wager if she and I were pitched against each other in a one-to-one wrestling match she'd have her knee on my neck in short order.

Having brought her back to her feet, Lucatz now took her off into a whispering huddle. This too annoyed me. The pair had evidently forged some kind of relationship from which I was excluded. But that would not do. I was the abbey's official representative. The nuns were as much my responsibility as theirs – a least until they were handed over to the abbey of Saint Gilles. A modicum of deference might not go amiss.

'Er, may I just interject?' I said raising what I thought was a rather vital point of order. 'Where are the other nuns? We were told there were nine of you.'

Dame Flora's snout twitched as though I had just soiled my britches.

'My ladies are in a secure place.'

My ladies. Now that was an interesting turn of phrase. Did I detect a certain proprietorial ownership?

'That's good hearing,' I said equably. 'When will we be permitted to meet them? As we shall be sailing together I thought perhaps now would be a good time to iron out any problems the sisters may have.'

The lady turned her icy gaze upon me. How many generations of Scottish hostility were frozen in that look, I wondered? It was the Battle of the Standard all over again. Maybe that explained her dislike of me - and at the same time her equanimity towards Lucatz. He was French; I was English. The Scots and the French have long been allies, whereas the English – well, we are the Auld Enemy, aren't we?

'I am their prioress. Their spiritual guide. Any problems my ladies may have they will bring to me - or to Brother Lucatz.'

'Then the sooner we meet the sooner I will be able to win their trust,' I said pleasantly.

She drew herself up defiantly.

'Perhaps it would be for the best, Dame Flora,' said Lucatz.

'But brother -' she began, but Lucatz insisted. 'As you wish, brother.' She turned her icy gaze upon me. 'My ladies at present are at their prayers. As soon as they are finished I will bring them into the church for your *inspection.*'

'I only wish to meet them, Dame Flora. Not examine their teeth.'

The lady hissed, hitched up her skirts and stomped off.

A quarter hour went by. A quarter more. At last the south door opened and in marched – and I use the word advisedly - a squad of eight black-robed magpies in two rows of four. Except for the shuffling of their feet they made not a sound as they entered the nave of the church and lined up before us with their heads lowered and their hands clasped before them in attitudes of modest supplication.

I have to say I was shocked by what I saw before me and not a little bemused. They were certainly dressed as nuns - habit, wimple, chin-barbe. But what was extraordinary was what they wore on their heads. Most nuns I had ever met, and those at Saint George's in Thetford were the most familiar to me, all wore black veils which covered their heads and hung down their backs as far as the waist. These nuns wore veils too - but what veils they were! More like wings. Vast white sails that covered not only the tops of their heads but the sides so completely that their faces were completely hidden unless seen full on from the front. So fantastical were these headpieces that I was seriously afraid of shutting the church door too quickly in case the draught caught them and carried them up to the rafters. They looked, in a word, preposterous. It was all I could do not to burst out laughing.

Leading the parade was Dame Flora and she did so with military precision. In her hand she held some kind of clicker. One click and the squad halted. Another click and the two lines turned to face forward. A third click and they went down on their knees. Casting her eye over them and nodding with satisfaction, the prioress then proceeded to name them by walking down the back of first one line and then up the other wagging a finger at each nun in turn as she went:

'Sister Theresa, Sister Ursula, Sister Prudence, Sister Rebecca, Sister Magdalene, Sister Mairi, Sister Federica, Sister Agatha,' each s-s-sister an exaggerated s-sibilant. 'There, are you s-s-satisfied?'

'Not quite. I should just like a quick word – if you don't mind, Dame Flora?'

She looked sharply at Lucatz who nodded. 'I see no reason to object.'

Dame Flora took a deep breath, stepped back and waited, clearly itching to get away. But I was determined to take my time and do the job properly. If I was to represent the abbey and take these young women into my care I wanted at least to make their acquaintance.

I took up position directly in front of the two lines – mostly so that I could see their faces inside those ridiculous veils. Not that they wished to see mine it seemed. Every eye was turned to the floor, not one dared to look up, at least not with Dame Flora glowering down at them. That was disturbing enough, but what shocked me more was their youth. They all seemed little more than children – all, that is, except the one called Agatha. She was clearly the matriarch of the troop old enough to be the others' mother – old enough to be Dame Flora's in fact. Of all of them she was the only one who dared to raise her eyes from the floor and smile before catching Dame Flora's eye returning her own to the floor again.

I could see this was going to be hard work. Still, *nihil ausi, nihil acquiritur* as the saying goes.

'Well now ladies,' I smiled adopting my most avuncular voice. 'How are we all? My name is

Brother Walter and I am a colleague of Brother Lucatz here.'

I indicated Lucatz just in case they hadn't noticed him.

'I don't know how much Dame Flora has told you but Brother Lucatz and I will be accompanying you on your voyage into the great unknown. We are going to be adventurers together,' I smiled.

I waited but there was no response. Young people I address normally laugh at my jokes, if only out of politeness. From these young women there was nothing. I tried again:

'Brother Lucatz and I will be looking after your welfare along the way, which is just as well for we are both physicians as well as monks.'

Still nothing. Not a titter from one of them, not even Agatha. In my experience nuns are a giggly lot. They will laugh at the least thing especially when being charmed by a personable fellow like me determined to win them over. But this lot kept their heads down and their lips tight. It was very disconcerting. Undaunted, I continued in a more businesslike fashion:

'So, if you have any particular health worries – or any other worries come to that – feel free to approach either me or Brother Lucatz at any time, we are here to help. Any questions?'

Still nothing. Their silence was beginning to irritate.

'You can look at me, you know? I won't bite.'

One or two did look up then, Sister Agatha for one. Behind me Dame Flora began to hiss impatiently.

'I think that's enough brother, don't you?'

I sighed and nodded. 'I suppose so. Thank you for your attention.'

Dame Flora moved quickly to the front. She clicked her clicker and all eight nuns got to their feet again. Another click and they turned in unison. A third click and out they all marched the same way they had marched in, two by two, like the animals into the Ark.

'Well,' I said to Lucatz when they'd gone. 'That went well I think.'

He pulled a painful face. 'Walter my friend, please don't be put off by Dame Flora's manner. She has a very great responsibility on her shoulders. These nuns have been under her exclusive care for some time. She is very anxious about the impending journey. And she has been waiting for us all day.'

'Waiting for *us?* Waiting for you I'd say. I seem to be excess baggage.'

'I am the one who has been in correspondence with her. It is understandable that she should look to me first. This is a huge undertaking for her and her nuns, leaving their familiar surroundings and travelling to a far-off land.'

'It's only the south of France, not Cathay.'

He frowned. 'You have seen the sisters. Dame Flora is like a mother to them.'

'More like their gaoler, I'd say. They are completely in her thrall. Did you know she was like this?'

'As I say, we only ever corresponded. I never met her until today.'

'Well now you have. Mind you, she seems happy with you. It's me she's taken against for some reason. In which case it might be best if I didn't come. Perhaps we should agree to say the handover has taken place. I'll return to Bury and you take the nuns on to Saint Gilles on your own.'

'And what do you think Prior Herbert would say if you were to return so soon, your mission unaccomplished?'

'I know exactly what he'd say – or rather do. He'd clap me in irons and send me off to some miserable rain-sodden island in the Outer Hebrides for half a decade.'

'That wouldn't be very fair, would it?' he smiled.

'Your concern is touching.'

'It isn't just that. Having met the nuns and Dame Flora I don't know if I can do this alone. I thought I might, but now I'm not so sure.'

'Don't tell me you find the prioress intimidating?'

'No no,' he frowned. 'But you've seen the sisters. They are so young, so vulnerable. I hadn't realised quite how vulnerable.'

'I don't think you've much to worry about. With those extraordinary veils they can always fly their way out of danger.'

'That's not all that worries me.'

He went to his satchel and came back with a huge bag of money which he let drop onto the floor of the nave with a satisfyingly metallic *thwump!*

'Good Lord!' I said picking it up and weighing it. 'How much is here?'

'Enough I hope.'

'For what?'

'To pay for our passage.'

I was stunned. 'You mean you haven't even found a transport yet?'

'That is what I have been trying to tell you. I wouldn't know where to begin.'

'What makes you think I would?'

'This is your country. Your language. An English ship with an English crew. It is all strange to me. You would be so much better at negotiating than I would.'

'I'm not at all sure that's true,' I said lifting the money-bag again.

'It is vital we find the right vessel, for the sake of the sisters. Nine young women on a strange vessel for a month. I'm sure I don't have to point out the risks.'

'You'll have Dame Flora. Worth three men in any scrimmage I'd say.'

'Walter, this is serious. You know what I'm saying is right. I can't do it without you. The two of us together again, just like the old days. What do you say?'

Chapter Six
A TICKET TO RIDE

Just like the old days. That's what people say when they want you to do something you might otherwise be reluctant to do - or is that just me being cynical? In any case, we did need to find a means of transport, and quickly or we wouldn't be going anywhere. To be frank I was a little disappointed in Lucatz. I couldn't believe he had organized this move to Bordeaux only to omit the rather vital detail of how we were actually going to get there. I would have hoped he had a bit more about him. But there was no point dwelling on it. Action was required - we would have to arrange transport ourselves. At least he'd had the foresight to bring the wherewithal with which to pay for it, which made it all the more extraordinary that he hadn't done so beforehand. But where does one start to look for a passenger-carrying ship? I had no experience of it either. There's not much call for ships in Bury. I supposed the obvious place to begin was the quayside.

Ipswich dock is a daunting place. Carts arriving and departing, men running about shouting in a dozen different tongues, cranes loading and unloading, everywhere noise and activity. Craft of all shapes and sizes lay at anchor, but they all looked like cargo vessels to me, and very intimidating. Those with masts seemed mostly to be cogs – the small craft that cross to the continent and back again carrying small loads. None looked as though it catered for human freight and even fewer appeared sea-worthy enough to make it as far as Gascony. Who should I ask? I approached several likely-looking types but my enquiries were met with blank stares. Many didn't even speak English. Lucatz and I walked up and down the quayside growing more and more frustrated.

'Why are you limping?' I asked him at last.

'I have the money bag concealed beneath my robe,' he replied in a low voice.

'Well try to walk normally. You're drawing attention to yourself.'

He continued to hobble. People were starting to stare. At this rate we'd be robbed before we were able to pay for a berth.

'Here,' I said. 'Give the bag to me.'

I pulled him into a side alley. As we lifted our robes to make the swap, two passing sailors nudged each other and winked.

I looked at Lucatz. 'I think we'd better find an ale-house.'

Taverns are not places that monks are supposed to frequent and least of all the type found in ports. But I thought it was our best chance of finding someone who might know of a suitable ship – and at least we could sit down. We picked the one that seemed the least rowdy and went in.

Inside it was dark and noisy. In one corner a group of men were playing some sort of a game with dice and very raucous. In another were sailors fresh off a ship with money in their purses and girls on their knees. They were rowdy too. The third corner contained a group of relatively sober-looking older men quietly supping their ale. We went over and sat down at the next table next to this group and ordered two measures of ale from the pot-man.

Lucatz took a mouthful of his and immediately spat it out again.

'What is this?'

I peered down into the dun-coloured liquid and scratched my chin. 'Flemish beer I think.'

'It tastes of wormwood.'

'That's the hops they put in to preserve it. It's not as sweet as ale, I grant you. You don't have to drink it if you don't want to.'

'Why do I have to have it at all?'

'Because this is a tavern. You can't just sit here without a drink. We'll be thrown out.'

'Then I will have wine.'

'In an English ale-house? You'll be lucky.'

The next time the pot-man went by our table I yelled my request above the din.

'You come to the wrong place, brother,' the man yelled back.

'But I was told this was where I could find captains of ship.'

'You can if it's to Flanders or Germany you be heading. No vessel here is Gascon-bound.'

I frowned my frustration. 'Can I hire one?'

'Not from here, brother. You picked the wrong port.'

The wrong port. Of course it was. No wonder those men on the quayside didn't understand me. It wasn't just that they spoke Dutch. It was because I was talking nonsense. How could I have imagined a little river port like Ipswich could send ships as far as Bordeaux? Vessels from here barely managed the few miles across the German Sea. They'd never make it along the Atlantic seaboard of France. Dover, Southampton - that was where we should be searching. And when I thought about it, Gascony was the centre of the wine trade. Those shipments being loaded on the dock were of wool and timber. What a fool I was not to have realised. We had been wasting our time. There was no point in staying.

'Drink up,' I said to Lucatz. 'We're leaving.'

'But I haven't finished my beer yet.'

'I'll explain outside.'

As we were about to get up I realised we were being watched. A sailor seated near the door - for now I'll call him "Beard" since that's about as much of his face as was visible - kept glancing furtively in our direction and looking away again. I motioned for Lucatz to sit down again.

'But you said we were leaving.'

'We will be - shortly. Just sit down and shut up.'

I stared purposefully back at Beard. He grinned, looked slyly about, then sidled over and sat down on the bench opposite. He took another guarded look around the room and lowered his head.

'Did I heard correct, you be seeking a passage down to Biksy Bay?'

From the way he said it you'd have thought he was selling children.

'We are looking for a ship going that way, yes. Why? Do you know of any?'

'Mebbe I do, mebbe I don't.' He looked slyly about him again. 'You got money?'

Beneath the table I jingled Lucatz's money-bag. He took a surreptitious glance under the table and nodded.

'Which port?'

'Bordeaux.'

He immediately sucked hard on his teeth. 'That be the divil of long way, brother. How many?'

'Eleven.'

He sucked his teeth again even harder this time and pulled a face. 'Who they be?'

'Nine are nuns plus me and my friend here. And please don't suck your teeth again.'

He shook his head and frowned at the impossibility of my request.

I was beginning to grow a little tired of this. I jangled the money-bag beneath the table again a little louder this time as inducement. One of the men seated on the adjoining table looked across at us quizzically.

'Do you know of a suitable vessel or don't you?' I asked the man pointedly.

Beard leaned closer and confided out of the side of his mouth: 'What you need is Dunning.'

I frowned. 'What I need is what?'

'Cap'n Abel Dunning. He be the master of a cog that might – I say *might* - be venturin' in that direction.'

'You mean this Captain Dunning might be prepared to take me and my friends to Bordeaux?' I said in my normal voice.

'Sssss!' he flapped his hand at me. 'Keep your voice down.' He looked anxiously about the room. 'You heard what that pot-man say?'

'I heard him. He said boats from Ipswich don't venture that far south. But why? The sea is all one beyond the estuary is it not? He can go which way he pleases - or have I got that wrong?'

Beard looked at me as though I were soft in the head. 'This be Ipswich brother. Here be rules and here be fees and them that sows t'one reaps t'other.'

It took me a moment to decipher his code but I gathered there was some kind of monopoly operating out of Ipswich with penalties for those who broke it. I'd heard of such trading syndicates before but they were usually German or Polish in origin. I wondered how real this one was and how much was invention by our friend in order to bump up the price. Time to get to the bone of the matter:

'How much?'

Beard stroked his beard thoughtfully. 'Eleven you say?' He did some elaborate calculating on his fingers and came up with a figure that made me burst out laughing.

He looked offended. 'If you can find anything cheaper, brother, you're welcome to it.'

'Maybe I can. Or maybe I'll just ask these gentlemen here.' I made a pretence of leaning towards the men seated at the next table.

Beard grabbed my arm. 'Let's not be hasty, brother.' He ran his hand over that luxuriant beard again. 'I can mebbe drop the price a smidge, seein' as how you be men of the cloth.'

'How big a smidge?'

He mentioned a lower price. Again I snorted. 'I can hire a barque for less than half that from Portsmouth.' I had no idea if that were true but it sounded good.

But it seemed I'd miscalculated. Beard's eye started to glint. 'Portsmouth you say? Well now, that be three, maybe four days ride away. These is dangerous times, brother. I heard robbers swing monks from trees for a purse o' silver, or higher if

71

they have none. Assuming you make it there with your cargo. Assuming you find a barque to take you. Assuming they don't cut your throat and toss your body o'er the side soon as they get out of sight of land. Sounds like you got a job of work to do, brother. I wish you well wi' it.' He got up to leave.

Lucatz who had been listening to all this now started with alarm. 'Walter my friend?'

'You heard his price,' I told him. 'He's trying to rob us.'

He looked at me in desperation. 'But Walter!'

By now Beard was half way to the door. The thought of going back to Saint Mary's and face spending another day with Dame Flora and her coterie of juvenile magpies persuaded me.

'Wait!' I called to him. 'All right.'

He came back and sat down again with a knowing grin. 'Half now, half when you board.'

Under the table I counted out the pennies into his bag. 'How do I know I can trust you? How do I know you won't simply take my money and disappear?'

He looked offended. 'You have the word of an honest English tar, brother.'

'Yes, but can I trust it?'

He looked about. 'See them salts yonder?' he said indicating the table of sailors with their girls on their laps. They were laughing and having a good time. Splendid fellows every one of them I had no doubt.

'If they or their mates gets wind of what we been discussin' it won't be just linen danglin' from their mastheads. It be your balls and mine. We in this now, brother. We hang together or we hang separate.'

I let go the purse. 'When and where?'

'Be at the dockside tomorrow morning, daybreak. Dunning's cog is the *Gretchen*.' He got up to leave.

'Why so early?'

He looked back at me as though I were stupid. 'High tide, brother. You'll be wantin' to float to Bordeaux I take it?' he chuckled and went off shaking his head and chortling into his beard.

'Can we trust him?' asked Lucatz.

'I don't think we have any choice.'

'But do we have a sail?'

'We'll find out tomorrow.'

Predictably, Dame Flora was less than impressed with my efforts. I'd have been disappointed if she had thought otherwise.

'You expect my ladies to expose themselves on the say-so of a man you met only an hour ago?'

'"Expose" is a little extreme, Dame Flora.'

'What's your word for it? We are to board a vessel you haven't seen, captained by a man you've never met and crewed by criminals.'

'You do them a disservice, madam. These are *merchant* seamen. It's the navy that's manned by cut-throats.'

Her eyes narrowed dangerously. 'Who will protect my ladies when they are mauled? You?'

'Ladies do not get mauled on English ships.'

'English ship,' she smirked. 'Called *Gretchen*?'

I supposed she had a point there. "Gretchen" is the German form of "Margaret." Was the crew German? Was Captain Dunning Flemish? I hadn't really thought about it. Most of the seamen I'd spoken to so far had been one or the other.

Dame Flora hadn't quite finished with me yet: 'Why did you hand over good coin to a complete stranger when you had no guarantee of a passage?'

I shrugged. 'I trusted him.'

'Then you are a fool.'

'Would you prefer I hadn't? Wait for another vessel that meets with your approval? That could take weeks and there's no guarantee we'd find one. Besides, it was Brother Lucatz's money and he was happy to pay.'

'Walter only gave him half the purse, Dame Flora,' defended Lucatz. 'This Beard will be wanting the other half promised him. I am confident the *Gretchen* will be ready to sail tomorrow morning.'

'You have known many sea captains in your time, brother?'

The prioress gave Lucatz the same kind of look she had been giving me before snorting with contempt and storming off back to "her ladies".

'Now we're both in trouble,' I told Lucatz watching her go.

He frowned. 'I will apologize to Dame Flora.' He started to stride after her, but then faltered, bit his thumbnail and came back. 'Maybe later.'

I nodded. 'Very wise.'

For the rest of that day we got ready for the coming voyage. Such preparation is not merely physical but emotional and spiritual as well. A journey by sea is no small undertaking. There are many dangers, natural and unnatural in the great blue yonder. The oceans are full of monsters and the seas filled with devils. Hardly surprising. If God had intended mankind to travel the seas he would have given us fins. To be on the safe side I decided to pay a visit to the shrine of Our Lady of Ipswich since it was close by and ask for her blessing on our coming endeavours. Lucatz declined to join me pleading exhaustion. I didn't bother asking Dame Flora.

The patron saint of sea travellers is actually Saint Brendan of Clonfert, the sixth century Irish apostle called "the navigator". Like us, he too set out to sail on the Atlantic Ocean, only in his case not in search of Bordeaux but of Paradise. What he actually found was an island bare of vegetation that turned out to be no island at all but a sea monster. A lesson to be learned there, I think. Still, a quick prayer to him couldn't do any harm along with another to the Queen of Heaven herself.

The Ipswich Madonna is similar to the one at Walsingham crowned in majesty, seated on a throne with the Christ-child on her lap. She looked beautiful in her red gown with her gold-painted crown and blue cape. The sight of her uplifted my spirit and reassured me that all would be well. What I prayed for above all was a calm sea – I'd heard how violent the storms can rage in the Bay of Biscay. I lit a small taper and dropped a coin in the poor box for luck.

Back at Saint Mary Elms, Lucatz and I settled down for the night in the nave for which we had the permission of the parish priest – a nervous young man with a squint. Meeting Dame Flora probably made the squint worse. She and her nuns were secured in the church rooms next door well away from us men. There was nothing more we could do that day. All now rested on the quayside tomorrow. I was nervous but full of confidence. I had good feelings about this trip. After an exhausting day and despite the hardness of the church floor I had no trouble falling asleep. If I'd known then what we were in for over the coming weeks, of course, I'd never have slept a wink.

Chapter Seven
ALL ABOARD

And so here we were ready to set sail, to hoist the mainsa'l, weigh anchor, slip our moorings and begin our journey across the ocean deep.

You see how *au fait* with the language of seafaring folk I'd become already despite having been among them for only a few hours? Oh yes, I was definitely getting my sea legs even before climbing aboard the boat – sorry, that should be *ship*. A "ship" is vessel with a sail while a "boat" has no sail and is rowed. A fine distinction which I got from the men on the quayside, and from them I learned much more of their nautical ways. For instance, did you know that despite being an ocean-going port Ipswich is actually on a river estuary a dozen miles from the sea? The river in question is the *Orwell* and though the same as any other river for most of its length at some point it becomes tidal. The larger sailing vessels can only penetrate as far inland as the bridge. Any further west and the river is too narrow and too shallow for them to navigate safely. East of the bridge is the quay where all the sea-going vessels dock to load and unload their cargo, and that is where we were due to pick up the *Gretchen*.

I can't pretend to know all there is to know of the lores that govern the ocean blue. For instance, that term "tidal". How do tides actually occur? As far as

I'm aware there's no more water in the sea today than there was yesterday, so why does the level go up? Rivers do add to the quantity, admittedly, but in that case why does it go down again? Where does the water drain to? Down some great well beneath the ocean floor perhaps? The answer I'm told has something to do with the moon although I fail to see how. One of those old fisherman's tales no doubt. The moon rose this day shortly after daybreak - hence Beard's instruction that we be on the quayside so early. The fact that he nominated any time at all gave me hope that he might be genuine, for if, as Dame Flora suspected, it was all a hoax and there was no ship then it would hardly matter to Beard what time we arrived. The later the better, in fact, to give him time to disappear. This thought gave me some encouragement as we waited on the quayside for our deliverer.

We must have looked a curious band sitting there among the carts, barrels and detritus of the loading docks. The nuns were huddled together in one corner and looking more than ever like a flock of hens in those ridiculous head-pieces with Dame Flora clucking over them and slaying with a glance anybody who dared venture too close. Lucatz had apparently made his peace with the lady after their little contretemps the day before but she still didn't have much time for me. I suppose the chivalrous thing to do would be for me to admit to being at fault and take the blame. Somehow I never got around to it. Instead I sprawled idly next to my bag while Lucatz sat on his.

'Which do you think is the *Gretchen?*' I mused squinting at the bewildering array of vessels moored in the harbour pool before us.

'One of the bigger ones I should imagine,' said Lucatz.

'Any look like the one you came over on?'

'I did not come by sea. I travelled overland as far as Wissant and caught a cog from there. I have no more notion of passenger ships than you, my friend.'

'Well, how about that one? Does that look like an ocean-going type to you?'

I was pointing to the mountain of a vessel that lay at anchor right in front of us. It was by far the grandest with a tall mast, miles of rope that was quivering in the morning breeze and with a well-tarred hull. None of the other barques looked anything like as grand or sturdy enough to be able to sail as far as Bordeaux.

'I can't see a name but it must surely be the *Gretchen*.'

'If such a vessel even exists,' Lucatz said.

'You've been listening too much to Prioress Flora. I shan't be sorry to have done our duty and handed her and her brood over to your abbot. Do you think once we've settled the sisters in their new home you and I might take time to visit some of our old haunts? Montpellier, Nîmes, Arles, Carcassone perhaps? I know I'm being selfish. It's just that I haven't been to that part of France since we graduated. I may never get another opportunity.'

'Much has changed since our day, *mon frère*. The war has destroyed many places. You may not recognize it. Or like what you see.'

I supposed he was right. But I still intended doing some sight-seeing before we returned.

'Excuse me, brother. Do you intend occupying the entire quayside?'

The voice was foreign and commanding. I swivelled round to see a grand matron glaring down at me.

'Forgive me,' I said jumping up and moving my satchel to one side.

'I see you have luggage,' she nodded. 'You are waiting for a ship also?'

'Indeed we are, madam.'

She nodded. 'Very wise, brother. Brother...?'

'Walter de Ixworth.' I gave a courteous bow. 'From the abbey of Saint Edmund.'

'Never heard of it. I am the contessa di Montefiore. You've heard of me, of course?'

'Erm...?'

She shook her head and tutted. 'That is the trouble with this race of mongrels. No sense of history. Montefiore is my ancestral name. My husband was the Comte d'Eu. You've heard of *him?*'

'Of course,' I lied. 'How is the, erm, comte?'

'Dead. Three months since. Left me in penury. Now we must return to the land of my forefathers or starve. At least we are able at last to leave this island of perpetual fog and rain.'

'We?'

She waved a hand in the direction of the young girl with her. 'My daughter, Carmela.'

I gave her a similar bow. She was a pretty girl of about eighteen summers I'd guess, and looked quite miserable.

'*Signorina,*' I said.

The contessa shook her head. 'No need. She speaks only English. That will change once we get to Italy.'

At that the girl burst into tears.

'Oh, stop snivelling girl,' frowned her mother. 'We haven't even left yet.'

I gathered the contessa's daughter wasn't quite so keen to be leaving these shores as her mother. And they didn't look particularly poor to me either. But then what passes for poverty among the aristocracy is often different from that of the rest of us.

'I have no sons, you see,' the contessa continued to complain. 'It's sons that perpetuates the bloodline, not useless girls.' She gave her daughter a contemptuous look.

'Ah, but Italy,' I twittered. 'Land of sunshine and olive groves... Er, where do you go first? Calais? Dieppe?'

'Bordeaux.'

'Bordeaux? Oh then that means you are sailing on -'

'The *Gretchen*.'

'Then we will be fellow passengers,' I beamed. 'How marvellous! In which case allow me to introduce Brother Lucatz de Saint Gilles who will also be sailing with us.'

Lucatz stepped forward and gave a very low bow. '*A votre service, signora. Je suis ravi de faire votre connaissance.*'

'French,' she sniffed approvingly. 'At least we may have some civilized conversation *en voyage*.' She gave a quizzical glance at the huddle of nuns.

'The rest of our party,' I explained.

The contessa grunted. 'I dare say we will meet in due course.' She twiddled her stick high in the air. '*Avanti!*'

The two women plus their manservant carrying the luggage continued to the end of the quay where they settled on a bench.

'Cause for encouragement do you think?' I suggested squinting after them.

'What do you mean?' asked Lucatz.

'Well, if *la contessa* thinks the *Gretchen* is real then perhaps it is. I dare say we'll find out when our man arrives.'

'It looks like you may get your chance.' He nodded towards the figure that was striding purposefully along the quay towards us.

'At last,' I said loudly enough for him to hear.

Beard was grinning all over his hairy face as he approached. 'You look worried, brother. Did ye think I wor leavin' you in the lurch?'

'I was beginning to wonder.'

'No need to wonder anymore. I's here.' He looked around at the others. 'We's all here. Good.'

'Is this it? Just fourteen passengers?'

Beard gave his most obsequious smile yet. 'Think of it as a select few, brother.'

I looked over his shoulder. 'Where's Captain Dunning?'

'Bless you brother, he been aboard for hours.'

'Then why are we freezing out here on the quay?'

'Soon as you settle, brother, you can board.'

'What? Oh, yes.'

I was still a little reluctant to hand over the second half of the fee. But it didn't seem very likely he'd snatch and run, not with the contessa and her group here as well.

By now the others had got to their feet and were slowly making their way towards the gangplank. It looked as though we were right and the ship we thought was the *Gretchen* was ours. I must say it was a thrilling sight. It rose high above us as it swelled and rode majestically on the rising tide. There was more activity as the sail was unfurled and billowed in the breeze making the vessel buck and groan like a war horse chomping for the off. I confess to a quiver of excitement at the sight of her.

'She's certainly impressive,' I said to Beard indicating the vessel.

'Aye, she is that.'

'She looks well able to carry us to the far corners of the earth.'

'Well able,' he agreed.

But even as we watched the great leviathan started to move slowly away from the dock.

'What the -?' I turned to Beard. 'What's happening?'

'Happening brother?'

'Well look man!' I said pointing to the widening gap between the ship and the quay.

Beard feigned surprise. 'Oh, I see. You thought that wor the *Gretchen*? No brother, that be not the *Gretchen*. That be the *Henrietta Marie* bound for Antwerp.'

'Then where…?'

'Yon be the *Gretchen*.' He nodded further down the quay towards another ship half the size of the first and twice its age.

'God in Heaven!' I gasped.

'Bootiful en't she?' he beamed, his chest swelling with pride.

'You mean that decrepit wreck is ours? You expect us to go all the way to Gascony, risk our lives across a thousand miles - on *that?*'

He looked offended. 'Why not? She done the trip a hundred times afore.'

'That's what I mean.'

The *Gretchen* was indeed ancient, even an ignorant land lubber like me could tell that. If it had been a horse it would have been put down years ago. And the old hulk seemed to agree. It creaked and groaned wearily in its moorings as though protesting it had had a long life and it was time to be laid to rest.

I turned angrily to Beard. 'You've cheated us.'

'I never said it wor the *Gretchen*,' he said nodding as the *Henrietta Marie* glided gracefully out into the harbour pool. 'You just assumed it wor.'

'You deliberately let me think it was. I'd never have handed over the money if I'd known the truth.'

He shook his head. 'It wor a fair price, brother. But the cap'n be a reasonable man. He don't like bad feeling at the start of a trip. So feel free to leave now if that's what you want – and half your money back.'

'*Half* our money? I want *all* of it.'

Beard shook his head. 'Can't be done, brother. Some's been spent already.'

'On what?'

'Improvements. The *Gretchen* be a winer, not for passengers. Passengers need cabins. Cabins have to be built. You want a bit of comfort, don't 'ee?'

'Comfort? On that?'

'What if we decide to stay?' Lucatz asked quietly.

Beard shrugged. 'A deal's a deal, brother.'

I continued to protest but as Lucatz pointed out we had little choice. It was the same argument as before. If we didn't take the *Gretchen* we would have to find another ship, and the thought of having to go through all that again made me wilt.

'How long to Bordeaux?' Lucatz asked him.

'If the weather be with us, three weeks.'

'And if not?'

The man shrugged. 'Three months.'

I groaned. 'Heaven defend us!'

By now the others were pressing to get on board and Lucatz and I had to stand aside to let Dame Flora pass with her "ladies". Beard took the opportunity to slip aboard effectively ending the argument. Finally came the contessa followed by her daughter and manservant. Something about this man seemed familiar. His face was hidden by the parcel he was carrying but then I happened to glance down at his feet.

'Wait a minute. I recognize those boots.' I spun the man round. 'Bruno!'

'Ho cousin,' he grinned.

'Christ in all his majesty, will I never be free of you? What are you doing here?'

'Working.'

'At what?'

But before he could reply the contessa's voice came fluting back: '*Oh Henri, vennez s'il vous plaît!*'

'*Oui madame!*' Bruno replied.

My jaw nearly hit the quayside. '*Henri?*'

He gave an embarrassed shrug of his shoulders. 'She prefers it to Bruno.'

'How? When?'

'We met in one of the inns. The contessa needed a manservant. I needed the money.'

'In return for what exactly?' I put up my hands. 'No. Don't tell me. I'd rather not know.'

'Well I had to do something, cousin. You left me no choice.'

'If Rowena ever finds out...'

'She won't unless you tell her.'

I opened my mouth to protest further but the lady called again, more impatiently this time: '*Henri, j'attends!*'

'*Oui madame, je viens!* Sorry cousin,' he shrugged and followed the contessa up the gangplank.

'Was that who I think it was?' asked Lucatz.

All I could do was nod.

'Why is he here?'

'Don't ask. But whatever the reason you can be sure it will not be a good one.' I groaned. 'Can things get any worse?'

There was no time to answer that. If we didn't board now the *Gretchen* would sail without us. We scrambled up the gangway which was then immediately withdrawn. Shouts were made, men ran to their stations and ropes were hauled. A tug rowed by half a dozen men hauled on the prow of the ship and another similarly the stern. Slowly the *Gretchen* began to move away from the dock and turn towards the mouth of the river. Once in the middle of the harbour the tugs were loosed leaving us adrift and on our own at last. More shouts followed, the sail filled and I instantly felt its pull. We were on our way. The Great Adventure had begun.

PART TWO

Chapter Eight
LIFE ON THE OCEAN WAVE

Our universe had now shrunk to the parameters of the *Gretchen.* Despite my continued indignation at having been duped by Beard there wasn't much I could do about that. Whether I liked it or not this was to be our home for the next few weeks so perhaps I should take a moment to describe this new wooden world of ours.

First and foremost it is a moving world. Nothing is ever still – the ship, the sea, the sky, and most of all my stomach. One moment it was in my mouth and the next it was in my boots. In the first two days I think I must have thrown up twenty times over the side of the ship.

(Incidentally, for future reference this is best done *with* the wind and not *into* it or like me you will quickly learn the true meaning of Hosea's dictum: Αυτοί που σπείρουν τον άνεμο πρέπει να δρέψουν τον ανεμοστρόβιλο - They that sow the wind shall reap the whirlwind. Fortunately I'd remembered to pack a spare robe.)

However, *mal de mer* does not seem to afflict everyone to the same extent. Lucatz must have had an iron constitution as indeed did Dame Flora judging from the smirk on her face every time she passed behind me with my head hanging over the bulwark. From the bucket she kept sluicing out, however, I'm guessing some of her charges were not so resilient.

But back to the *Gretchen*. It was, I'd say, about seven English yards in width and about three times that in length. Despite my earlier misgivings it was not an altogether inelegant beast. The front, or "prow", was raised to a pleasing apogee from whence was thrust the thickest beam of oak I had ever seen. Called the "carina", this giant wooden digit curved and arched its way the full length of the vessel forming the creature's spine or "keel" from which the rest of the ship sprouted. The rear or "stern" of the vessel was squared off below the aft-castle - of which more shortly.

So much for the lateral dimensions. In height we were three decks, the lowest being below the water-line. Down there in the bowels of the ship was a different world, a universe of perpetual night where the cargo was stored in water-tight barrels called "tuns". Normally these would be filled with wine from Gascony for shipment to England and on the return trip with other cargo – wool, ore, timber. On this journey, however, they were empty, the "cargo" being us, the passengers. That is not to say the lower deck was completely devoid of life. Ballast dredged from the sea floor compensated for the absence of cargo and contained every kind of disgusting creature that ever crawled, wriggled or slithered over God's good earth. I swear there was life down there that could be found nowhere else in creation. They lived off each other and whatever fell through the decking above. I shudder still when I think of it.

Above this deck and linked to it by ladder was the main deck of the ship where most human activity took place. This was permanently open to the skies and was the passengers' chief recreational area. Standing proudly at its centre and dominating all was the ship's mast, a magnificent fifty-foot finger of sturdy scotch pine anchored by lengthy "guy-lines" the longest and thickest of which ran from the top of the mast to the prow of the ship. This was known as the "fore-stay" and was the main brace of the ship keeping the mast erect even in the fiercest gale. Near the top was the suitably-named "crow's nest" wherein sat the "barrel-boy" whose job it was to keep lookout for any ships, rocks, islands and any other hazards that might potentially cause us damage. It was also his responsibility to make sure we never lost sight of land for if we were ever once to do so we would never be able to navigate our way back again.

Finally in this brief tour there was the upper deck, or "aft-castle", so-called because it lay at the rear of the vessel and extended out over the water like the turret of a castle. This was also known as the "quarterdeck" - presumably because that's what it was: a deck about a quarter the size of the main deck. It was the highest point of the ship below the crow's nest. Here our captain, Master Dunning, kept court and issued his orders via his second-in-command, a man called Benit. These two men were the monarch and chief minister of our little kingdom. Nothing happened aboard the *Gretchen* lest they say so. The quarterdeck was strictly off-limits to all except these two gentlemen – oh, and the "tiller-man" whose job it was to handle the "rudder" - the machine that steered our course as we ploughed our way through the water. This "rudder" was the *Gretchen's* great pride and joy and a new innovation. Set in the middle of the "stern" it replaced the more cumbersome steering-boards that other vessels had on either side of the ship. The great advantage of the rudder, apparently, was that it only needed one crew member to handle it whereas the old steering-boards needed two and so made the vessel less manoeuvrable.

How do I know all this? Hogtie – that was Beard's real name. He it was who took me on my guided tour. Despite our earlier skirmishes in the ale-house and on the quayside he seemed to have taken a shine to me. Or maybe it was out of pity as I leaned over the bulwark for the fifth time that morning and gave to the sea what remained of my breakfast.

'I don't think I'm ever going to want to eat again,' I groaned.

'You will, brother,' he assured me. 'Trust me. In a day or two you'll be wanting your dinner again like eve'yone else.'

The very thought made me want to retch again.

'I see'd yon party o' nuns on deck earlier.' He winked lasciviously. 'Some tasty horse-flesh there.'

'Yes, well just you remember they are brides of Christ.'

'Oh, I not be talking about them young fillies. I mean the Scotch mare in charge.'

I looked at him sideways. 'That Scotch mare as you call her is Dame Flora, the prioress, and she'll eat two like you alive for breakfast.'

Hogtie rubbed his hands together. 'I likes a woman with a drop o' spittle about her. Puts me in mind o' my wife.'

'*You* have a *wife?*'

'Course I have a wife,' he said indignantly. 'Back home in England. Why you think I be at sea?' he added with a grin.

'A pity you couldn't have brought her with you instead of lusting after others.'

He shook his head. 'Wives b'ain't allowed on board ship, brother. Cap'n Dunning be very partic'lar about that.'

'He sounds a bit of a tyrant, our captain.'

'No worse than many. Better than most.'

'What about his lieutenant? What's he like?'

That sent Hogtie into further paroxysms of mirth. 'Bless you brother, Mister Benit be no lieutenant. He be the first mate. Mister Benit more or less run the ship – following the cap'n's orders acourse.'

'And what's your function on this fine vessel of ours - when you're not fleecing honest passengers of their hard-earned silver, that is?'

He stuck out his chest. 'I be the axe-man.' He proudly patted the hand-axe which I now saw was stuck prominently in his belt.

'What does he do?'

'Axe-man be the most important man on a ship - after the captain and first mate, acourse.'

I looked at him blank.

He explained: 'If there be a blow and the *Gretchen* look likely to take a roll, it be the axeman's job to fell the mast.'

I was appalled. 'Fell the mast? Are you mad? That would be suicide, surely.'

'Better than sinking, brother. Least that way you'd stand a chance of swimming ashore.'

'I can't swim.'

'Neither can anyone else.'

'But you're sailors. You must be able to swim.'

He shook his head. 'No crewman aboard the *Gretchen* can swim, brother. Cap'n Dunning prefer it that way. Concentrates the mind, see? If they can't swim they can't desert.'

'Has anyone ever tried?'

'None that's lived to tell the tale.'

I glanced hesitantly at his axe. 'Have you ever had to use it?'

'Only once. When we was off the top of Jutland where the Skagerrak and the Kettegat do meet.'

'The what and the who?'

He sniggered. 'The Skagerrak and the Kettegat. That be what them Scandies call the waters twixt the German Sea and the Baliatrics that don't much like each other overly. It can get mighty rough when them two boys is fightin'.'

This was beginning to sound like another old fisherman's tale.

'Go on, I'm listening.'

'The sea wor a-roaring, see? Waves as big as mountains lashin' at us from ev'ry which way. We was being tossed this way and that. Tiller-man couldn't hold his course and the sail wor torn and useless. We was in danger o' keelin' over. So the cap'n orders me to strike the mast to keep us off the rocks.'

'Did it?'

He shook his head. 'Too late. We was already holed midships and takin' in water fast.'

'So what happened?'

He shrugged. 'Ship went down with all hands.'

I gasped which was evidently the reaction he was hoping for. He grinned with satisfaction.

'Hang on a moment,' I said. 'If *all* hands went down with the ship, how come you're still here?'

For answer he merely winked and his grin grew even wider.

I was beginning to get the measure of the man. He liked to spin a yarn and wouldn't let awkward facts get in the way of a good tale. But at least it made me forget about my sea-sickness.

'Course, there is other things a cap'n can do to make the ship more stable,' he said with a twinkle in his eye.

'Like what?'

'He can make the ship ride higher in the water by ditchin' dead weight overboard.'

'By dead weight I take you to mean the sand and gravel below deck?' I said remembering the stinking midden in the belly of the ship.

'Aye, ballast be the first to go.'

'The *first* to go? Why, what else is there?'

'Horses be next.'

I'd heard of this before, horses being thrown overboard from ships *in extremis*. I cringed at the thought of those poor creatures struggling to stay afloat and finally succumbing to the waves. But he said they were the next to go. What was left, I wondered?

'The women.'

I looked at him askance. 'Now I know you're jesting.'

He shook his head solemnly. 'Women be no use on a ship. They just extra weight. Best they go overboard with the horses.'

'We don't have any horses.'

'Aye, that we don't.'

I looked across at the Sisters of Grace who were squatting in a corner of the deck oblivious to the possible fate that awaited them.

Hogtie chuckled again at my horrified face. 'You're right, brother, I do be jestin'. Cap'n Dunning wouldn't throw them young'ns overboard to drown. That would be a cruel and un-Christian thing to do.'

'I'm relieved to hear it.'

'No. He cut their throats first.'

To conclude my brief tour of the ship: At the back of the ship beneath the quarterdeck and sheltered by it were the passenger cabins. Despite Hogtie's insistence that they were expensively built these were little more than screens put up in a temporary manner with the very minimum of privacy. The walls were so thin, in fact, a fart in one of the cabins could be heard it in all the others.

There were essentially three cabins: The largest took up the entire left-hand side of the deck was reserved for the nuns and Dame Flora. The one furthest back was for the contessa and her daughter while the third, the smallest, Lucatz, Bruno and I shared. Not that we saw much of Bruno who seemed to spend most of his time in the contessa's hutch. And some very disturbing noises were coming through the walls from that quarter, I can tell you:

Contessa: *I will require your special services this evening, Henri.*

Bruno: *My lady, I'm not sure I will have the energy this evening.*

Contessa: *I do not pay you for your convenience but for mine. Will you be able to perform this evening or no?*

Bruno (sighing): *As your highness wishes.*

Contessa: *Then please present yourself in my hutch immediately after supper.*

Bruno: *And the signorina Carmela?*

Contessa: *She will not be participating tonight. However, if she wishes she may stay and observe.*

Stay and observe? Her own daughter? Outrageous! Poor Rowena. If she ever got wind of what her husband was up to she would surely die from the shame.

Later when I found Bruno alone, I remonstrated with him.

'We all have to earn a living, cousin.'

'There are some things no man should lower himself to do for any reason.'

'Beggars can't be choosers, cousin. Of course, if I had another source of income...'

I shook my head. 'Never give up do you, Bruno?'

'What would you have me do, cousin? Starve?'

'What I would have you do is come to confession, declare all to God and beg his forgiveness. But above all *go and sin no more!*'

But he just shook his head: 'I am my own man. I do as I please.'

He was right, of course, I couldn't force him. But after this he could give up any hope of profiting from my mother's estate.

Chapter Nine
THE FIRST SHALL BE LAST

Bruno apart, life aboard the *Gretchen* passed tolerably well. We soon settled down to a regimen that was more or less the same every day: We would sail only in daylight, the French coast being deemed too treacherous to navigate in the dark. There were no lights on the shore so we had no way of knowing how close or how far away we were, and without a moon the shore was virtually invisible in the dark. So at sunset we would drop anchor and retire for the night leaving half a dozen men, those with the keenest ears and the sharpest eyes, on watch. The oarlocks would also be engaged so that if we did need to run in a hurry we would be ready to do so. Then at sunrise the oars would be stowed again, the sail unfurled and off we would set on the next leg of the journey. In this way we would cover perhaps fifty miles in a day, depending on the strength and direction of the wind, of course.

For the first couple of days we were in the narrowest part of the Channel within sight of both England and France. On the third day we passed the port of Boulogne. Here the Channel widened considerably and England finally disappeared from view. It was a bright clear morning and on a whim I decided to climb the mast to the crow's nest in order to get a final glimpse of the old country while it was still possible to do so.

'Do you think the captain would object?' I asked Hogtie squinting up at the figure on the quarterdeck. I still hadn't spoken to the man yet.

Hogtie thought about it for a moment. 'I don't see why. No, you go ahead. Cap'n Dunning won't mind.'

I should have realised by now that any assurances of Hogtie's were about as worthless as a tin penny but I was so keen to gaze one last time on the old country that I needed little encouragement.

Actually, I had another reason for wanting to climb to the top of the mast and it was to do with something Abbot Samson had once told me years before. When he was a young man and still subsacrist, Samson had gone with Abbot Hugh to inspect King Henry's new castle at Orford which he'd recently completed on the Suffolk coast. This castle was the very latest design put up in less than eight years to counter the growing strength of earl Bigod of Norfolk, a powerful local baron who had built his own castle nearby at Framlingham.

The central feature of Orford Castle is its magnificent keep which rises ninety feet above the ground with commanding views all along this part of the coast. It seems Samson and the abbot were gazing out at sea when suddenly and without warning Samson had raced to the top of the tower, much to the abbot's consternation. When he came back down the abbot asked him what in the world he thought he was doing to which Samson made some lame excuse about the weather and tides. It was only years later he told me the real reason for his extraordinary behaviour. It seemed he had spied a fishing boat off the shore which at ground level suddenly disappeared from view. Seeing this Samson had raced to the top of the tower in the hope of seeing it again. Sure enough, from ninety feet up the fishing boat had miraculously reappeared.

Now, my reaction when I heard this tale was the same as everyone else's: that the fishing boat had simply sailed out of sight and then sailed back in again. But Samson insisted it was because the world was round and the boat had slipped below the horizon. At the top of the tower he claimed he was able to see that little bit further, "over the edge of the earth" as he put it, and so he saw the boat again. He even drew a sketch to show me.

If anyone else had told me this tale I would have dismissed it as fantasy, but Samson had been right about such things before. Whether or not he was right this time was impossible to prove since Bury is far from the sea and there are no fishing boats sailing over the horizon. I had long harboured a desire to repeat his experiment and see for myself but I'd never been in a position to do so before. Here on the *Gretchen* was a unique opportunity to do just that and one I couldn't pass up.

Encouraged by Hogtie's assurances, then, I shinned up the rope ladder to the crow's nest as fast as I could before anyone could stop me. At the top the barrel-boy, a lad of about fifteen or sixteen summers, looked horrified.

'I'm not sure you should be up here, brother. The captain is very particular about that.'

I gave him my most avuncular smile. 'Let me worry about the captain. If he asks, blame me.'

I went on to explain to him what I was about, Samson's theory and so on, not that I thought he understood a word of it. To him it was perfectly natural that he should be able to see further from up here than down on deck. That, after all, was why he was up here. But sure enough along the starboard horizon the thin smudge of the English coast that had disappeared at deck-level came back into view just as Samson's theory predicted. And there was no chance of England sailing out and back into view. Therefore Samson's theory was proved correct. I was sure the old trickster would have been impressed with my efforts. I was overjoyed when I saw it and clapped my hands with glee.

'Remarkable!' I said thumping the boy roundly on the shoulder. 'Simply remarkable!'

'If you say so, brother.'

But now there was another problem that I hadn't anticipated. The wind was picking up. Down on deck the motion of the ship was bad enough, but up here it was far worse. Like a spinning-top when it starts to lose its momentum the top of the mast was swaying about quite wildly from side to side. My sea-legs were better than they had been a few days before but not yet quite up to this. I was beginning to feel distinctly nauseous again.

'I think I'd better return below,' I said much to the boy's obvious relief.

However, going down is not the same as going up. Climbing a ladder one tends to look up. Going down you have to look down which was when I discovered my mistake. While the crow's nest was only fifty feet above the deck from up here it looked twice that distance. I had barely gone more than a few rungs of the ladder when I froze unable to carry on down or to climb back up again. I was stuck almost literally half way between Heaven and the

Deep Blue Sea. Then I heard a yell from below me that very nearly made me lose my grip altogether:

'Get that man down!'

It was Captain Dunning. But yell all he liked there was no way I was going to move. I was frozen to the spot.

It was Hogtie who came to my rescue. He must have anticipated something of the sort for he had remained at the bottom of the mast and now climbed the rope ladder beneath me.

'Hogtie, I can't move,' I whimpered.

'Yes you can. Just don't look down that's all you have to remember. I'm right behind you. I won't let you fall.'

It took an age and many more words of encouragement from Hogtie but eventually, rung by excruciating rung, we inched our way to the bottom. There on the deck First Mate Benit was waiting to escort me to the captain.

'Have you taken leave of your senses?'

I was still feeling shaky from my descent, and the captain's booming voice wasn't helping.

'My apologies, captain. I meant no harm. I thought I had permission.'

'Permission? From whom?'

From Hogtie of course, though I could hardly tell him that.

'I just assumed it would be all right.'

'Passengers are permitted on the main deck of the ship and in their cabins only. You should have been told that.' He looked quizzically at Benit.

'I instructed the passengers as soon as they came on board, captain,' the first mate confirmed looking at me. 'As always.'

Now I thought of it, I did vaguely remember something of the sort but at the time I'd been too concerned with Bruno and getting the nuns settled to take much notice.

'I can only apologise again, captain. It won't happen again.'

'You're right. It won't.'

Damn the man! Who was he to dress me down like I was one of his crew? I was the one paying the piper. I should be the one calling the tune.

'While you're here captain might I have a word about cabins?'

'Accommodation is Mister Benit's province. Speak to the first mate about cabins.' He started to leave.

'I'd rather speak to you, if you don't mind.'

Dunning came back. 'Well?'

'Brother Lucatz and I have been allocated a hutch barely big enough for two yet you have put three of us in it. I should have thought for the price we are paying we should receive more amenable accommodation.'

'The *Gretchen* is a cargo ship, brother, not a passenger ferry. Space is limited.'

'But we are not sardines. And Brother Lucatz and I have our daily offices to recite. You would agree, I hope, that the success of your endeavours depends upon the correct prayers being said?'

First Mate Benit leaned over and whispered something in the captain's ear.

'The third person in your cabin is your cousin, I believe.'

'So?'

101

'Mr Benit tells me he spends very little time in his own cabin preferring that of the contessa di Montefiore.' He raised a sardonic eyebrow.

I felt the colour in my cheeks rise. 'Bruno is the contessa's manservant. It is natural he should spend most of his time with her.'

'But while he is in the contessa's cabin he can't be in yours taking up space.'

'He doesn't sleep in the contessa's cabin,' I insisted, although I wasn't entirely sure I was right about that.

'You are welcome to share with the crew, if you prefer,' said Benit.

'Oh? Where do they sleep?'

'On deck in leather bags.'

My jaw fell open. 'I'm not paying a king's ransom to sleep out in the open in a sack!'

Dunning shrugged. 'Then you will have to put up with the arrangements as they are. Now, if there's nothing else?' He started to leave again.

'As a matter of fact there is. The food.'

'What about the food?'

'There isn't any.'

'Did you not bring your own?'

'No of course we didn't bring our own! Call me naive, but I was expecting to be fed as part of the price of our passage.'

Dunning shook his head. 'We can't afford to carry food, brother. Food takes up valuable cargo space.'

'You're not carrying any cargo.'

'No, not if we have to carry food as well.'

'But you've just admitted you're not carrying any food either!' I said with exasperation.

'There has to be food, brother. The crew have to eat.'

We were going round in circles.

'We will be putting into port in a day or two,' said Benit. 'You will be able to buy all the provisions you need there.'

'And what do we do until then?'

Benit shrugged.

'As it happens we will be dining tonight,' said Dunning. 'Assuming, that is, you accept my invitation.'

'Invitation?'

'The passengers are invited to dine at the captain's table as his guests,' said Benit. 'It's a tradition of the ship.'

For a moment I didn't know what to say. 'That's … very generous.'

Dunning gave a curt nod of his head. 'In that case I'll expect you at eight bells. And in the meantime I'll be obliged if you will stay out of my crow's nest.'

Thus ended my first meeting with Captain Dunning. Not the most propitious of introductions.

Chapter Ten
A DINNER PARTY

I cornered Hogtie later on deck:

'Thanks for dropping me in it.'

'Droppin' you in it, brother?'

'With the captain. You knew perfectly well he wouldn't agree to my going up to the crow's nest. Why did you tell me he would?'

'You wanted to meet him,' he chuckled. 'Seemed an ideal opportunity.'

'I meant under salubrious circumstances. Not as a delinquent.'

'Brother, you'd ha' shimmied up that ladder whatever I said. I could see it in your eyes. Besides, I knew the cap'n wouldn't have you flogged. He have too much respect for men of the cloth.'

'I'm relieved to hear it. But it didn't feel much like respect.'

'That's just his way. He used to talking to the likes o' me not a man o' culture like you.'

'I'll try to remember.'

I spent the rest of the day trying to avoid catching Dunning's eye – not easy when he's up on his quarterdeck looking down on us all the time. The trouble is there isn't much to do on board a ship. Once you've strolled round the deck half a dozen times and inspected the horizon, that's about it. After a while waves start to lose their fascination. The crew were all right: they had their scrubbing and their mending and their splicing to do, whatever that is. For the passengers there was nothing but hours of unrelenting tedium. I did think of inviting Lucatz and the nuns to a period of prayer and contemplation. If nothing else it would fill up an hour or two. But when I broached the subject with Lucatz he was less than enthusiastic. He didn't think Dame Flora would be very keen.

'Do you want to ask her?'

I grimaced. 'On second thoughts, let's forget the idea.'

I went back to my strolling. It's times like this that I envy the endurance of the ascetics. Take Saint Simeon Stylite for instance. He stood alone atop his pillar of rock in the desert for thirty-three years without once sitting down even to sleep. Not to be outdone his disciple, Saint Daniel, remained upright on his pillar for thirty-three years and three months thus beating Simeon's record by ninety days. Neither seemed to have been bored by the experience. Such feats – not to mention *feet* – of endurance are to be admired. Monks like me and Lucatz are mere novices by comparison. But then, Benedict didn't devise his Rule for extreme eremites like Simeon and Daniel but for ordinary men and women who wish to lead a Christian life. I did spend some private time in prayer, naturally, but however well-intentioned the mind does eventually start to wander.

I wondered how my fellow passengers were coping with the tedium. I had a good idea about Bruno and the contessa, but the least said about that the better. As for the nuns, I don't know what they did with themselves cooped up in their rabbit hutch all day. It can't have been healthy in there. The young need to get out to breathe fresh air and stretch their limbs. But I hardly ever saw them emerge from their cabin and rarely on their own. If I did happen upon one of them they would scurry away like frightened mice before we had a chance to speak. Whenever they did appear in public it was always in their regimented lines and always with Dame Flora at their head. They would march around the deck a few times with their heads bowed and their eyes lowered inside those comical winged veils, and then disappear back inside again much to the amusement of the crew whose cat-whistles Dame Flora studiously ignored. And woe betide any who came too near. Anyone who dared would instantly be turned to stone by one of the prioress's ferocious glares. I suppose I couldn't blame her for being protective of them. They were for the most part young, vulnerable women on a ship full of men – and some of the basest men at that. But it did seem to me she applied her duties a little over-zealously at times. It would be nice to catch one of them on their own and find out a little more about them.

'Do you know anything about the sisters?' I asked Lucatz after one of these perambulations. 'You're more intimate with them than I am.'

'What is it you wish to know?'

'Oh, I don't know - how did they come together? Were they part of a single community before they came to Ipswich?'

'I believe so, yes.'

'Somewhere in East Anglia?'

'Further afield I think.'

I waited. 'Well go on then, further afield where? England? Europe? The Shahdom of Khwarizm?'

Lucatz just smiled and shrugged in that exasperating way the French have. Getting information from him was like trying to squeeze milk out of a turnip.

But then I happened to be leaving my cabin just as Sister Agatha, the oldest of the sisters and the one who had secretly smiled at me at Saint Mary Elms, was returning to hers with a sluice bucket. Of all the nuns she would surely be most approachable. This time, however, she wasn't smiling. On the contrary, she looked rather pale and sickly.

'Are you all right, sister?' I said going up to her. 'You don't look very well.'

She was startled by my presence but quickly recovered herself and waved a dismissive hand. 'It's the motion of the ship, brother. It will pass.'

It didn't look like sea-sickness to me, more like exhaustion. She started again towards her door but stumbled as the ship rocked and slipped to one knee. I instinctively reached out to catch her arm and was shocked at how thin it felt.

'Here, let me help you.' I eased her down onto the floor. 'Can I get you some water?'

'No, thank you brother. I will be fine in a minute.'

'Would you feel better on deck? At least you will see the next wave coming.'

'We are not permitted on deck.'

That annoyed me. 'Who does not permit it?'

No need to answer that one. Dame Flora.

'As well as your chaperone I am also your physician. And as such I prescribe a little more air and a lot more food. You're as thin as a stick. No wonder you're weak.'

'Brother Lucatz is our physician.'

'That's your choice, of course. But I'm a doctor as well – at least, my brother monks tell me so.'

At that she did smile. 'I know you are being kind, brother, but there is no need to fuss - truly.'

I couldn't force her to take my advice, of course – even my paying patients don't always do that. And she had a perfect right to choose who her physician should be. But I thought I might have a quiet word with Lucatz later on her behalf.

'May I ask how long you've been a nun? I don't wish to pry but you are somewhat older than most of your sisters.'

'I was widowed in the spring. With my children gone...'

I nodded. 'I understand. A convent is a good place to retire.'

She gave me a stern look. 'Oh, I shan't be retiring, brother.'

'No, of course not,' I said. 'Forgive me. I know the good work the nuns do even with just their prayers.'

Agatha shook her head. 'No, you don't understand.'

'I think I do. You're not the first nun I've met, you know? There are the sisters of Saint George in Thetford with, if you don't mind my saying, a far more amiable custodian in the guise of Mother Odell, the prioress there.'

Agatha frowned. 'You should not judge Dame Flora too harshly.'

'Your loyalty does you credit sister, but I can only speak as I find. And what I find is that you are not taking proper care of yourself. If I may say so, you're no longer a young woman and this is quite a journey to be embarking upon for a woman of any age.'

'It is God's will, brother.'

'You believe God has called you to undertake this journey?'

'We all must go where the good Lord sends us, brother. And now I must get back.'

She struggled to rise and I helped her up feeling again how thin she was. She was as light as a feather, practically skin and bone.

She braved a smile. 'I'm feeling much better now.'

'Well, if you need me you know where I am.'

'You are very kind,' she nodded and was about to go but stopped and said: 'It's been nice knowing you, brother.'

I returned her smile. 'It's a pleasure knowing you too, sister.'

It was a strange thing to say although at the time I didn't think any more of it. But it wasn't long before her words would come back to haunt me.

And so to the captain's table. To my surprise Dunning did us proud. A trestle table had been set up on the deck with benches down either side. There was a table-cloth and salt-cellar, even finger-bowls – all redolent of a feast in some great lord's hall, which I suppose was the idea. He'd also moored the ship in a small cove in order to reduce the swell and make the experience more pleasurable – not to mention preventing the food from sliding off the table. Two of the youngest and least unwholesome-looking members of the crew had been scrubbed up and stood waiting to serve. And the food they served up was excellent, although not all of it provided by the ship's cook. The contessa made great play of a couple of pheasant she had provided from the cages she had stored in the hold.

Initially there were just six of us seated along one side of the table: Captain Dunning was in the centre with the contessa on his right. Next to her was Carmela and at the far end sat First Mate Benit. On the captain's left was Lucatz followed by me and finally Bruno. Together we filled up one bench. The bench opposite thus far was completely empty being reserved, I'd imagined, for Dame Flora and her flock of magpies who had yet to arrive. While we waited the rest of us engaged in polite conversation. I flatter myself I managed to smooth over my earlier misunderstanding with the captain. Loquacious by nature, the wine was making me bolder than usual. I drained my cup and had it refilled while we waited. And we waited. And still we waited. I scowled at one of the serving boys who had his finger stuck up his nose. By now the conversation was beginning to sag as doubtless also was the food. I was beginning to wonder if we were ever going to eat. At last Lucatz excused himself and went to see what the delay was.

Eventually there came the sound of a door slamming and Dame Flora stomped in alone and sat down heavily in the middle of the bench opposite with a face like thunder. Lucatz whispered something in the captain's ear and retook his place next to me. It seemed we were not to be honoured by the presence of the other eight sisters after all. The captain rose to his feet.

'Now we are all here,' Dunning began, 'may I, on behalf of the company and crew of the *Gretchen,* welcome you aboard and pray that you may have a pleasant and an incident-free journey. I now call upon one of the brothers to say the grace.'

All eyes fell on me. After three cups of wine I'd already begun to feel a little light-headed and hoped

Lucatz might do the honours, but to my annoyance he declined. If someone didn't say grace soon we'd never eat.

'Oh, all right.' I pushed myself up and made a perfunctory sign of the Cross: '*Benedictus benedicat,*' I intoned and sat back down again – rather more heavily than I intended.

At last the two servers were able to start serving the food and not a moment too soon as far as I was concerned. I tucked in heartily. After days of being unable to keep anything down I was ravenous. The contessa immediately engaged the captain in a lengthy discussion about the finer points of pheasant cuisine, how it should be killed, how long it should be hung, the various methods of cooking and so on. I couldn't care less how it was cooked so long as we got to eat it. Opposite the prioress just sat scowling. To my addled brain she looked comical just sitting there. Maybe it was the wine but I couldn't resist having a go:

'Are you not eating mother prior?'

She glared back at me. 'No.'

'That's a little ungracious isn't it? The captain has gone to a great deal of trouble.' I broke a leg off one of the pheasant and began chewing on it. 'What about your sisters? Will they not be joining us?'

'They have already eaten in their cabin, thank you.'

'The sisters are shy,' Lucatz explained. 'They are not used to the company of strangers. I'm sure Captain Dunning will understand.' He gave a polite nod in Dunning's direction.

'Well it's up to you what you do, of course,' I smiled. 'But do the sisters have no say in the matter?'

111

'I've already told you, brother. They have already eaten. I have a store of biscuits.'

At that I let out a snort. 'You expect them to survive on just biscuits?'

'Abstinence is good for the soul, brother.'

'A little less abstinence and a little more sustenance might not go amiss. When I saw Sister Agatha she looked ready to faint for lack of a decent meal.'

At that Dame Flora shot a look across at me. 'You've spoken to Sister Agatha? When was this?'

'Earlier today. She stumbled out of her cabin – literally. Naturally I offered her a helping hand.'

'My ladies need no help from you or anybody else. And I would be grateful if you did not accost them behind my back.'

Now, normally I would let a comment like that flow over me, especially in such a gathering as this. But I suppose the combination of wine and an empty stomach were affecting my mood somewhat – and my better judgement.

'What would you have me do? Ignore her? The poor woman was clearly in distress. Small wonder if all she has to live on is dried up old biscuits.'

From a dried up old biscuit barrel, I could have added.

'These young girls,' said the contessa from further along the table. 'So concerned about their figures, they starve themselves one minute and then wonder why they faint the next. Carmela is exactly the same. The slightest distress and she quite swoons away. The count and I were at a constant loss of what to do about it.'

'Maybe she'd feel better with a little more wholesome living,' I mumbled into my cup.

'Hm?' smiled the contessa. 'What was that brother?'

'What Brother Walter means,' put in Lucatz quickly, 'is that the stomach is a cauldron in which wholesome food is cooked, the liver providing the heat for this combustion. Naturally if there is not enough fuel in the stomach the fire goes out, hence the cold, clammy appearance of the patient. The body temperature drops, the brain is deprived of blood and the patient faints - isn't that right, brother?'

I grunted into my cup.

'By wholesome food you mean like these fine pheasant of mine,' the contessa purred. 'From my own estate in Norfolk.' She smiled indulgently round the table.

'Carrion,' sniffed the prioress.

The contessa shot her an indignant look. 'I beg your pardon, mother prioress. I'll have you know *my* pheasants were alive not two hours since.'

'Exactly. What the girl needs is a good purge. Get rid of all this poison.'

'Poison?' gasped the contessa.

'For once I agree with the prioress,' I said. 'A good purge, and not just of her bowels either.'

'I'm not sure I follow you, brother,' said the contessa.

'Do you not?'

'Wal-ter,' warned Lucatz beside me.

I ignored him and leaned towards the contessa: 'There are certain things, madam, that no young woman should have to witness. I think we all know what I'm talking about.' I glared at Bruno who at least had the good grace to lower his eyes.

'Walter please,' begged Lucatz.

By now Carmela was starting to look a little green around the gills. 'Mama…' she said plaintively.

Her mother pushed her away, drained her cup, held it out for a refill and then leaned across the captain towards me.

'What "things" are you referring to brother?'
'I hardly like to say, madam.'
'I think you should.'
'Mama…'
'I would if good manners did not prevent me.'
'Bugger good manners.'
'In that case ask your daughter.'
The contessa turned to her. 'Carmela?'

But Carmela wasn't able to tell. There was another swell of the ship. The girl heaved and covered the front of her mother's gown in a thick yellow bile.

The contessa shot to her feet, drew back her hand and gave the girl a tremendous slap across the face. 'You stupid girl!'

Lucatz was instantly up on his feet. 'Signora!'

Carmela was too shocked to say anything. She fled in tears holding her stricken face. Bruno glared at me and went off after her followed by Lucatz and the contessa. Dame Flora gave a satisfied smirk and then she too departed leaving only me, the captain and First Mate Benit still seated. Judging by the expression on the captain's face he was enjoying the entertainment enormously and doubtless judged his dinner party a huge success.

Why can I never learn to keep my mouth shut? The trip had barely begun and was already turning into a disaster. I had made enemies of Bruno, the captain, Dame Flora and now the contessa. This wasn't what

I'd intended at all. I had so much wanted this evening to be a success yet here I was the chief offender.

My head was spinning and I needed some air. Out on deck the night air was cool. I took some deep breaths. It was a clear night, not a cloud in the sky. A thin sliver of moon was rising in the east. In the darkness I could vaguely see the outline of a figure standing by the bulwark. It was Carmela.

'My child,' I said going over to her. 'Are you all right?'

'I like the night, brother, don't you? I find it comforting. Like a great blanket enveloping you.'

'I'm not sure it's safe for you to be out here alone at night. I would be happier if you went back to your cabin. Is your mother there?'

'You've seen what she's like. What she is capable of.'

'I'm sure she meant nothing by it. It was just the wine talking. We only chastise those we love.'

She looked up at the stars. They filled the blackness like a huge dome from horizon to horizon. 'They say there is a star for everyone. I wonder which is mine.'

I sighed. I knew she wasn't as keen as her mother to be leaving England. I wondered if perhaps she had a special reason for wanting to stay. A young man perhaps?

'What will you do when you get to Bordeaux? Have you spent much time in Italy?'

'Most of my mother's family are there. I believe she has it in mind that I should marry a Tuscan count, grow grapes, some olives and *bambini* - lots of *bambini*.'

'And you?'

She gave a secretive smile. 'I may have other ideas.'

I went back to my cabin. I would have liked some company to commiserate with but nobody seemed to be about. Bruno was probably giving his own brand of solace to the contessa. I didn't know where Lucatz was. I felt in need of some spiritual solace myself and by "spirit" this time I meant the liquid sort. One of the others must have had the same idea for I found a flask of brandy-wine open on the small table in the hutch. I admit it was tempting for I am particularly partial to brandy-wine although I'd probably had enough to drink for one day. There was no bung for the flask to be found anywhere in the cabin and some of the contents had already been spilled with the roll of the ship.

I poured myself a cup - just enough to prevent more of the precious nectar from slopping on the table and being wasted. It had an instant warming effect and I felt better for it. It was also an excellent vintage. I wondered where it had come from and who had opened it. I poured myself another cup. That was even better. And then a third. Gradually the world was seeming a much nicer place.

Chapter Eleven
THE FIRST DEATH

'Brother, wake up!'

'Hm? What?'

Someone was violently shaking me. I opened my eyes. Vague shapes swam before me. Was I awake or dreaming? I decided dreaming and went back to sleep again.

'Brother, please! You must wake up!'

I opened my eyes again and this time saw a face staring anxiously into mine. The face seemed vaguely familiar. I pulled back trying to focus.

'Sister Rebecca?' I blinked. 'What is it? What's wrong?'

'Brother, you must come.'

I groaned. 'Sister, it's the middle of the night. Can't it wait till morning?'

'It's not the middle of the night. It's the middle of the day.'

'What? Middle of the day?' I sat up quickly. Bad idea. My head pounded and I felt nauseous. 'Oh…' I held my head and tried to think. 'What is it? What's happened?'

'It's Sister Agatha. She needs you.'

'Sister Agatha?'

'Yes, Sister Agatha. Oh please hurry brother before it's too late.'

'Too late for what?' I shook my head trying to wake up. 'All right. I'll come.'

With great difficulty I swung my legs over the edge of the bunk and tried to get to my feet but immediately sat down again. My head swam and my knees wouldn't hold me. What was the matter with me? Why did I feel so giddy? After a moment the nausea subsided enough for me to stand again and with Rebecca's help I managed to stagger across to the nuns' hutch.

Sister Agatha lay on her cot surrounded by her other sisters. I had to admit she didn't look too well. She was delirious, tossing and moaning incoherently, apparently unaware of her surroundings. I sat on the edge of the cot as much for my own sake as hers and took her pulse. It was thin and weak. Her brow felt cold and clammy.

'How long has she been like this?'

'Since yesterday.'

I frowned. 'But she was all right when I saw her this morning.'

'That was yesterday morning, brother.'

'*Yesterday* morning? Why wasn't I called?'

None of this was making any sense. Was I still dreaming? I looked round the room.

'Where's Dame Flora?'

'With Brother Lucatz. Please hurry brother,' said Rebecca wringing her hands. 'You must perform the rite to give her a good death.'

A good death. I knew what that meant. The application of the sacrament of Extreme Unction administered by a priest to a dying person - essential if the soul is to get through the dangerous last stages of life on earth and make it safely into the afterlife. It is the final act before death. But Sister Agatha wasn't going to die.

'She will die,' insisted Rebecca. She *wills* it.'

'Wills it? You mean she *wants* to die?' I looked incredulously at Rebecca's face and those of her sisters. They all nodded in earnest.

'Please brother. The sacrament.'

I took Agatha's pulse again. It was weak, possibly getting weaker. I still wasn't convinced she was about to expire but as far as administering the last rite it didn't really matter. The patient may well recover and receive the anointing all over again at a later date. After all, nobody can know for certain when the moment of death comes. It's better to be on the safe side and assume the worst rather than delay and risk sending the patient off into afterlife shorn of the Church's immaculate armour. Getting the process right was what mattered.

I tried to clear my head. All right Walter, focus. There are several stages which must be conducted in the correct sequence for them to be effective. Get one thing wrong or in the wrong order – say "Son, Father and Holy Ghost," instead of "Father, Son and Holy Ghost" for instance - and the entire procedure is void.

First things first then: Confession. Clearly a full and contrite confession from Agatha was out of the question, she was too far gone for that. I would have to improvise.

I leaned closer. 'Sister, can you hear me?'

Her eyes swam away from me.

'Do you renounce the Devil and all his works?'

Agatha mumbled something incoherent which I took to be a yes.

'Do you believe in the scriptures according to the teachings of Holy Mother Church forsaking all heresies and errors condemned by the Church? Are you sorry for the sins you have committed by thought, word and deed and by what you have left undone?'

Her head fell forward as though nodding.

'That's the confession out of the way. So far so good. Next, communion. Damn!'

'What is it brother?'

'I haven't any wafers.'

Rebecca glanced quickly about. She reached behind her and thrust something into my hand. 'Will this do?'

It was one of Dame Flora's rock-hard biscuits. I suppose they had their uses. I quickly blessed the thing making the sign of the Cross over it and crumbled a few pieces into Agatha's gaping mouth.

'The Body of Christ.'

Agatha coughed out most of it, but enough went in I think. I pushed the few crumbs between her lips. What next? Anointing with oil. But I didn't have my satchel containing my emergency phial. I was about to ask Rebecca to go and fetch it from my hutch when there was a noise behind and I turned to see Dame Flora standing in the doorway with a look of outrage on her face. All the other nuns gasped and instantly shrank away leaving me alone beside the cot.

'What do you think you are doing?' Flora bellowed.

'What does it look like I'm doing? I am administering the Last Rite to this dying woman.'

'You have no right.' She began grabbing my arm. 'I've told you before my ladies do not need your help.'

'I think I'm the best one to decide that,' I said snatching my arm back. 'Besides, my presence was requested.'

'By whom?'

'Sister Rebecca.'

Flora turned and glowered ferociously at the girl who instantly fell to her knees in an attitude of abject subjugation.

'Forgive me, mother. I meant no harm.'

I was astounded – and disappointed. I had thought of all the nuns Rebecca might have stood up to Flora's bullying. Older than the rest, Rebecca seemed to be made of sterner stuff. But I was forgetting just how much in awe the nuns were of their prioress and how much they were in her power.

'We will have words later, sister,' Flora hissed at her.

'Don't blame Rebecca,' I defended. 'She did absolutely the right thing by calling me. Sister Agatha needed a priest and I was on hand.'

'Brother Lucatz is the sisters' chaplain.'

'Brother Lucatz wasn't here.'

'He is now.'

She stepped to one side. Sure enough, Lucatz was standing behind her.

'Lucatz, tell this woman I am acting in accordance with the Holy Laws of the Church. Lucatz?'

I might have expected his support but he merely shrugged one his infuriating Gallic shrugs again and kept silent. Had he now fallen under the Great Gorgon's spell too? I was about to say something further when behind me there was a gurgling sigh.

121

One of the nuns leaned over and placed her cheek against Agatha's lips. She felt her pulse and then her forehead. She then stepped back.

'She is gone.'

The others now joined Rebecca on their knees in their usual military uniformity just as I felt something drop from my hand. I hadn't noticed but in my confrontation with Flora I had crumbled the remainder of the biscuit completely to dust. It showered from my hand like snow onto the cabin floor.

Seeing it, Flora smirked. 'Well, even you must now admit your services are no longer required, brother.'

I dusted the crumbs from my hands. 'That's all right. I completed the ritual. As far as I'm concerned Agatha died a good death. I am satisfied.'

I wasn't, but I was damned if I was going to let Flora see that. Having done as much as I could I marched out of the nuns' cabin and back to my own.

In truth I wasn't sorry to be out of it. I had more or less completed the ritual. Under the circumstances it was a good death – or good enough. I was sure God would not deny Agatha entry in to Heaven simply because I had failed to perform the rite strictly. A great many others dying on battlefields or alone in their hovels never achieved even that much. What troubled me more was that comment of Rebecca's that Agatha had wished to die. What had she meant by that? But I couldn't think about it now. My head was pounding, I was feeling woozy again and wished nothing more than to lie down on my own cot – which I did and instantly fell back into a deep sleep.

Dreams are funny things, aren't they? They are not real in themselves but reflect what is happening in the real world. Like a glass window that had been smashed and the pieces put back together by some alien hand ignorant of the original. All the parts are there but arranged higgledy-piggledy. The picture that emerges may not be the original but corners that were otherwise ignored assume greater importance, as though the mind was trying to tell you something. Unimportant things loom large while what you thought was important fade into obscurity. In my dream biscuits and pheasants jostled with Agatha's smiling face repeating over and over: "It's been nice knowing you, brother. It's been nice knowing you, brother." And right in the middle of it all was a giant bottle of brandy-wine that grew bigger and bigger until it burst and I awoke to find Bruno's face leering down at me.

'Ah, awake at last.'

I pulled back. 'Bruno. What are you doing here?' I looked about me. 'How long have I been asleep?'

'Days. I was beginning to think you'd never wake up. Here.' He proffered a bowl of something under my nose.

'What is it?'

'Soup.'

I sat up smartly nearly knocking the bowl away.

'Careful cousin!' he tutted.

'Thank you Bruno, but I'm not hungry.'

'You must be. You haven't eaten in days. Here, try it. I made it myself.' He scooped up a spoonful of the steaming brew and proffered it to me.

I pushed myself back even further into the corner. 'I don't want it.'

'You're weak. You're not thinking straight. This time I'm the physician and I'm prescribing for you to eat!'

He lifted a spoonful up to my lips again just as the door opened.

'Lucatz!' I said with relief. 'There you are.'

'Are you all right Walter?'

'I am now. Bruno - do you mind?'

Bruno sighed and reluctantly lowered the bowl. He looked up at Lucatz and shrugged. 'Very well.' He stirred the spoon in the bowl. 'Tell you what, I'll leave it here in case you change your mind.' He put the bowl down carefully onto the bench. 'I hope you're feeling better later.' He nodded to Lucatz and left.

'That looks good.' Lucatz lifted up the spoon to his mouth.

'Don't touch it!' I said and knocked the spoon out of his hands sending its contents spilling onto the floor.

'Oh!' Lucatz tutted at the mess. 'What did you do that for?'

'I think it may be tainted.'

'Tainted? How?'

I looked anxiously at the door and lowered my voice. 'I think Bruno may be trying to poison me.'

Lucatz scowled in disbelief. 'Why would he want to do that?'

'Why do you think? Have you forgotten? My inheritance.'

'And you think he would poison you to get it?'

'Why not? You've heard how desperate he is. My mother's estate is substantial. Men have murdered for less. What better opportunity to do it than on board the *Gretchen*? People die all the time on boats from exotic diseases no-one's ever heard of or knows the cure for. Then they get buried at sea and no-one is any the wiser.'

'Bruno's your cousin.'

'By marriage. Only by marriage. Besides, I have proof.'

'What proof?'

'He opened a flask of brandy-wine and left it for me to find. He knows I'm partial to brandy-wine and guessed I would take a cup. I'm sure it was tainted.'

Lucatz frowned. 'Where is this flask?'

'It's here somewhere.' I looked around the hutch but couldn't see it. 'Hah! Gone. See? He's disposed of the evidence already. Very clever.'

'I think you're letting your imagination run away with you. You probably dreamt it.'

'You're right, I did dream about it. I saw it all clearly in my sleep.'

'Well there you are then. You've been asleep for too long.'

'How long?'

'Two days.'

'*Two days?* Did you not think to wake me?'

'I tried. We all tried. It was impossible.'

'There, you see? He tried to poison me with the brandy-wine. My dream was warning me. That failed and now he's trying again with soup.'

Lucatz scowled. 'Walter, you're being ridiculous.'

'Why else would he worm his way onto the boat?' I gasped. 'Yes, that's it. Think about it. He has no reason to go to Bordeaux. You wait. One morning you'll find my lifeless body lying on the cot next to you. Then tell me I'm wrong.'

He shook his head. 'I didn't come here to listen to this.'

'What did you come for?'

'I came to apologize. For not speaking out the other day. Over that business with Sister Agatha I mean.'

'Yes, well I could have done with your support.'

He grimaced awkwardly. 'I know. And you were right. You were only acting in accordance with your priestly vows. But Dame Flora was also right. I am the nuns' chaplain and I should have been there for her. If it's anybody's fault it's mine. I didn't say anything at the time because I didn't want to create any more fuss.'

'It seems to me a fuss is exactly what Dame Flora needs. Something to shake her up. That woman is a menace. It was a good thing Rebecca came to fetch me. If it wasn't for her Agatha would have died unshriven.'

'Well, you'll be pleased to know she received a proper sea burial. While you were asleep. Captain Dunning presided.'

'Pity. I should have liked to have seen the body first.'

'To what purpose?'

'I don't know. But something about her death wasn't quite right. My dream again. She seemed perfectly all right when I saw her last. A little thin perhaps. No,' I corrected myself, 'not a *little* thin. Positively emaciated. That's down to Flora as well with this ridiculous biscuit diet she has the nuns on. I think that's the secret of her control. Starve a dog and it will cower to you.'

Lucatz shook his head. 'You're reading too much into this, Walter. Agatha died of natural causes. She was old. The sea voyage was too much for her, it's as simple as that. These things happen.'

'It's not just that. It's something Agatha said to me when we parted company that last morning. She bade me farewell.'

'Isn't that what people say when they part?'

'Not as she did. It was too final. As though she knew she wouldn't see me again. As though she knew she was going to die. And that's another thing. Rebecca said she wanted to die.'

'Maybe she knew her time was near. Maybe she was suffering. In any case, it's too late now. I am more concerned with the living – specifically you. Even physicians get ill sometimes.' He put his hand on my brow. 'You are a bit hot. Do you have a headache?'

'Yes.'

'Drowsiness?'

'That too.'

'Nausea? Dry throat?'

'All of those. Symptoms of poisoning perhaps?'

He shook his head. 'Symptoms of *mal de mer*. As your doctor I advise you to avoid heavy meals, keep away from confined spaces and above all no alcohol.'

'Too late for that.'

'You're strong. Things will improve in the next few days. I promise.'

But he was wrong. Things didn't improve. They just got worse.

Chapter Twelve
SHOOTING THE DUCK

For the next few days I avoided Bruno, as far as it was possible to avoid anybody on board a ship. Fortunately he spent much of his time in the contessa's hutch from where those embarrassing noises continued to emanate. At least it kept him out of my hair – during daylight hours at any rate. At night he returned to our hutch to sleep, although I made sure Lucatz lay between us.

As for my delirium, I had no way of proving it was caused by something Bruno had given me since the suspect brandy bottle had mysteriously vanished – to the bottom of the English Channel I imagined. After a few days I was feeling better and when there were no further incidents I began to relax a little. However, during my torpor I had completely lost track of time and had no idea where we were on our journey. Fortunately Hogtie was on hand to assist:

'We be off the coast of Normandy.'

I groaned. 'Is that all? I was hoping we'd be further on by now. How long have we been at sea?'

'Ten days.'

'Ten days and not yet through the Channel?'

'We be making decent progress,' he assured me. 'Weather's been fair. I've known it take this long just to get to Calais. See that?' He pointed to a hazy smudge off the starboard bow. 'That be Jersey island. And that wi' the pennants flying atop the cliff be Gorey Castle built by King Johnny when the Frenchies stole the rest o' Normandy from him. That bit of rock and the few others scattered here about be all that's left of his daddy's empire,' he chuckled gleefully.

'I'm quite sure our new king, *Henricus Tertius*, will recover his father's rightful possessions in the fullness of time,' I nodded indignantly.

Hogtie shrugged. 'Aye, mebbe. Once he growed up a bit.'

I frowned and looked at the island again. 'We seemed to be getting closer. Are we stopping?'

'Aye. The cap'n'll be callin' in to fill up with fresh water and supplies.'

'That at least is good hearing. And a chance for some decent food, I hope. I'm sick of pottage. It will be good to feel solid land underfoot again.'

'Oh, we won't be docking. We get in close as we can and they floats our needs out to us - and anything else they can sell us. You can float back wi' 'em if you've a mind but I wouldn't advise it.'

'Why not?'

He pulled a face. 'Pirates.'

'What? In these waters? This is the English Channel not the Barbary Coast.'

'You can scoff brother, but there be plenty o' pirates in these waters. Ever heard of Eustace the Monk?'

I looked at him sceptically. 'Is this another of your fanciful tales?'

He shook his head. 'No tale brother. Eustace wor a real pirate hereabouts during the recent troubles. I'm surprised you han't heard of him being a monk yourself.'

'Not a real monk, surely?'

'As real as you. Left his abbey in Calais to avenge his father's murder, took to pirating and never looked back.'

'A monk who's also a pirate?' I shook my head. 'I don't believe you.'

He crossed his heart. 'God strike me dead if it be a lie. And monk weren't all he wor, neither. They do say he studied the black arts from the moors of Spain then menaced these lanes from his castle on Sark – that be another o' these craggy rocks hereabouts. They even say he helped ferry Prince Louis to England to steal King John's throne from him.'

'I suppose next you're going to tell me you knew him.'

'I knew him right enough. Where you think I learnt my sailin'? Me and old Eustace, we was like that.' He twisted two fingers together and nodded.

I looked at him askance. 'I never know when you're being serious.'

'You'd know if you felt the tickle of his sword-blade on your windpipe. And being a monk hisself, he wouldn't pay no heed to your naked pate. Cut your throat as soon as look at you.'

My hand went automatically to my throat and I glanced nervously about. 'Is he still at large, this erm, pirate monk?'

'Not since the English parted his head from his body. But they do say his ghost still ply these waters.'

'Ghost!' I snorted. 'Anyway, we've nothing to interest pirates. The *Gretchen* carries no cargo – this trip at least.'

'Don't you believe it. There be plenty aboard the *Gretchen* pirates want.'

'Like what?'

'Any of the crew they can persuade to join them to start with - to replace them as got kilt harryin' some other crew.'

'Who'd want to join a band of privateers?'

'Them that wants to keep their heads. They that dissn't join voluntary-like gets they throat cut,' and to emphasise the point he pulled his finger across his windpipe.

I swallowed hard feeling my Adam's Apple ride up and down.

'All right. So that's the crew. What about the passengers?'

'The men they ransom – them that's worth ransoming. As for the rest -'

'Don't tell me.' I ran a finger across my throat.

Hogtie merely grinned.

'And the women?'

'Ah, well now, the women be another story. The young'uns they use for their pleasure then sells on to the moors. The rest they throws overboard.'

'There you go again with your throwing women overboard.'

'I told ye before. Women be no use on a ship, least of all a pirate ship.'

'Pirates!' I snorted. I looked at him. 'Have you, erm, ever seen his ghost? Not that I believe a word of anything you've said.'

'No. But they do say them Northern Lights seen in the sky be the restless spirits of folk he done murdered.'

By now we had sailed right up to the island. Several rowing boats had already come out to greet us selling wares and exchanging badinage with the crew. I was impressed with the way Master Dunning skilfully guided us in slackening off the sail at just the right moment so that we glided effortlessly into the little make-shift harbour below Gorey Castle which stood high up on the cliff-top above us. Even before we dropped anchor we were surrounded by a flotilla of little boats laden with all manner of goods to sell: food mostly, but also more exotic ware – like a group of lightly-clad ladies in one of the row-boats calling out and waving. As you may imagine, these created much interest among the crew. There was a lot of whistling and cat-calling between them, the men leaning out over the rail to touch the women while they were doing their best to entice the men down.

'Any man who steps across the bulwark needn't think to return.'

This from First Mate Benit. It was the first time I'd heard him address the crew and he was impressively commanding. He stood with his feet planted solidly apart twitching a swagger stick at his side. Who among the crew would dare cross him, I wondered? Or passengers come to that.

Meanwhile the serious business of replenishing our supplies got under way. Some of the more substantial traders were allowed to board in order to negotiate directly with the captain. These were a select bunch and no doubt coin changed hands for the privilege. No doubt also they made this up by charging higher prices. Of course we paid – what choice did we have? It was either that or starve. Remembering Captain Dunning's earlier admonition about providing our own food, I bought poultry -

some very scraggly-looking capons and a couple of layers. Lucatz bought beans, leeks and onions.

'Is that all you want?' I tutted. 'Bordeaux is a long way.'

'I'm still suffering with stomach cramps,' he said rubbing his belly. 'This will do me for now. There'll be other opportunities to buy later in the trip I'm sure.'

I shrugged. 'Just as you wish. But you can sleep downwind tonight.'

Nearby the contessa was doing some lively haggling with a very doubtful-looking character over the price of a pair of guinea fowl in a cage. He initially asked for eight deniers at which the contessa scoffed and started to walk away. The man then asked for six deniers. The contessa offered two. They finally settled on four.

'Hey, that's a good price,' I said, impressed. 'I'll have a couple of guinea fowl for four deniers.'

'*Non*,' said the man firmly. 'For you we start again. Eight deniers.'

One of the lightly-clad women in the dinghy now called up to Lucatz and me:

'*Ho-la, mes garçons! Tarif spécial pour les membres du tissu! Hooh-hooh! Comment aimez-vous les jumeaux?*'

'What's that she's saying?' I asked Lucatz. 'Special rates for members of the cloth? Something about twins? What twins? What's she selling?'

'Well, it's not guinea fowl,' he nodded as the woman cupped her breasts provocatively.

'What? Oh, yes. Very nice, madam!' I called back. 'But not today thank you!'

The woman shrugged and muttered something inaudible to her companions who laughed.

133

These "Jersey toads" or *crapauds*, as these charming young ladies were known, were not the only entertainment to be had in the island's waters. If you threw a silver penny over the side boys would swim under the ship, retrieve the coin and swim up the other side holding the coin aloft which they would then keep. I wouldn't have thought it possible to hold one's breath long enough but they did it time and again, to much applause from the crew – and profit to themselves. I envied their agility and secretly vowed to learn to swim when we returned to Bury.

It was while all this was going on that our complement of nuns - now reduced to seven since the death of Sister Agatha - made an appearance led, as ever, by the prioress. This was the normal time for the nuns to emerge for their daily circumambulation of the deck and Flora would stick to her routine come what may. You'd have thought she might have waited at least until we had upped-anchor and were sailing away before subjecting the sisters to possible ridicule and humiliation, but that wouldn't have been in Dame Flora's character. She wasn't going to allow the minor inconvenience of a few dozen jeering islanders to disrupt her routine. Out they marched, the entire troupe in their familiar double lines. As ever they were robed in their magpie uniforms, much to the amusement of *les damoiselles de crapaud* who screamed abuse as soon as they saw them. Dame Flora ignored them and marched her company relentlessly twice round the deck and then back again to their cabin.

Hogtie watched her with adoring eyes. 'En't she magnificent?' he sighed. 'She can click her clicker at me any time.'

I looked at him with dismay. The man was clearly delusional.

As soon the ship's stores were replenished we were ready to get under way again. The Jersey toads and the diving-boys returned to their onshore lairs to await the next unsuspecting prey to visit the island while we up-anchored and turned once more into the wind. Slowly the *Gretchen* eased out of Gorey Harbour leaving Jersey island with its dubious delights behind.

The waters off the east and south coast of Jersey are notoriously treacherous and it's easy to run aground and tear the bottom out of even the shallowest draught, so instead we passed round the north of the island where the water was deeper and headed straight for the Brittany coast. This took us across the widest stretch of open water we'd met so far but the weather was clear and the sea calm so Captain Dunning was willing to take the risk.

Lucatz and I were out on the main deck together enjoying this period of calm when the contessa approached. We hadn't spoken since our little spat during the Captain's dinner, and she evidently had no intention of doing so now. She spoke only to Lucatz entirely in French and ignoring me. But I got the gist of the conversation. She wanted a mass to be held for the benefit of the crew and passengers. Apparently after her experience of Jersey island she was concerned that morals aboard the *Gretchen* had lapsed – a notion I thought was a bit rich coming from someone who engaged in Heaven-knew-what with Bruno in her hutch every night. But if she wanted Lucatz to indulge her she was to be disappointed:

'I would like to help, contessa. Alas I cannot hold a mass. I am not a priest.'

'But you are a monk. Surely all monks are priests.'

'By no means. Ordained monks are unusual. However, Brother Walter is and I am sure he would be only too pleased to oblige you.'

The contessa hesitated but I was determined if she wanted my assistance she was going to have to ask me directly – and in English.

'Well brother?'

'Hm? What was that? I'm sorry my lady, I wasn't paying attention.'

She pouted. 'I was asking Brother Lucatz if it would be possible to have a mass said for the benefit of the passengers and crew.'

I looked around innocently. 'Are you asking me?'

'I suppose I am.'

I gave her my broadest smile. 'My lady, I would be honoured. As a matter of fact, I have been thinking of approaching Master Dunning with the same idea. We are clearly thinking along similar lines. Shall we say tomorrow?'

'Tomorrow will be fine,' the contessa agreed and turned to go but added as an afterthought: 'Thank you.'

'Can you imagine what that "thankyou" must have cost her?' Lucatz chuckled once she'd gone.

'She'll survive. To misquote the prioress, humility is good for the soul. Besides, what I said was true. I had been thinking of asking the captain for a mass. In memory of Sister Agatha as much as anything else. But why did you tell her you're not a priest? You were ordained just as I was.'

'I thought if you did it it might get you two talking again after your fiasco at the dinner. And it worked.'

'I see,' I nodded. 'Ever the diplomat.'

'You'll have to clear it with the captain first, of course.'

'You mean I'll have to go and talk to him too. More diplomacy?'

'Well, you were wanting to restore harmony on the ship.'

'You're a sly old dog, Lucatz de Saint Gilles.'

He smiled. 'Are you sure you want to do this? I wouldn't want to force you into doing anything you didn't want to do.'

'Of course I'll do it – though not for the reason the contessa thinks. For Sister Agatha. Let's just hope the captain agrees.'

He did agree and went out of his way to accommodate us arranging for a makeshift altar using one of the trestle tables to be set up on deck for the purpose. However, not everybody was as keen on the idea. I thought I heard Lucatz remonstrating with Dame Flora who doubtless was reluctant to be preached at by me. No surprises there. Meanwhile I got to work on my homily.

Preaching is not something I do very often anymore. In Bury the abbot or the prior lead on Sundays and feast days while the rest of the time it is the younger monks who needed the practice. But I was determined to make a decent fist of it. I thought I'd take as my theme something appropriate to our situation: the story in Mark where Jesus and his disciples are crossing the Sea of Galilee when a storm blows up and Jesus calms the wind and the waves with a mere wave of his hand. The moral of the story is clear. If Our Lord was able to rescue the disciples from the storm how much more was he able to rescue us from the storms of everyday life? It was a call to the faithful keep the faith in the face of temptation – a point not lost on Bruno and the contessa, I hoped.

I was quite pleased with the result. And judging by the reaction of the passengers and crew they liked it too. When I summoned up the image of the storm, graphically describing the waves breaking over the boat, you could have heard a pin drop. I had in mind Hogtie's description of the storm between the Skagerrak and the Kettegat though with less drastic results. The description was very realistic, even the contessa was impressed and congratulated me afterwards. I also put in some special prayers for the soul of Sister Agatha which was my main purpose for the mass and to make up for my missing her committal to the deep. Not exactly a requiem but a moment to remember her by.

The one person who was not impressed, predictably, was Dame Flora. She hardly waited for the final blessing before rounding up "her ladies" and marching them back to the protection of their hutch. Ah well. You can't win them all.

While I was packing up the altar I caught sight of Lucatz having an animated discussion with one of the nuns. At first I couldn't see which nun it was because of those ridiculous veils they all wear hiding their faces. Then I realised it was Rebecca, the sister who had called me to Agatha's bedside. But as I approached they ended the conversation abruptly and Rebecca started to hurry away.

I quickly caught up with her: 'Ah sister. I was hoping to have a word. We haven't had a chance to speak since Agatha's death. I wanted to ask you about what you said. About Agatha willing her own death.'

Rebecca glanced quickly at Lucatz then back at me. 'I'm sorry brother, I spoke out of turn. I meant nothing by it.'

'Well you must have meant something or you wouldn't have said it.'

'I think you misunderstood me.'

I frowned. 'I don't think so. I know I was a little bit woozy that day but I was wide awake when I saw Sister Agatha. You were quite specific. You told me Agatha wished to die. She said so herself.'

'I don't remember saying that.'

'Well you did. Why are you being coy now?'

'I'm not being coy, brother. Everyone knows Sister Agatha died of natural causes.'

'Don't be tiresome, Walter,' said Lucatz. 'If Rebecca says you were mistaken then you were mistaken. Thank you sister. You may go.'

Rebecca did a quick curtsey and hurried off before I could stop her.

I turned to Lucatz. 'What did you do that for? I hadn't finished speaking to her.'

'You were bullying her.'

'I most certainly was not. I was asking her a simple question.'

'Walter, you frightened her, surely even you could see that? And as their chaplain I have a duty of care to all the nuns.'

'As do I.'

'Fine. Let's leave it at that,' and he started to walk away.

'What were you two talking about?'

'Talking?'

'Just now before I came over. You and Rebecca were talking. Quite animatedly.'

'It was a private matter.'

'About what?'

'If I told you that it wouldn't be private, would it?'

'You don't want to tell me?'

'No.'

So saying he marched off leaving me feeling frustrated and confused.

Rebecca frightened? She didn't look frightened to me. Or if she was it wasn't me she was frightened of. Why had she changed her story about Agatha? And what was the private matter she was talking to Lucatz about? Maybe I'd get a chance to speak to her another time on her own when neither Lucatz nor Dame Flora were around, not that there had been too many opportunities to do that. But there was plenty of time before we reached Bordeaux. I was in no hurry. After all, none of us were going anywhere, were we?

Boredom was now the order of the day once more. After the elation of my sermon I was feeling a bit flat. I've said already that there isn't much to do on board ship and even less so when the weather is becalmed. At such times even the crew find they have time on their hands. Some of them sleep, some mend nets, but others play a game called "shooting the duck".

This is just a bit of diversionary fun. A handful of stones are scooped up from the ballast as sling-shot and aimed at a target tethered off the ship's bow. This is the "duck". Bets are laid and the nearest to the "duck" scoops the pot. The "duck" on this occasion was a pig's bladder blown up to the size of a man's head, tied off and let out on a rope fifty yards or so off the bow. Passengers are invited to join in if they want.

Now, it's been a long time since I've thrown anything other than a temper-tantrum so my aim wasn't very good. But a challenge from Lucatz resurrected the old competitive rivalry of our youth. I couldn't turn it down. Egged on by the crew it was soon a contest between our two abbeys. The honour of Saint Edmund and Merry England pitted against that of Saint Gilles representing *la belle France*. Naturally being mostly Englishmen themselves, the majority of the crew were rooting for me and I was still riding high on the success of my sermon. Mister Benit refereed.

So we began: Lucatz aimed first. Hopeless. He lost his footing, slipped on the wet boards and his missile went straight up in the air and plopped two feet away into the water to much jeering from the crew.

My turn. All I had to do was lob my missile a foot closer than Lucatz had to the "duck" to win. The prize was practically in the bag.

Unfortunately it never got that far. I rolled back the sleeve of my robe with great aplomb, swung my sling-shot around my head only to be halted before I could loose it by a cry from above. The boy up in the crow's nest was shouting down something and pointing out to sea. I couldn't hear what was being said but after a brief exchange with the first mate, Mister Benit turned and ran up the ladder of the quarterdeck to the captain's station. Something was amiss, that was for sure. But what?

'What's that?' Lucatz was squinting and pointing out at sea in the direction the barrel-boy had been pointing.

I shielded my eyes. 'Our duck.'

He shook his head. 'No, further out. Can you see? Something bigger. Something floating on the surface.'

I shrugged.

More shouting now. Men running. The sail was lowered, the sea anchor dropped and a dinghy was rapidly lowered over the side. Five men clambered in accompanied by First Mate Benit and rowed towards the mysterious floating object. It was all very bewildering. A short while later they had retrieved whatever it was out there and were on their way back. By then it was clear what they had found. And it wasn't a duck.

Chapter Thirteen
A LADY VANISHES

'Rebecca? You're saying it was Sister Rebecca they found? Sister *Rebecca*?'

Lucatz shrugged. 'As far as we can tell.'

'What do you mean as far as you can tell? Was it her or not?' Then a horrifying thought struck me. 'Dear God! You mean the body was so badly mutilated as to be unrecognizable?'

'No. I mean there was no body.'

I frowned. 'No body? Then what did they fish out of the water?'

'Her robe.'

'Her *robe*?' I shook my head. 'I'm not following this. You say it was just a robe they fished out of the water?'

'Yes.'

'Not a body?'

'No.'

'Then how do you know it was Rebecca's?'

'Because,' said Dame Flora impatiently, 'Rebecca is missing. She is not in the cabin.'

'That doesn't mean anything. She might be elsewhere on the ship. Have you looked?'

'Of course we've looked!' Flora snapped. 'Do you think we are fools? She is nowhere to be found.'

'All the other nuns are accounted for,' explained Lucatz. 'The robe can only have been Rebecca's.'

'That still doesn't mean anything's happened to *her*. She might have removed the robe herself.'

'For what reason?'

'I don't know. Why do nuns remove their robes?'

'My ladies never remove their robes,' insisted Dame Flora. 'For any reason.'

'Well Rebecca clearly did or she'd still be wearing hers, wouldn't she?'

Flora shook her head. 'This is exactly what I had feared. It is why I insisted my ladies never leave the cabin alone.'

'Oh, and you think that without your constant supervision the sisters are likely to fall overboard? That they are incapable of standing on their own two feet?'

'No brother. I think they are eight innocent young women on a vessel filled with men.'

'So therefore one of them must have attacked her. That's the only possible explanation?'

'It has to be considered, Walter,' said Lucatz.

I still wasn't convinced. 'I'd like to see this robe.'

'To what purpose?' asked Flora.

'If Rebecca was attacked there might be indications. She struck me as a doughty young woman. I'm sure she would have given good account of herself. Or are you going to continue to insist on your precious inviolability, Mother Prioress?'

'I can't see that it will do any harm, Dame Flora,' said Lucatz still playing the diplomat.

Flora pressed her lips together. 'Very well. You may examine the robe.'

Rebecca's robe, or what was reputed to be Rebecca's robe with its great white wings now rinsed of their starch by sea water and floppy like a puppy's ears, was laid out on a trestle table to dry. I inspected it minutely under the watchful eye of Dame Flora and Lucatz. I don't really know what I expected to find: a knife-wound perhaps or some blood, although the salt water would probably have washed that away too. As it was I found nothing. It was just a robe like all the other nuns' robes if a little damper. No snapped tie-cords. No tears in the fabric. It was as if it had been simply removed and dropped in the sea.

Dame Flora watched my fruitless examination with smug eyes. 'Satisfied?'

'There's no sign of a struggle,' I conceded.

'As I told you.'

'Which puts paid to your theory that she was attacked.'

'Not at all. She could have been knocked out first.'

I couldn't see the sense of that. If Rebecca had been ravaged as Dame Flora clearly thought, why would they bother to remove the robe so completely and so neatly? No. I was sure something else was going on.

'I want to interview the other nuns.'

Dame Flora shook her head rigorously. 'Out of the question. Examine the robe if you must but the ladies themselves – no. I absolutely forbid it.'

'Why? They may be able to shed some light on what happened to their sister. Isn't that what we all want?'

'I have already spoken with them. They know nothing.'

'Maybe you didn't ask the right questions. Or maybe they told you what they thought you wanted to hear.'

Lucatz frowned: 'Walter, you insult the prioress with your accusations.'

'Then I apologize. I just think another voice may prompt them to remember something they might otherwise have forgotten, that's all.'

'What makes you think they will tell you what they wouldn't tell me? They are not used to the company of men.'

'They're used to mine. I've spoken to them before. You can stand guard outside the door if you so wish. The walls are thin enough. You'll be able to hear when they scream.'

'When they -?'

'I think Brother Walter is jesting,' said Lucatz.

'On the contrary, I'm deadly serious. The prioress will be able to hear every word. She just won't be able to … interrupt.' I meant "interfere". 'And Brother Lucatz will be on hand to offer his protection too if needed.'

Lucatz turned to the prioress. 'Dame Flora?'

She pouted. 'Five minutes. Not a moment longer.'

Inside the nuns' hutch it was even more cramped and oppressive than our own. Nine nuns - eight now with Agatha dead - all crammed into a space hardly big enough for three. With Rebecca and the prioress also absent there were only six facing me.

I'd forgotten how young they were. Agatha had been the oldest by far but Rebecca was the second oldest. Those remaining all looked little more than children. They clearly regarded me with trepidation, six pairs of innocent eyes gazing up at me. Fortunately they had removed those preposterous winged head-pieces. I tried to put them all at ease straight away by smiling and addressing them as I would a classroom of novice monks at the abbey:

'You all know who I am, yes? Brother Walter from the abbey at Bury. You remember we met first at Saint Mary Elms in Ipswich, and again later at Sister Agatha's bedside.'

They made no response.

'Come now, I'm not such an ogre am I?' I pulled a funny face. Still nothing. This was going to be harder than I thought.

'We are not supposed to speak to you,' said one at last.

I frowned. 'Who told you that? Your prioress?'

'It's not just you, brother,' said another. 'We are not supposed to speak to anybody.'

'Well I'm not just anybody. And Dame Flora has given her permission for me to speak to you today. You can ask her if you're worried. She's just outside the door.'

Still no response. I was using up my precious few minutes. I tried another tack:

'What's your name sister?' I asked the first nun who had spoken:

'Magdalene.' She blushed and lowered her eyes.

'Magdalene,' I nodded. 'A fine Biblical name. It's the name of Our Lord's closest woman friend. Is it the name you were Christened with, or did you adopt it when you took the veil?'

'It was the name I was given.'

'And where was that? Where is your home?'

She shook her head.

'What, you don't remember? Surely you remember your home?'

She looked at me blank.

I turned to another. 'What's your name? Ursula isn't it?'

She nodded.

147

'From the Latin meaning "bear". You don't look much like a bear to me. More like a goat. Who thinks Ursula looks like a goat?'

At this there were a few giggles. Progress at last.

'Now, let me see if I can remember the rest.' I went through them one at a time: 'Theresa, Prudence, Marie and Federica – have I got it right?' I smiled encouragingly around them. 'Well now let me tell you why I'm here. I want to have a little chat about Sister Rebecca - trying to find out what might have happened to her. Does anybody have any ideas?'

I looked round encouragingly. Blank faces and silence.

'Perhaps she's been unhappy,' I suggested. 'I know what you young girls are like, you share secrets. Who was Rebecca's closest friend? You Magdalene?'

The girl shook her head.

'How about you, Marie?'

She did the same.

'Well she must have spoken to someone. Where did she sleep?'

They pointed to a mass of webbing above our heads.

'Hammocks,' I frowned. 'Yes, I see. Not much opportunity for girly chit-chat there.'

'We're not allowed to speak after dark.'

'The rule of silence,' I nodded. 'We have the same rule at the abbey. But no-one takes much notice of it. I dare say you don't either. I bet you whisper under the bed-clothes. Was there something troubling Rebecca? Some little secret?'

They all just stared back at me. This was getting us nowhere and time was running out. But then I remembered something else:

'When Sister Agatha lay dying, it was Rebecca came to fetch me – you remember that? She wanted me to perform the last rite, to ease Agatha's final hours. She was very insistent as I remember.'

'She shouldn't have done that,' said Ursula.

I turned to her. 'Why not? Sister Agatha was passing from this life to the next. We all need the services of a priest at such times. I'm sure you were taught this in novice school.'

'Brother Lucatz was here,' said Magdalene.

'So was I.'

I looked at the six sets of eyes staring placidly back at me. This was getting nowhere and my time was nearly up. I had one last throw of the dice:

'Can anyone remember anything that Rebecca said or did that might help us understand what happened to her?'

They shook their heads. I realised that even if they had seen anything they may not have understood its significance. And now it was too late to continue. I could hear Dame Flora making noises outside.

'Well, thank you for your attention.'

I was about to leave when Sister Ursula suddenly stepped forward. 'Brother, did you mean what you said?'

'Said child? When?'

'At the service this morning.'

'The mass, you mean? Yes of course I meant it. What a strange thing to ask.'

She nodded and stepped back into line.

I waited. 'Is that it? Nothing more?'

No-one said anything else. I took one last look round the other faces. I was sure I was missing something but I didn't know what question to ask to

149

get at it. And even if I did I wouldn't have had a chance for Dame Flora already had the door open. As I came out, she went in.

Lucatz was still waiting outside and this time Captain Dunning and First Mate Benit were with him.

'Well, brother?' said Dunning. 'Did you discover anything?'

I shook my head. 'The sisters could offer no explanation as to what happened.'

'As I suspected. It was probably misadventure. It happens all the time at sea. Most likely she slipped on the wet deck and fell overboard.'

'In that case when did she remove her robe? Before or after she fell in the water?'

He conceded the point. 'You examined the robe. Did you find any evidence of foul play?'

'No, none. And without a body we're never likely to know.'

'I had some of the men scout about but they found nothing other than the robe,' said First Mate Benit.

'Shouldn't we extend the search further. Rebecca could still be alive out there somewhere.'

'Unlikely. No-one survives in the sea for very long. Take it from me brother, if she fell overboard she is beyond our help. We could search for a month and never find the body. It could wash ashore anywhere on the coast of England or France.'

I was shocked. 'Good Lord! It could travel so far?'

'The sea is a big place,' said Benit. 'Tides and currents can move a body over long distances.'

'There's nothing more to be done here,' said Dunning. 'Best we up anchor and get under way.'

'There is something I'd like to do,' I said. 'I'd like to speak to your men. I may be able to discover something.'

'As you did with the sisters?' Dunning shook his head. 'The crew are nervous enough as it is. I can't have you upsetting them further. They never liked the idea of so many women on board. They think it's bad luck.'

I scoffed. 'That's just superstition surely?'

'Call it what you will, brother. My primary concern has to be my ship. An unhappy crew is a problem crew and we've still a long way to go before we reach Bordeaux. If they start thinking the ship is jinxed we may never get there. In the absence of any other evidence, therefore, I will declare the nun's death a tragic accident and leave it at that.'

'What's troubling you?' asked Lucatz when the captain and Benit had gone.

'It's those young women. There's something odd about them.'

'Odd in what way?'

'I can't put my finger on it. They're not like ordinary nuns.'

'They are very young. Who knows what they really understand of the mass or anything else.'

'Why did you mention the mass? I didn't tell you Ursula asked about the mass.'

'She mentioned it to me. I shouldn't worry about it. Once they get to Languedoc they will change. I'm sure they will develop and mature with time.'

I was sure they would too, but into what?

151

Chapter Fourteen
THE BODIES BEGIN TO MOUNT UP

Day fifteen of our journey and we at last rounded the headland off the coast of Brest and entered the Bay of Biscay, that great bite out of the corner of Europe where sea and weather collide in one great hurly-burly of nature. We could expect some rough seas and strong winds from now on – or so Hogtie informed me. As for me, my mind was in a hurly-burly of its own going over again what had happened to the two sisters.

Of the two deaths Agatha's was the more easily explainable. She was old and weak and the stresses of a sea voyage had simply proved too much for her. At least, that's what I had assumed at the time. Now I wasn't so sure. I know I wasn't fully alert when Rebecca summoned me to Agatha's bedside but I was sure I heard her say Agatha had willed her own death. I wasn't dreaming it. So why would she later deny it? And then there was that parting comment of Agatha's: "It's been nice knowing you, brother". So final, as though she knew we would never see each other again. The sort of thing someone might say if they were deliberately starving themselves to death. But why would she do that? Self-murder was as much a crime as murdering another. Life was given to us by God, it is for Him alone to take it away.

And now Rebecca gone too. She certainly didn't starve herself to death. Of the remaining nuns Rebecca was by far the most mature. So how does a healthy young woman in the prime of life simply fall off a ship? The Channel had been calm for days. Nothing to jolt anyone into losing their footing. And if she had gone overboard what had happened to the body?

There was another obvious answer to Rebecca's disappearance of course, the one favoured by Dame Flora, that someone – some *man* presumably – had forced himself upon her and the resulting tussle had ended in tragedy. As much as I resisted the idea Lucatz was right, it couldn't be ruled out. But who amongst us was capable of such an evil act?

'Still trying to work it out, *mon frère*?'

'Hm?'

I turned to see Lucatz standing behind me.

I shook my head. 'It's an impossible conundrum.'

'Accidents happen at sea, Walter. Can you not accept that?'

'I could except this one doesn't make any sense.'

'What is there to make sense of? Rebecca fell overboard and drowned. Captain Dunning said as much himself. A tragic but all too common event.'

'I would agree - except for one thing: her robe. How did she lose it?'

He shrugged. 'It came off in the water in her struggle.'

'The way those nuns are trussed up? It'd take a tempest.'

'Perhaps she removed it herself despite what Dame Flora asserts to the contrary.'

'And then threw it in the sea after her?'

He nodded. 'So then you think someone else removed it - by force presumably. But in that case there would be signs of a struggle. And we've already established there weren't any.'

'No, not if she was knocked out first.'

'That was Dame Flora's suggestion. I thought you'd pooh-poohed the idea.'

'Then let's try it and see.'

'What?'

'Yes, come on,' I said suddenly galvanized. 'I'll be the attacker. You be Rebecca.'

'Oh no Walter, please.'

'We want to see if it's possible don't we?'

'You just want to prove Dame Flora wrong.'

'I want to find out what really happened.'

He sighed. 'Oh, very well. What do you want me to do?'

'I've been thinking about it. If she was attacked it would have to have been at night. If it happened during the day someone could have seen it. Very well, it's night-time. I see you standing alone by the bulwark. I creep up behind you and hit you over the head – *Bosh!*'

I made pretend to hit him on the back of the head.

'You collapse onto the deck.' I paused. 'Well go on then, collapse.'

He wrinkled his nose. 'You want me to lie down on this filthy deck?'

'Sorry if it offends you delicate French sensibilities.'

He grumbled something inaudible but started to ease himself down onto his knees.

'Not like that,' I frowned. 'You've just been whacked on the head not invited to a prayer meeting. You *fall* down heavily with a thump.'

'Unless her attacker caught her on her way down.'

I nodded. 'Good point. All right, let's assume he catches her and lays her down gently on her back.'

Lucatz did so.

'He removes her robe - it's all right, you can leave yours on. He has his evil way with her – I won't do that either,' I grinned.

'Undergarments,' said Lucatz.

'What?'

'If he's going to ravish her he will have to remove more than just her robe.'

'Yes, quite so. Well, assuming he manages to get through that lot he then drags her unconscious body over to the bulwark, heaves it up over the side, drops it in the ocean and throws her robe in after her.'

I went through the motions.

'Well, what do you think?'

Lucatz shook his head. 'Not very likely. Not without arousing the suspicion of the men of the watch keeping their eyes and ears open for the slightest disturbance.'

'And they'd have to be deaf as well as blind not to have noticed,' I agreed.

'Then we are back to it being an accident again. Rebecca, for whatever reason, simply fell overboard.'

'In which case why didn't she scream?'

Lucatz shrugged and shook his head.

'There's something else,' I went on. 'Captain Dunning said the body must have been swept away by the ocean currents.'

'So?'

155

'So how come the robe didn't get swept away with her? It remained yet the body didn't.'

'Maybe it sank.'

'Bodies don't sink, they float. I've seen enough of them to know.'

'In rivers and ponds perhaps. This is the ocean.'

I shook my head. 'Makes no difference.'

'Well I don't know,' he said getting back up on his feet. 'Maybe she got eaten by sharks, or giant octopuses.'

I gave him a disparaging look.

'All right, maybe not giant octopuses. But if it wasn't an accident or foul play, what else is there?'

'Only one other possibility.'

'Which is?'

'She never left the ship.'

He looked aghast. 'No,' he shook his head vehemently. 'She must have done. The robe was in the water.'

'But not the body.'

'Then where is she? This isn't a big ship. There aren't too many places to hide a body. Dame Flora and I searched and found nothing.'

'Maybe you didn't search hard enough. At the time everything was a bit confused. You could easily have missed something.'

'I sense you are going to search yourself?'

'I think I must.'

'Then, *bonne chance, mon frère.*'

Having talked myself into it I suppose I had better get on and search the ship. But where to begin? Lucatz was right, the *Gretchen* wasn't a very big vessel. There weren't too many places to hide a body. The main deck was open to the skies and the hutches could barely conceal a smile never mind a body. The obvious place to look was the lower deck. I have to say the thought of searching down there filled me with revulsion. I hadn't enjoyed my first venture into this foul netherworld and had hoped I would never need to go there again. But I owed it to Rebecca to try. As I gazed into the gaping opening to the lower deck the *Gretchen* seemed to groan like a great whale daring me to enter. There was nothing else for it. Hesitantly, with my robe held across my mouth and nose, I descended into the bowels of the monster like a latter-day Jonah.

It was certainly dark down there. It was also cramped and the stench was overpowering even with my robe over my nostrils. Being below the waterline there were no openings to let in daylight and the animals were deliberately kept in permanent darkness in order to keep them subdued. I groped my way about hoping my eyes would get used to the dark eventually constantly aware of various shapes moving around – rats, beetles, cockroaches, toads, and Heaven alone knew what else. The floor beneath my feet felt squidgy and mobile and the air was foul and hot. Despite the heat I shivered.

I soon realised I was on a hopeless quest. No-one alive could survive down here. If there was a body concealed here it would take more than a casual inspection to find it. The entire lower deck would have to be systematically searched. I was wasting my time. Then something snorted close to my ear. Startled, I raised my rush-light and saw a pair of eyes blinking back at me.

'Rebecca?'

Another noise.

'Who's there?'

Something barged past me. I lost my footing, struck my head on a beam and fell. The last thing I remember before the world flashed away in a blaze of pain and light was a pair of eyes staring down at me.

I awoke in my hutch with Lucatz leaning over me and a cold wet compress on my brow.

I sat up with a jolt. 'Aow my head! What happened?'

'You were knocked out.'

'Again?'

'You do seem to be making a habit of it. It's lucky you didn't drown.'

'How long was I out for this time?'

'Only a few minutes. Your cousin Bruno found you.'

'Bruno? What was he doing down there?'

'Looking for you.'

'*Looking* for me? Or *following* me?'

'He was concerned about you.'

I snorted. 'The only thing Bruno is concerned about is my money.'

Lucatz went over to the bench to wring out his cloth. 'Did you manage to find anything?'

'No half-naked nuns. No bodies. I managed to search most of the lower deck before I was ... incapacitated.'

'So that's it then? You've finally given up the idea of finding a body?'

'Not quite yet. There's still one last place. The master's cabin.'

Lucatz spun round. 'Walter, you're not serious? Captain Dunning will never permit you to search his quarters.'

'I don't intend asking him.'

'You remember his reaction last time you were somewhere you shouldn't ought to be? Are you willing to risk his wrath again? His own cabin?'

'I don't think we've any choice. It's the only place we haven't tried.'

'We?'

'Well, you wouldn't want me to go in alone,' I grinned.

'Oh no Walter, *je refuse. Absolument. Non!*'

'You won't have to do anything. Well, not much anyway. Just keep watch for me while the captain's out of his cabin. I'll be in and out before you know it.'

'And if he returns while you are still in there?'

'Whistle a warning.'

'I cannot whistle.'

'Well sing then.'

'Sing what?'

'Anything. The Te Deum.'

'I don't know the words.'

'Don't be ridiculous. Every monk knows the words to the Te Deum. Oh come on Lucatz, this isn't like you. Where's your sense of adventure? Of course, if you'd rather I was caught…?'

'You *will* get caught. I guarantee it.'

'Then you know what to do to prevent it.'

I stood up – rather too quickly and had to put out a hand to steady myself. Maybe the whack on the head was worse than I thought. There was movement on the deck above our heads. I glanced out the cabin window as a shadow went by.

'Look, Dunning's leaving his cabin. Here's our chance. Come on. I'll be in and out before you can say "nun".'

'Walter, wait!'

Before he could object further I was out the door and making my way towards the stairs connecting the main and the quarterdecks. Behind me Lucatz made a noise like a strangled tomcat - clearing his throat ready to sing, no doubt.

I don't know what I expected to find inside Dunning's hutch but I was much surprised. It was more spacious and more permanently built that the passenger accommodation, but with so many accoutrements there was hardly any spare room, certainly not enough to hide a body. It gave me a fascinating insight into our captain. His hutch was certainly better ordered than I'd imagined. There was the sort of paraphernalia you'd expect to find in a sea-captain's quarters: a sleeping cot, a stool, many strange items from exotic lands and bits of animal I couldn't put a name to. Everything was carefully stowed as you'd expect from someone used to living on a permanently moving world. There were also, to my surprise, books. Not many but some of the titles were surprising. Books on natural philosophy, theology, astrology. I have to say I was impressed. I'd never have had the master of the *Gretchen* down as a literary fellow.

So absorbed was I with Dunning's library that I didn't hear Lucatz's warning - assuming there was one. It was while I was leafing through a copy of *Geographia* by the second century Greek mathematician, Ptolemy, that I caught sight of something bright and shiny behind me.

Quick as a flash and using Ptolemy as a club, I swung round and with all the force I possessed I clouted my assailant across the head with it. He let out a yelp and fell to the floor dropping the knife as he did so. I raised Ptolemy to have another go at him when I saw who it was:

'Bruno! Again?'

He was sitting on the floor looking up at me, dazed and rubbing his head. 'What was that for?'

'What do you think? You attacked me.'

'I did not.'

'You did. You had a knife.'

'Of course I have a knife. Everybody has knives.'

'Not unsheathed they don't. And what were you doing in the lower deck earlier? Don't deny it. Lucatz saw you.'

'I was looking out for you.'

'Pah! Looking out for me! Looking to do me harm more like.'

'Why do you always say things like that? I don't want to harm you.'

'Not much you don't.'

But there was no more time to argue. A shadow went past the louvre window. Captain Dunning was returning.

'Quick!' I said to him. 'Get up!'

He was still staggering to his feet as the door opened and Dunning appeared looking … what? Shocked? Angry?

'Ah, ha-ha, captain, there you are. We were just looking for you. No doubt you are wondering why we are here.' So was I. I would have to think quick.

'I know why your cousin's here,' said Dunning nodding at Bruno.

'You do?'

'He came to shave me.'

'To *shave* you?' I looked at Bruno in astonishment.

161

'That's what I was trying to tell you,' whispered Bruno. 'That's why I had the knife.'

'Since when were you a barber?' I whispered back.

'Since I needed money.'

'So brother,' said Dunning. 'That's why he's here. Why are you?'

'Me? I came ... to assist.'

I quickly bobbed to the floor and retrieved the tin bowl which I had knocked out of Bruno's hand when I hit him. Water had splashed all over the floor – and over poor Ptolemy.

Dunning leaned forward and peered into the bowl. 'It's empty.'

'So it is.'

The situation was farcical and I could see no way out and retain my dignity. Fortunately just at that moment Lucatz appeared at the door saving me from further embarrassment. I was still furious with him for not having warned me of Dunning's approach, but from the look on his face he had something else on his mind.

'Captain, you must come at once. You too, Walter.'

'Why? What's happened now?'

'There have been two more.'

'Two more what?'

'Nuns.'

We all bundled out of the cabin and onto the quarterdeck. A sea mist had come up and hung like a veil over everything so that it was difficult to see clearly. But hanging from the yard-arm it was just possible to make out two figures, their arms outstretched in a grotesque imitation of the crucified Christ. Even through the mist there was no doubting from their robes they were two of the sisters although it was impossible to tell which ones – both had those ridiculous veils shielding their faces. On the deck below several members of the crew had gathered to gaze up at them in wonder. Some had even fallen to their knees and were adopting attitudes of prayer.

For a moment no-one moved or said anything, we all just stared up at the appalling sight above us. But then the sail flapped momentarily taking the two figures out of sight. When it flapped again a gasp went up from the crew. The space where they had been was empty. The two nuns had vanished.

Chapter Fifteen
SPIRALLING DOWNWARDS

Captain Dunning, First Mate Benit, Lucatz, Bruno and I held a crisis meeting in the captain's cabin. An air of incredulity bordering on panic permeated the place. Losing one nun was bad enough. Losing two more in full view of the entire ship's company was potentially disastrous. These the captain couldn't simply brush off as a freak accident.

'Where did they go?' he asked with incredulity. 'Did anyone see?'

We all shook our heads.

'One moment they were there,' said Lucatz. 'The next -' He opened his hands like a conjurer performing a magic trick.

'Well someone must have seen something. They can't simply have vanished. Mister Benit?'

'I've spoken to the men,' said the first mate. 'They all say the same. No-one saw the nuns climb up. No-one saw them climb down.'

'What about the barrel-boy?' I suggested. 'He was closest.'

Benit shook his head. 'In this fog. You don't always see what you think you see. It plays tricks on the eyes.'

'Conveniently,' said the captain.

'Or deliberately,' said Bruno.

We all looked at him. Frankly I didn't know why Bruno was there other than the fact that he happened to be in the captain's cabin when Lucatz brought us the news.

Bruno coloured, unused to the attention. 'I j-just meant that if I wanted to disappear I'd pick a day like today to do it,' he stammered. 'That's all.'

'There speaks the voice of experience,' I sneered.

Bruno glared at me.

'No, he's right,' said Benit. 'A foggy day. It's an ideal time to disappear.'

'But why would they want to?'

'Some kind of female hysteria?' suggested the captain.

I shook my head. 'That theory has been discredited. The idea that the womb – or to give it its Greek name, the *hystera* – wanders around the body causing temporary insanity is now dismissed by most medical schools,' I nodded sententiously. 'That's the latest thinking at any rate,' I blushed.

Now it was Bruno's turn to sneer.

'Maybe they had no choice,' suggested Lucatz.

'Go on,' said Dunning willing to consider any theory.

'Well, you hear of such things, don't you? A ship found floating in the open sea, things left casually lying about: a book open at the last page read; a meal half-eaten on the table. All seems perfectly normal - except there is no-one on board. It's as though everyone had suddenly got up and left. Except this is a ship at sea. There is nowhere to go. I do not know what this is in English but in French we call it *un navire fantôme*.'

165

'A ghost ship,' I translated. 'You really think that's what's happening to the *Gretchen*? That we are all going to be spirited away starting with the nuns?'

'I'm simply saying stranger things happen at sea,' said Lucatz. 'I'm sure the captain will bear me out. Mister Benit mentioned the fog and the tricks it can play. We know demons can conjure such things and shroud themselves in order to carry out their evil deeds.'

I looked at him with incredulity. 'You're suggesting demons caused the nuns to disappear? Lucatz, are you being serious?'

'It is what some of the crew are saying,' agreed Benit. 'They never liked the idea of so many women aboard. They think they are a bad omen.'

'That's nonsense,' I said firmly. 'And dangerous nonsense. Women travel all the time on ships. Look at the number of women pilgrims who travel to the Holy Land.'

'Nevertheless,' said Dunning, 'notions like that can have unforeseen consequences.'

'What consequences?'

'Consequences,' he repeated.

A noise from the door interrupted our deliberations. Dame Flora was standing there. She must have been there for some time listening to what was being said. She now came in and glared around the table at each of us in turn.

'So,' she nodded slowly. 'This is where the conspirators congregate.'

'Conspirators madam?' frowned Dunning.

'What else would you call it? Men sitting around discussing my ladies, making decisions about them no doubt. Why was I not invited?'

'It wasn't deliberate,' said Dunning. 'We just happened to be here when the nuns ... when they ...'

'You have no word for it, captain. Then let me suggest one: Harassment.' She then glared around the table settling at last on me. I might have guessed sooner or later it would come back to me.

'The prioress thinks it's my fault the nuns have disappeared, captain,' I sighed wearily. 'Isn't that right, Dame Flora?'

'You were the one interrogating them.'

'I didn't interrogate them. I merely invited the sisters to respond to some questions I had about Sister Rebecca - who, I would remind Dame Flora, had already disappeared *before* I spoke to the others.'

'Aye,' she nodded. 'And now two more are missing.'

'Who is it this time?' asked Lucatz. 'Do we know?'

'Ursula and Magdalene. The very two Brother Walter catechized.'

'Catechized,' I snorted. I looked round at the others who were all now staring accusingly at me. 'I admit it was Ursula and Magdalene I spoke to. Or rather, they spoke to me. They were the only ones who dared. The others were too afraid.' I returned Flora's glare.

'My ladies are afraid of nothing,' insisted Flora.

'Nonsense! They're terrified of you. You can see it in their faces. Small wonder they want to jump off masts.'

'Please,' said Lucatz. 'Can't we stop this bickering? It helps nobody.'

'Brother Lucatz is right,' agreed Dunning. 'We should present a united front – for the sake of the crew if nothing else. But Brother Walter is also right. Talk of omens is dangerous. It's like a canker if

167

allowed to spread. What we need is to do something positive to show we are on top of it.'

'Left to me none of this would have happened,' insisted Flora.

'Could we not try to recover the bodies?' Lucatz suggested. 'They must be out there somewhere.'

Benit was shaking his head. 'We could go round in circles for days and still not find anything.'

'I tell you what we are going to do,' said Dunning decisively. 'In two days' time we are due to pick up supplies in Saint Nazaire. We will inform the French authorities there and they can look for the bodies - or not, as they see fit. This is their country after all. In the meantime we should all keep our heads. And please, try not to lose any more nuns.'

When the meeting broke up Lucatz took me to one side:

'Be careful how you handle the prioress, Walter my friend. She is very *agité*. Understandably after what has happened.'

'I'm not the one making wild accusations.'

'No. But it would be best if you avoided each other, for the time being at least. Just until we know more about what has happened to the sisters.'

'Do you think we will?'

From the look on his face I think I could guess the answer.

I still had some unfinished business with Bruno. I found him skulking alone in our cabin.

'Remembered where you live then?'

'I needed to lie down,' he frowned rubbing a bump on the side of his head where I'd struck him. 'I'm injured. You really hurt me, you know?'

'Here, let me see.'

I examined his head. There was a lump. Quite a palpable one, too, I was pleased to see. Good to see Ptolemy being useful for once. But the skin wasn't broken, or the bone underneath as far as I could tell, more's the pity.

'You'll live,' I told him. 'Lucky for you you've got such a thick skull.'

I infused some animal fat with aniseed and began rubbing it into the lump.

'We didn't finish our earlier conversation. You were going to tell me what were you doing in the lower deck.'

'Like I said. I was looking out for you.'

'How did you know I was down there?'

'I didn't. I followed Lucatz.'

I stopped rubbing his bump. 'Lucatz went onto the lower deck? When?'

'Just before you.'

'That's odd. He'd already searched down there. Did he say why he was down there?'

'I didn't ask.'

I finished rubbing the infusion into Bruno's scalp and then bound it with a bandage soaked in another infusion made from a deer's anal gland that I normally use to soften the hard skin on the soles of shepherds' feet. I also used it to keep rats away. Nothing to do with bumps on the head.

He sniffed. 'God, that stuff stinks.'

'Does it? Good. It might keep you out of the contessa's cabin for a while.'

'Thanks very much.'

'Don't mention it.'

I went out on deck in order to try to clear my head. A pointless exercise. There was no air. The fog was still lying thick and with no wind it wasn't moving, and nor was the ship. The sail hung limp and useless in the rigging. In all likelihood the bodies of the two sisters were floating just a short distance away and on a clear day they would be easy to recover. But with this fog I could barely see a dozen yards beyond the bulwarks. It was so frustrating.

I could, however, see a change in the mood of the *Gretchen's* crew. Normally a cheerful bunch ready with a bit of good-humoured banter, they seemed more subdued than usual and reluctant to meet my eye. This was worrying. Four of them were sitting now on a pile of ropes looking morose so that I felt obliged to say something:

'You men think because of what has happened here today this ship is cursed – am I right?'

They exchanged embarrassed looks between themselves.

'Well I can tell you it is not. There is a simple explanation for what happened and I assure you we – that is Captain Dunning, First Mate Benit, Brother Lucatz and I – will discover the answer.'

'Not before we are all murdered,' said one.

'No-one is going to be murdered,' I assured them. 'I know at the moment you feel powerless and fearful but you must not despair. We live in an age of reason. We are in control of our own destinies. So therefore I say unto you trust in yourselves, your ship and your captain, but most of all trust in God and all will be well. In light of which I would ask you to join me now in a short prayer.'

God, I sounded pompous. But it's how one has to address the lower orders. Besides, someone had to maintain authority on this wretched ship. I waited. Reluctantly, one by one, they got to their feet and took up an attitude of suitable humility. Once all were up I laid my hands on the heads of two of them and closed my eyes:

'Oh God of the sea and of the land, guard and protect these thy servants. Give them peace and a calm voyage and bring them wholly and safely to port, for thy Son's sake.'

They responded with a reluctant "*Amen*".

I then made a perfunctory sign of the Cross. '*In nomine patris et filii et spiritus sancti.*'

'That wor a nice a little speech, brother,' grinned Hogtie from the bulwark.

I went over to him. 'I thought someone ought to say something. This talk of omens is unhealthy. It's depressing the men. And you're no help with your talk of throwing women overboard.'

'I did warn 'ee. Sailors be a superstitious guild. Specially where women is concerned.'

'Enough for one of them to do something about it?'

'You mean one of the crew threw them nuns o'erboard?' Hogtie shook his head. 'Don't rightly see how. There weren't no-one near when they two little nuns vanished.'

'You were closer than most. Did you see anything?'

'They was strapped to the yard arm. The sail filled. They was gone.'

'Into thin air,' I nodded. 'That's what we all saw. Or maybe something a little more solid.'

He eyed me sideways. 'You should be careful, brother. You don't want no dangerous talk.'

'I have to consider every possibility. An attack by one of the men. It's a reasonable assumption. A group of young women at sea for a month guarded only by two monks. It must be a temptation.'

'Not with a dragon worth two o' thee,' he grinned. 'I think you be safer to believe it wor a sprite, brother.'

'What do you believe?'

'What I sees with my own eyes.'

'And what's that?'

He nodded towards the French coast about half a mile distant. Through breaks in the fog it was possible to make out a figure on the shoreline sitting astride a donkey that seemed to be keeping pace with the ship. I could tell he was a monk of some description, his distinctive black and white robe was plain to see. But it was not an order I recognized.

'He been following us for two days now,' said Hogtie.

'Any idea who he is?'

'Well, he be no sprite, that's for sure.'

There was one person who'd been even closer to the nuns than Hogtie when they disappeared. Someone with a bird's-eye view of the world - literally. The barrel-boy was one of the youngest members of the crew. Young eyes see clearer and further than older ones. If anyone should be in a position to see what happened to the nuns surely it must be he. Captain Dunning had forbidden me to climb to the crow's nest after my last attempt and I was no keener to be up after my little wobble. But these were special circumstances. I felt it my duty to explore every possibility. And if I was quick in this fog no-one would see me. Taking my courage in both hands, therefore, I shinned up the mast before anyone could stop me.

At the top the barrel-boy looked nervous as I heaved my leg over the side.

'You shouldn't be up here, brother,' he said backing away. 'Last time I got in trouble.'

'Don't worry. No-one saw me. And if they did I'll take the blame.'

'Come to do some more experimenting?' he asked hopefully.

'In a way. I've come to test your powers of observation.' I peered out to the horizon. 'You can see everything from here, can't you? You have a unique vantage point.'

'If you say so, brother.'

'What about the shore? It's a little hidden by the mist today I know, but most days you must be able to see it, am I right? Villages on the shoreline? Church towers? That sort of thing?'

He nodded cautiously.

'And the coast road? You can see that from up here too?'

He nodded again.

'What about people on the road? The reason I ask is because there's been a report of a man on the coast road the past few days. I wondered if you'd noticed him at all. He'd be dressed like me in a monk's habit. Sitting on an ass, possibly keeping pace with the *Gretchen*. Do you think you might have seen someone like that?'

'Only monk I seen is you, brother. And Brother Lucatz.'

'Yes of course,' I smiled. 'So there's nothing you can tell me about this man?'

The boy shook his head.

I sighed. 'Never mind. It was just a wild shot. What I really wanted to ask you was about the two nuns.'

At their mention he immediately clammed up. 'Don't know nothin' about them nuns.'

I was taken aback by his sudden vehemence. 'But you did see them. You must have done. Everyone else did even from way down on the deck. You were barely ten feet away.'

'I didn't see nothin' brother.'

I frowned slightly annoyed. 'Has someone been speaking to you? Before you answer, remember who I am. Lying to a member of the clergy is a serious matter. It could imperil your soul.'

The boy looked frightened. He lowered his eyes. 'We been told not to talk about it.'

'By who? Who told you that?'

He just shook his head. But it didn't take much guessing did it? First Mate Benit. The boy was clearly confused and it wasn't fair to bully him. Besides, I wasn't sure who he was more afraid of, God, me or Mister Benit. I'd have to try something else.

'I tell you what. You don't have to talk about it. Let's play a game instead.'

He looked up warily. 'What sort of game?'

'A simple question-and-answer game. I ask you a question. All you do is shake your head if the answer's no. If the answer's yes you say nothing. A bit like "O'Grady Says".'

He looked at me blank.

'You must have played "O'Grady Says" when you were a child. No? What a sad childhood you must have had. Well, never mind. Let's give it a try anyway. Are you ready?'

He nodded cautiously.

'First question: Is my name Brother Lucatz?'

He gave a lopsided grin and shook his head which meant no.

'Is my name Brother Walter?'

No reply which meant yes.

'There, that was easy wasn't it?' I nodded encouragingly. 'You're good at this – well done! Now, let's try another question. Did you see the nuns climb up the mast?'

He looked at me hesitantly.

'Oh come on, it's a simple enough question. Did you see them, yes or no? Shake your head if the answer's no.'

He shook his head. Pity. I was hoping he could tell me how they got up here.

'But you did see them when they were up here?'

No response. So he had seen them.

'Did they speak? Did they say anything at all?'

He shook his head again.

'You've no idea why they were here?'

Again no.

'All right. Now this is the big one. We all saw them disappear. The question is did they jump or did they fall? Sorry, that's two questions. Start with the first: Did they jump?'

He shook his head.

'Then they fell?'

Again he shook his head.

I frowned. 'Well they must have done one or the other. They certainly didn't climb down. Perhaps they were pushed?'

The boy's face contorted with frustration and confusion again. He'd clearly seen something and wanted to tell me what it was. I could probably bully

175

it out of him but I didn't have the heart. And now the fog was starting to dissipate. Stay here much longer and someone down below would notice me.

'All right. Don't distress yourself. I'd better climb back down anyway, if I can stomach it.' I put my leg over the side of the barrel and started to climb out.

'They didn't -' the boy began.

I stopped half in and half out. 'Didn't what?'

He hesitated. 'What you said - jump or fall.'

'So someone did push them?'

'Not that either.'

'Then what did they do?'

The boy's eyes widened with awe. 'They flew.'

I frowned. 'They what?'

'It's like I told Mr Benit. They spread their wings and -' He held his arms out wide either side. 'And they just flew away.'

Back in my cabin I tried to make sense of what the boy said. First omens, then ghost ships and now flying nuns. The stories were becoming more bizarre by the hour. Clearly the nuns did not fly. The boy had misinterpreted what he'd seen somehow. Maybe Lucatz was right and the sea was having a strange effect on everybody. Or Benit was right and it was the fog. To make matters worse my head was spinning again and wasn't helped by the noises coming from the next hutch. I could hear laughing and screeching. Bruno and the contessa at their exercise again.

'Henri, you're doing it wrong.'

'Perhaps if we were to change places, my lady?'

'No no, I am comfortable as I am. In any case it's your turn this time. Take hold of your piece! Put it here. No, not there, here! Good God, am I to do all?'

Take hold of his piece? Change places? Had they no shame? Well, this was one aberration I was determined to put a stop to. Angrily, I stamped out of my own hutch and burst in to the contessa's expecting to catch the two of them *in flagrante delicto* -

And stopped.

Bruno, still with his bandage wrapped around his head, was facing the contessa across the little bed. Between them was a wooden board on which was inscribed some lines together with some counters. I'd seen this game before. The novices play it in the abbey cloisters where the board is even scratched into surface of the stone bench. Nine Men's Morris it is called. A childish game. All perfectly innocent if a little juvenile. Even Samson used to join in sometimes.

Bruno was holding his "piece" – his counter - in his hand ready to play his turn.

He shrugged when he saw me. 'I learnt to play as a child. I'm very good at it.'

'To while away the hours,' added the contessa with a smirk. 'Care to join us, brother?'

Chapter Sixteen
SAINT NAZAIRE

Day nineteen of our journey and we entered the mouth of the River Loire. This, I am reliably informed, is France's longest river rising somewhere in the south of the country and flowing north and west for several hundred miles before emptying into the Atlantic. At this end the river forms the border between the duchy of Brittany and the county of Anjou which is the county from where the present king's grandfather, Henry Plantagenet, emerged to become first Duke of Normandy and then King Henry II of England. Five miles up the estuary on the northern shore lies the port of Saint Nazaire which was where we were scheduled to pick up more food supplies and drinking water.

Most of what I know about this town I learnt subsequently but the name itself held a certain piquancy for me, and no doubt for Lucatz as well, for Nazaire is the name of the saint to whom the cathedral in Béziers was dedicated. Béziers – may its name be forever etched in infamy - is a city some forty miles south west of Montpellier where Lucatz and I were medical students together. Those were happier times when a man's religious beliefs were his own and nobody asked questions. But then Pope Innocent III ascended the throne of Saint Peter and unleashed his war on the Cathars of Languedoc that still continues to this day. Ten years ago almost to the day Béziers was the location for one of the most shameful episodes in that war.

The story goes that on the twenty-second of July 1209 the pope's legate, Abbot Amalric of Citeaux, arrived at Béziers with his army and prepared to lay siege to the town warning that anyone who did not submit would be put to the sword. The bishop of Béziers tried to save the Catholic population by sacrificing the heretics, but to their credit the Catholics refused to hand over their Cathar neighbours. The bishop then offered to lead the Catholics out of the town in person and leave the Cathars to their fate, but this too they rejected reasoning that since Abbot Amalric could not distinguish Cathar from Catholic he would spare them all. Alas they were wrong. When Béziers finally surrendered Amalric ordered the massacre of everyone in the town, Catholic and Cathar alike, leaving it to God to sort out which was which. Thousands of Bézieries were slaughtered that day, the town torched and the fine cathedral of Saint Nazaire burnt to the ground.

None of which has any bearing on the port of Saint Nazaire in Brittany, of course, but I could not help recalling the tale as we approached the dock. Unlike in Jersey we had little difficulty in sailing the *Gretchen* right up to the harbour wall as here the river is deep enough to accommodate her draught. Once again the crew were refused permission to disembark this time for fear that they might desert which in light of recent events was a distinct possibility. Naturally the embargo didn't apply to the captain, Lucatz, Dame Flora and me who were to comprise the delegation to the town magistracy. Our mission was to persuade the mayor to send out a search party to recover the bodies of the three nuns, Rebecca, Theresa and Magdalene.

This was the first time we had docked since leaving Ipswich and I have to admit to a grudging admiration for the skill of the crew and of Captain Dunning who handled the vessel as though it were a child's toy on a duck-pond. We were not alone. Dozens of other vessels of every size and description were anchored near the sands all vying for the safest berth. Captain Dunning did well to secure one of the best.

I should perhaps just mention that ships from England have not always been welcomed in the ports of Brittany. Twenty years earlier when King John was endeavouring to succeed his brother Richard to the throne of England, Bretons favoured his nephew, the Prince Arthur, who was also their duke. As the son of John's older brother Geoffrey, Arthur had at least as good a claim to the throne as his uncle. In the ensuing succession struggle Arthur was defeated and his subsequent disappearance has left a lingering suspicion that King John had had him murdered. John is no longer around but Breton memories are long. As an English delegation, therefore, we did not know what sort of reception we would get.

When we got to the mayor's office my heart sank. There was a long queue of people outside the door, everyone from poor fishermen stinking of fish to elegantly-dressed burghers with pomanders and we had to wait our turn along with the rest. But a quiet word from Lucatz in the ear of one of the guards and we were miraculously ushered to the front of the queue.

'What did you say to him?' I whispered to Lucatz.

'I'll tell you later.'

Despite our misgivings Saint Nazaire's mayor turned out to be an affable sort of fellow albeit a wily old burgher with a business brain at least as acute as that of Abbot Samson. I recognized the type immediately. On the face of it he was all smiles and full of sympathy for our problem. He listened with compassion to our tale of disappearing nuns tutting and nodding in all the right places. And when it came to our request for assistance he could not have been more accommodating:

'*Mais bien sûr, nous allons vous aider à trouver ces femmes tragiques* – ah, forgive my poor English, she is not so good. Of course we will do all we can to help you find these tragic women,' he nodded profusely.

I could hardly believe our luck. Could it be he was actually going to help us look for the bodies? It seemed too good to be true. But then came the thunderbolt:

'Naturally you will wish to pay for this service.'

The four of us exchanged glances.

'We are but a poor fishing village, *mes amis*,' the mayor went on quickly, 'not a great trading port like Lon-Don. Recovering dead bodies for us is a costly business,' he smiled.

Gold buckles on his slippers; silver braid trimming his cap and enough gemstones on his fingers to sink a flotilla - he didn't look particularly poor to me.

'How much?' asked Dunning.

The mayor's forehead wrinkled painfully. 'Three bodies you say? This would require several boats. One would hardly be sufficient...'

'How much?' Dunning repeated.

'Then there are the wages of the crew. My staff in their supervision. They would have to forego their usual occupations of course...'

'How much?' said Dunning again.

The mayor sucked his teeth. '*Dix livres*.'

Dunning's eyes nearly popped out of his head. 'Ten pounds? I could commission a new ship for that!'

'As indeed you are perfectly at liberty to do, *mon capitaine*,' smiled the mayor. 'Of course such a vessel would take up berthing space required by other ships. Some of the other captains might object. There could be difficulties. Expensive difficulties...'

I was beginning to see what it was Lucatz had said to that guard that got us in early. Funny how the mayor's English improved when it came to the knotty subject of money.

'I think we should pay,' said Dame Flora turning to the captain in all seriousness. 'My ladies deserve to be recovered whatever the cost. If we delay there may not be much left to find.'

'There is that as well of course,' agreed the mayor shaking his head sadly.

'Do you have ten pounds, madam?' Dunning asked Dame Flora through gritted teeth.

'No of course not.'

'Neither do I.'

So saying, he stood up abruptly and made a sort of gurgling noise in his throat before storming out followed in some disarray by the three of us.

The mayor shrugged and turned his attention to the next waiting supplicant.

'I suppose we could try hiring a boat of our own,' I said to Lucatz once we were outside again. 'It must be cheaper than bribing the mayor. Isn't there some legal procedure in such circumstances?'

But Lucatz just shook his head. 'Do not even think of it, *mon frère*. This is not England. The king of France is a long way away. Here the mayor is all. Nothing gets done without his say so.'

'Unless you grease his palm. How much did you promise him?'

'Clearly not enough.'

'So that's it then? We do nothing?'

'I fear so.'

'But we can't just leave them. Three bodies just abandoned.'

'What do you suggest? You heard the first mate. We could go around in circles and never find them. Captain Dunning has a responsibility to the living as well as the dead. We must continue our journey.'

I was disappointed. This wasn't the Lucatz I knew. In the old days he would have relished a challenge like this.

I looked round. 'Where is the captain? And the prioress? We seem to have lost them.'

'The captain went off in something of a choler. I did not see what happened to Dame Flora. I will look for them.' He started to walk off.

'I'll come too.'

'No. Better you go back to the ship in case they return. We will all meet later.'

So saying he disappeared into the crowd before I could follow.

I got back to the quayside as the *Gretchen* was finishing loading up our supplies. This was the first opportunity I'd had since leaving Ipswich to see the ship from the outside. I realised now my impression of a rickety derelict was far from the truth and I felt a grudging admiration for the builders. How long is a cob like this supposed to last, I wondered? Five years? Ten? This one must be at least that. It had been patched and repaired several times but its underlying construction looked sound to my untutored eye. For nineteen days this leviathan had been our home. Only a few days more if Hogtie was to be taken at his word. Three weeks he had estimated it would take to get us from Ipswich to Bordeaux. Well, three weeks would be up in two days' time and I for one would not be sorry when they were. While my feelings for the old girl had softened somewhat the thought of adding more days to our journey in the probably fruitless search for the bodies did not appeal.

As I approached the gangplank I could see First Mate Benit standing guard at its foot – to discourage any would-be deserters, no doubt. I'm sure it would work. The sight of Mister Benit toying with his whip would deter any who might be thinking to abscond. He would certainly put me off. I have to say I found difficult to like our first mate. I was sure he was excellent at his job but there was no humanity to the man. I supposed that's what it takes to be second in command of a ship like this. Still, like him or not, there was no reason to abandon the normal civilities. I gave him good day as I approached.

'You are alone brother?' he said glancing about me.

'The others decided to do some last minute shopping,' I quipped.

'Your cousin too?'

'Bruno?' I groaned. 'Don't tell me he went ashore.'

'As soon as you were out of sight.'

'I asked him not to. I hope he doesn't delay us,' I said peering over the heads of the crowds.

'He won't do that,' said Benit. 'If he isn't here by the time the captain is ready to weigh anchor he will be left behind.'

'That may not be an entirely bad idea,' I mused.

'How went your meeting with the mayor?'

'Let's just say we didn't get all we were after.'

'They refused to send out a search vessel?'

'Oh, they would have done – for a price.'

He nodded. 'That sounds like the French.'

'Unfortunately without the bodies we are unlikely to know what happened. I, erm, don't suppose you have any ideas about that?'

Benit shook his head.

'Clearly not the barrel-boy's explanation.'

He gave me a steady look.

'Flying nuns?'

He continued to eye me steadily. 'You've spoken to the boy?'

I nodded. 'Two days ago. Up in his nest.'

'You went up there again? Despite Captain Dunning's orders? I wonder what he would say if he knew.'

'Are you going to tell him? If so I would have to mention that you ordered the boy to keep quiet about what he saw. I wonder what he'd think to that.'

Benit took a step closer to within a few inches of me. I have to admit I found him intimidating and his breath overpowering, but I was determined to stand my ground. He lowered his voice:

'Brother, I have a dozen men under my command. They already think the ship is cursed and this business with the nuns has unnerved them further. Some are even calling for the remaining women to

185

be put ashore. How do you think they would react if they started hearing stories about flying nuns?'

'Mister Benit, someone aboard the *Gretchen* is manipulating things,' I said equally quietly. 'Someone less ethereal than ghosts and spirits. I intend to find out who it is and when I do it will be more than Captain Dunning's displeasure they will need to fear.'

'Is that a threat, brother?'

'If you like.'

He took breath to say more, but before he could we were interrupted by some disturbance further along the quay. Lucatz had evidently found Dame Flora and the captain and all three were hastening back to the ship. They seemed to be in quite a hurry.

Dame Flora was first to arrive. She barged past me up the gangplank without a word. Next was Dunning barking his orders to Benit to cast off even before he was properly on board. Last came Lucatz.

'We must leave.'

'Why the rush? What's happened?'

Behind him I could see a crowd following. They looked angry.

'Not now, Walter. Just get aboard.'

I didn't argue but clambered after him. As soon as I was on board the gangplank was pulled up after me. But then I stopped:

'Wait! Bruno. Is he with you?'

'No – why, did he go ashore?'

'I don't know. Yes, I think so. We can't leave him.'

'We will have to. Look, the sail is filling. We are already moving.'

He was right. The gangplank had been withdrawn, the anchors weighed. First Mate Benit was barking orders, Captain Dunning was at his post on the quarterdeck. The ship was moving away fast from the dock even before the gates were fully shut. But where was Bruno? The mob on the quayside looked murderous shouting and waving their fists. Whatever I said to Benit I couldn't simply abandon him to the mob. But there was no way to stop the *Gretchen*. He had missed the boat.

Then I saw him. He was running along the quay and looking for somewhere to jump aboard. But there was nowhere. By now the gates had been closed and we were gathering speed and pulling further and further away from the dock.

'He's not going to make it,' I gasped.

It didn't stop him trying. At first he managed to keep pace with us while the crew were cheering him on. As we increased speed he was falling further and further back. Then – disaster! He stumbled and fell. The mob rushed towards him.

My heart was in my mouth. 'My God, they'll kill him!'

But then he was up and running again, and with one final desperate leap he hurled himself against the ship's webbing. My heart was in my mouth. There he hung suspended between life and death. I felt a surge as the rudder was hauled. The captain could not stop. The great ship swung and rolled dangerously half-keeling over. Bruno disappeared beneath the water and I gasped again. Surely he must have been swept away in the swell. For several moments he remained out of sight beneath the water. I was sure he would be gone, drowned or crushed beneath the hull. No-one could hold their breath for that long. But when the ship righted again, miracle of miracles, he was still there clinging on looking like a half-drowned rat. I crossed myself twice.

Willing hands now grabbed him and held him tight as the great ship swung again, its weight slewing the other way. At last he was hauled aboard to much applause from the rest of the crew and much angry jeering from the crowd on the dockside. Among them I couldn't help noticing were several guards from the mayor's office not looking at all pleased at having lost their quarry. Now facing into the harbour mouth a gust of wind caught the *Gretchen's* sail billowing it out. The great leviathan surged into the middle of the estuary and we were at last heading towards the open sea still being chased by smaller vessels. As my heart continued to pound I looked down at the panting, sodden Bruno lying on the deck. He was filthy, grazed and choking, but still alive - just.

Chapter Seventeen
A CONFUSION OF HABITS

We weren't out of the wood yet, to use an entirely inappropriate and non-nautical metaphor. We had left the quayside but were now being chased by a dozen vessels of all shapes and sizes each determined to stop us if they could. But they hadn't reckoned on Captain Dunning's skill as a navigator or the seamanship of his crew. Oh yes, we English aren't an island race for nothing! My chest swelled with pride as we dodged and weaved past every obstacle placed in our way, the tiller-man bearing down on the rudder first this way then that. I could appreciate now the advantage of a single central rudder as opposed to the cumbersome steering-boards of our pursuers. With every man working as one pulling on ropes, heaving on oars we raced for the harbour entrance. In this we were assisted by Dame Nature for the Loire estuary broadens very quickly towards its mouth giving us more room to manoeuvre than in the crowded confines of the harbour. We were soon speeding out into the wide-open Atlantic Ocean and leaving our pursuers far behind. A cheer went up from the men as it became clear we had managed to evade our would-be captors. Even the contessa, no particular friend of the English, was jumping up and down and screaming abuse in a most unladylike fashion. I was full of admiration. This is what can happen when we all pull together. One little English ship can defeat the entire French fleet. Eventually the last of our pursuers gave up the chase and was left behind in our wake. We had escaped. Time now to find out what we had escaped from. I started with Bruno:

'All right. What have you done?'

He looked up at me from the deck. 'Me? Nothing. Why is it always me?'

'Because you were the one being chased by half the town.'

'Not just me. They were after all of us.'

'Yes, but in your case probably for good reason.'

'You don't know that,' he scowled. 'How can you know that?'

'Bruno, I know you. You attract trouble like flies to a midden.'

'I was the one nearly drowned.'

'Pity you weren't. What were you doing ashore anyway? I told you to remain on board.'

At that he grew red in the face. 'I don't have to answer to you. I go where I please.' So saying he stormed off back to the cabins still dripping wet and wrapped in a blanket.

Lucatz frowned watching him go. 'You are a little hard on him at times, Walter.'

'It's only what he deserves. Anyway, you've changed your tune. Three weeks ago you were calling him a boor.'

'I don't think this time it was Bruno's fault. He was nowhere near when the trouble began.'

'What trouble? What happened in Saint Nazaire that put half the town in uproar?'

'Kismet. We happened to be in the wrong place at the wrong time.'

'I think you'd better explain.'

He led me over to a coil of rope and sat down.

'After our abortive negotiation with *monsieur le maire*, you remember we all got separated.'

'That's right. You went off to find the others while I returned to the ship.'

Lucatz nodded. 'Well, I found the captain and the prioress at the very moment that *une clameur* – how do you say? A hue-and-cry - went up. A man had been murdered nearby.'

'Good lord!' I said, truly shocked. 'And they thought you had done it? Is that why they were chasing you?'

'It would appear so, yes.'

'Ha! What a ridiculous idea! You murdering a man indeed!' I looked at him. 'You didn't did you?'

'No, of course not,' he frowned. 'I just happened to be closest to the body, that's all - and my being a foreigner...'

'Just a minute. A foreigner? But you're French.'

He gave a sardonic smile. '*Mon frère*, this is *Bretagne*. Here even Frenchmen are foreigners.'

'Why didn't you stay and proclaim your innocence?'

'I could have done so, it is true. I could have stood and argued my case with the mob. And no doubt in the fullness of time I would have been exonerated – posthumously of course.'

I saw his point.

'So you ran?'

'In the circumstances it seemed the sensible thing to do.'

'Thus confirming your guilt in the eyes of your pursuers?'

'*Inévitablement.*'

A spontaneous round of applause and cheering went up among the crew. By now the oarsmen had been stood down, the sail slackened off and the order was given to ease-to. I was pleased. All thought of mutiny now surely must be abandoned. A new spirit of comradeship seemed to have broken out among the men. I just hoped it would last. Gradually the ship slowed and Captain Dunning came down from the quarterdeck.

'Captain,' I said as he approached. 'May I congratulate you? The way you handled your ship was most impressive.'

'Much good it'll do us.'

'What do you mean? We escaped didn't we?'

'Yes, and now every ship the length of the French seaboard will be looking for us. We'll be lucky if we make it to Bordeaux.'

'Oh but surely they won't chase us that far. The authorities in Saint Nazaire will soon discover who really killed that man and you will be cleared of blame.'

'Assuming they bother trying.'

'Why would they not? For all his guile the mayor struck me as a man who would jealously guard his town's reputation. He won't want a murderer to go unapprehended. Bad for trade if nothing else.'

'You don't know these people, brother. The mayor is probably delighted we ran. It gives him an excuse to do nothing.'

I shook my head. 'I don't follow.'

'Isn't it obvious? Why waste resources hunting for an unknown murderer when they have one conveniently out at sea? I wouldn't be surprised if he allowed us to escape.'

'You're being modest. He couldn't catch us if he tried – and he did try.'

'Am I? All the mayor need do is spread the word and the next time I or one of my crew show our faces in Saint Nazaire we'll be arrested. All right for you, of course, you'll have left the ship by then. I have to continue to ply these waters. The *Gretchen* will never be able to dock in Saint Nazaire again.'

'I'm sure the real murderer will have been caught by then,' I tried to reassure him. 'Who was the victim? Do we know?'

'Another one of you lot.'

'Us lot?'

'A monk.'

A slight shiver ran down my spine. 'You're saying the murdered man was a monk? What sort of monk?'

'What do you mean what sort of monk? How many sorts are there? He had a tonsure and wore a monk's habit.'

'A habit like mine? You can tell a man's religious order by his habit. Brother Lucatz and I are Benedictines so our robes are black. What colour was this monk's habit?'

'Brother, we were being chased for our lives. I didn't stop to note the colour of the man's garb.'

'I understand, but it's important. Please try to think. Was it perhaps white with a black hood?'

He shrugged. 'It might have been. Yes. White with a black hood.'

'You're sure?'

'No brother, I'm not sure. And you'll forgive me but I have more pressing matters to worry about at the moment.' So saying he marched off back to quarterdeck.

'I don't suppose you noticed what colour his robes was,' I said to Lucatz when he'd gone.

'I'm afraid not, for the same reason as the captain. But I have seen this habit you describe, white with a black hood. In Toulouse. Their wearers are followers of a former Spanish priest called Dominic of Caleruega. They are a new order of mendicant preachers who call themselves "friars". They have been spreading fast in the south of France but I didn't think they had reached as far as Suffolk yet. I'm curious to know how you knew about them.'

'We aren't all ignorant country bumpkins, you know?' I said indignantly. 'In any case, I've seen him, or someone like him, following us along the shore. I don't suppose you've noticed him?'

He shook his head. I didn't like to say, but if these so-called "friars" are such a rarity this far north and he was the same man who Hogtie had seen following the *Gretchen,* then it was a pretty astonishing coincidence that three of our number should have been in the vicinity just as he got himself murdered.

We were interrupted by a blood-curdling cry came from the passenger accommodation.

We looked at each other. 'Now what?'

We ran over to the hutches to find Dame Flora on her knees on the floor clutching one of the nuns' robes to her breast and rocking backwards and forwards. She looked so distraught that for once I felt genuinely sorry for the woman.

'Gone,' she moaned.

'Not another!' I said. 'Which one this time?'

'Theresa, Prudence, Mairi and Federica.'

'But that's all of them.'

Of course it was. How did I imagine it would be otherwise?

'I should have seen this coming,' I said mostly to myself.

Dame Flora glared up at me with a look of what I can only describe as raw hate. 'You! You wanted this from the start. You never wanted this mission to succeed. You have done everything you can to undermine my authority and turn my ladies against me. Well, now you've succeeded.'

I was truly shocked by her words but there was no point arguing with her. She was beyond reasoning.

The scene inside the hutch was macabre to say the least. There were the last four bunks each with what looked at first sight to be a nun lying there which was probably why Flora had only just noticed. Just like Rebecca their robes were intact with no sign of any struggle. It was as though their bodies had been removed leaving only their robes behind.

And now we had another problem. Unnoticed by any of us the ship's crew had quietly gathered around the door and were looking in goggle-eyed. They too had heard Flora's cry and had come to see what was going on. Dunning's initial impulse was to order them back to their posts, but Benit put a restraining hand on his arm.

'The men are concerned,' said the first mate.

'So am I,' agreed the contessa who had also emerged from her cabin and now pushed her way to the front. With her were Carmela and Bruno so that for the first time the entire ship's complement of crew and passengers – those of us who were left - were gathered together.

'Eight gone. Who will be next?' the contessa was asking.

Dunning was quick to reassure her: 'Contessa, you are quite safe. I assure you, nothing is going to happen to you whilst aboard my ship.'

'That's easy for you to say, captain. You are a man. Have you not noticed yet? It is we women who are being attacked.'

'"Attacked" is hardly the right word,' frowned the captain irritably. 'As far as we know no-one has been injured.'

'Are we then to wait until someone is?'

To that question no-one seemed to have an answer.

Chapter Eighteen
THE VOYAGE OF THE GRETCHEN

How can I best describe the atmosphere aboard ship now? "Tense" would be an understatement. The unease following Rebecca's disappearance had become anxiety after Magdalene and Ursula and with the latest batch was now approaching panic levels. Who was doing these dreadful things? Everyone suspected everyone else though nobody came out and said so. If we met on deck we glided around each other like skaters on a pond carefully trying to avoid a collision but looking back over our shoulder to see who had fallen on their arse. Even Bruno and the contessa seemed to have suspended their noisy frolicking, which was one good thing I supposed.

That last comment of the contessa about women being the target continued to haunt me. She had only been pointing out the obvious. Of the original eleven women who joined the ship at Ipswich only the contessa, Carmela and Dame Flora were left. Were they next? And after them would it be the turn of the men?

There was no point dwelling on it. Life had to go on, a ship does not sail itself. Everyone tried to maintain an air of normality - everyone, that is, except Dame Flora who barely emerged from her cabin of which she was now the sole occupant. I was tempted to go in to see how she was but I doubted I'd be welcomed. Her agonized moaning could be heard all over the ship like the grumbling of distant thunder.

Meanwhile a real storm was brewing out at sea. This is not unusual, apparently. The Bay of Biscay is a vast *cul-de-sac* into which the Atlantic Ocean is funnelled and then rages like a trapped animal trying to escape. Eventually the creature lashes out in a sudden violent squall, or so said Hogtie who appeared to be the only person unfazed by the change in the weather. On the contrary, he seemed to relish the oppressive atmosphere – the human as well as the climatic.

'So brother,' he grinned, 'who do you favour?'

I feigned ignorance of his meaning: 'I'm sorry? Favour...?'

He gave me a knowing look. 'I'm talking about them nuns, acourse. Who did for them?'

'I can't say I've given it much thought. And you shouldn't either. Speculation only leads to false accusation and we don't want any of that, do we?'

He snorted. 'Don't tell me you han't been specklatin'. I seen ye a-walkin' and a-mutterin' to yourself. An' I knowed for a fact you been chattin' to young Bobbie-o.'

'Who?'

'Yon barrel-boy aloft.' He nodded to the crow's nest. 'An' he must have told 'ee summit 'cos the first mate had him down in the wastes for a right bollockin'.'

Oh dear. I was afraid something like that might happen.

'Benit didn't hurt the lad, did he?'

'Not so's he'd notice. But I'm right, en't I? He did tell 'ee summit?'

'Nothing of any significance. He certainly didn't see anyone with the sisters, if that's what you're getting at. So you can spread the word on that one.'

'I'm sure the murderer will be reassured,' smiled Hogtie dryly. 'Still, someone must be involved. They nuns didn't vanish of they's own accord.'

'I thought that was exactly what you were suggesting the last time we spoke. Hexed away by some water-sprite wasn't it?'

'That's what the men be sayin'. Personally I see a human hand in it. And I got an idea whose.' He eyed me knowingly.

'I said just now speculation was a dangerous game and I meant it. The wrong man, or woman, gets accused and before you know it we have a vigilante killing on our hands.'

He shrugged. 'Fine, if you don't want to know, suits me.'

I looked at him. 'Go on then. Who do you think is the murderer? But whisper it. I don't want to be overheard.'

He leaned forward. 'It be obvious. That French monk acourse.'

My jaw fell open in astonishment. 'Lucatz? Don't be ridiculous! What on earth makes you think it was him?'

'He's French.'

'And that's your reason?'

'En't it enough?'

'I'll have you know I've known Brother Lucatz practically all my life. The idea of him killing anyone is absurd. He's the one who arranged for the nuns to be here, for Heaven's sake. Why would he kill them off?'

'Seems a good way to do it to me. Plenty of sea out there to lose them in.'

'That's insane. Lucatz as the murderer indeed! You're just prejudiced because he's French.'

'Not prejudiced brother, just logical. Sprites have no shadows. But people does.'

'What's that supposed to mean?'

'I say no more than that. I don't want to be accused to spreading false accusations. But if I was lookin' for a villain, that's where I'd start.'

The man was infuriating but he was right about one thing: if a human hand was involved it would have left some trace – some "shadow" as he called it. Not that I thought for one moment that he was right about Lucatz. But there was something that had been bothering me, something that I had been trying to ignore. It was probably nothing at all but like an itch that needed scratching I couldn't ignore it. Best to dispense with it and put my mind at rest. Willingly or not, therefore, I found my feet being drawn towards the passenger accommodation.

Even in the middle of the day it was always dark in those cabins, but there was just enough light coming in through the small louvre window for me to see my way around. I wouldn't have much time so I'd better be quick.

Where would he have put it? There weren't too many hiding places. Under his bunk perhaps? No, not there. On the bookshelf perhaps? Not there either. Where else..?

'Are you looking for something, brother?'

'Eh? What? Ah, Lucatz. I was just looking for you.'

'Well you won't find me up there,' he said indicating the shelf. He went over to a corner of the hutch where he retrieved something from under a pile of rags. It was a monk's robe exactly like the one he was wearing. Only this was his old one. He had changed it shortly after returning to the ship in Saint Nazaire. That's what I had noticed.

'It got torn during the chase,' he explained. 'Fortunately I had a spare.'

He held the old one out for me to see. There was indeed a large tear in the breast. There was also an incrustation of what looked like dried blood.

'Whose is that?' I asked.

He examined it as though he hadn't noticed it before. I expected him to say he'd cut himself shaving, or something banal like that. But he didn't.

'It's the murdered man's I expect.'

'So you admit it.'

'Of course I admit it – although I query "admit".'

'How did it get on your robe?'

'How did it get on my robe if I wasn't the murderer, you mean?' He smiled. 'I told you. The man was injured. I tried to help him. I haven't entirely forgotten my Hippocratic Oath. But he was already too far gone. There was nothing I could do for him. And the mob was gathering.'

It made sense, but I wanted more.

'Talk me through what happened. From when you left me outside the mayor's office.'

'Am I a suspect now?'

'Please. I'm tired. Just tell me.'

He gave me an indulgent smile. 'If you remember after we parted I went to look for the captain and the prioress.'

'And did you find them?'

'No.'

'But you all got back to the ship at the same time. You must have met up somewhere.'

'I heard a cry for help and I ran towards it. I imagine Dame Flora and the captain did the same. That's where we met.'

'So the friar was already in the vicinity?'

'I presume so.'

'Why? What was he after? Why was he following the ship?'

'That you would have to ask him.'

'Unfortunately he's dead.'

Lucatz shrugged.

I thought for a moment. 'You said he was from Toulouse.'

'No, I said his robe was the same as that used by friars from Toulouse.'

'But assuming he was from there, you are the only one with any connection to that part of the world.'

He shook his head. 'The contessa is Italian. The *Gretchen* makes regular trips to Gascony. Even you were once a student in Languedoc. Are you going to accuse us all?'

'All right. Forget about the friar for now. The nuns. All that nonsense you spouted about cursed ships. You don't believe that any more than I do. Why were you trying to muddy the waters?'

He sat down heavily on one of the cots. 'I said it because I didn't want to tell what I suspected really happened to them.'

'Which was what?'

He looked at me gravely before answering. 'Suicide.'

My jaw dropped open in shock. 'What? Which ones?'

He shrugged. 'All of them.'

'Are you being serious?'

'You said yourself Rebecca thought Agatha had willed her own death.'

'And later denied it.'

'Well she would, wouldn't she? If she was about to do the same thing.'

'Rebecca didn't starve to death. And neither did any of the others. A little thin perhaps from Flora's preposterous biscuit diet, but not emaciated like Agatha.'

'Maybe they preferred something a little quicker.'

Now I sat down on the cot too. 'I can't believe this. Why would they?'

'It's a not uncommon trait among closed communities. You have commented to me more than once how isolated the sisters were. A community like that often feels friendless with no way out other than the ultimate one. They feed on each other's fears and develop a kind of collective insanity.'

'I've never heard of such a thing.'

'I have. You remember Béziers?'

'How can I forget? The very name conjures up dreadful images even for those who weren't there.'

'As it happens, I was.'

'You were at the siege? You never told me that.'

'Because I was ashamed. You see, I was with Abbot Amalric's army.'

'You were one of the besiegers?' I said, shocked.

He nodded. 'You recall the details of course. How Amalric offered safe passage out of the town for all

Catholics and any Cathari willing to convert. None did preferring martyrdom instead.'

'But martyrdom is not the same as suicide.'

He smiled patiently. 'It's true most were slaughtered by Amalric's troops after the siege was lifted. But a few did not. Twenty-three burghers threw themselves from the battlements before the soldiers entered the town.'

'What? Why?'

He shrugged. 'Who knows? As a demonstration of defiance perhaps. Or the hope of assuaging Amalric's blood-lust. Or maybe knowing they could not survive they preferred to take their own lives rather than let others take them from them. All I know is that it is infectious. One does it and the notion spreads rapidly.'

I had an idea of what he was talking about. It brought to mind a story Joseph once told me about the Jews of York during the reign of King Richard. It was a time of religious fervour just before Richard departed for the Holy Land. They were holed up in a tower while outside the mob waited. There was no escape. It was hopeless. Knowing they wouldn't survive the men first killed their children then their wives and then themselves.

'But what has this to do with the nuns?' I asked him. 'They weren't under siege. There's no mob baying for their blood.'

'All I can tell you is that I have the same feeling now as I did at Béziers. First one goes, then the others follow his example in a kind of compulsive imitation.'

'If that's what you thought, why didn't you get Captain Dunning to lock them up? Or at least tell Dame Flora of your fears?'

'Do you think they would have believed me?'

It was a colourful picture he was painting but I wasn't convinced. Those burghers of Béziers would have done what they did in the heat of battle under imminent threat to life and limb. The nuns were never in any danger of that kind. Nor was it a final act of hopeless desperation like those Jews of York. What happened aboard the *Gretchen* was measured and took place over a period of days.

I didn't know how much credence to put on his explanation. It sounded plausible but then he was good at that. I wanted to pursue the matter further but before I could First Mate Benit appeared at the door. He looked first at Lucatz then at me.

'The captain's compliments, brothers. Would you join him on the main deck.'

'What right now?' I asked irritably. 'What's the urgency?'

'The captain will explain.'

Everyone was on deck – all barring Dame Flora that is. The crew were drawn up on one side while the passengers were on the other. Lucatz and I joined the passenger side. Captain Dunning stood on a box between us so that he could be seen by all. When silence was achieved he addressed us:

'I have gathered you all together in the light of recent events. We are all fearful for the future and suspicious of each other and this is bad for morale and the smooth running of the ship. I therefore wish to put your minds at rest.'

He turned to face the crew.

'You men know me. We have sailed together many times before. I have always tried to be a fair master. I have never lied to you. If there was anything particularly hazardous on any voyage I would be the first to abandon it. You also know the *Gretchen*. She is a fine ship. She has withstood gales and rough seas and has always brought us safely to port. And so it will be this time. The best way to achieve that is to do your work well and with God's help we will all arrive safely at our destination.'

'What about the nuns?' came a voice from the back of the crew.

Dunning put up his hand. 'I know there has been talk of dark goings-on. This is dangerous talk and plainly not true. I assure you, there is nothing supernatural going on.'

'We never had so many womenfolk in one sailing before,' came the same voice.

A murmur of agreement went round.

The captain frowned. 'We've carried women before.'

'Never so many,' the same voice persisted.

'The women be the cause all right,' said another.

'Aye, the women,' said a third.

More noisy agreement and nodding of heads. They were working themselves up into a frenzy.

'By all the injustices,' seethed the contessa next to me under her breath. 'We women are the victims here and yet we are to blame.'

'The captain's right about one thing,' said Lucatz. 'There is an explanation for all this. The problem is he can't give them one that will satisfy them.'

The mood among the men was growing darker by the minute. Dunning's words were meant to lighten it but they seemed to be having the opposite effect. He needed something else to reassure them. He consulted with First Mate Benit while the men continued to grumble among themselves. Eventually he put up his hand for silence and addressed the men again:

'I can see there doesn't seem to be anything I can say to satisfy you. Very well. We are half a day from La Rochelle. If any man wishes to leave he may do so there and no fear of reprisal. But until then I expect every man to do his duty.'

'He's hoping the mood will have changed by the time we get to Rochelle,' said Lucatz.

'He may well be right,' I said.

'So long as there are no more deaths in the meantime,' said the contessa. 'A wish with which I fully concur.'

Having delivered his morale-boosting speech – not entirely successfully in my opinion - Dunning nodded for Benit to get the men back to work. But they didn't look happy. It was plain to me that the only thing that would pacify them would be to give them a culprit - a live, human villain.

There was nothing else for it. I went up to Dunning. 'Captain – might I have a word? I think I know who the murderer is.'

Chapter Nineteen
THE MURDERER REVEALED?

I followed the captain to his cabin. Lucatz came too. Once inside Dunning closed the door and turned to face us.

'I'm listening.'

I began by listing the entire ship's complement of passengers and crew one by one and giving my reasons why each could not be the murderer. Half way through the captain interrupted:

'I thought you were going to tell me the identity of the murderer. So far you've told me who didn't kill the nuns. You seem to have exonerated everyone.'

'Not quite everyone.'

'Walter please,' said Lucatz softly.

'I'm sorry, my friend,' I said to him. 'I can't help it. There's far more at stake than the liberty of one man. I have to do this. My conscience won't permit me to remain silent any longer.'

'Very commendable,' said Dunning. 'So - who is it? Who is the murderer?'

I took a deep breath. 'Me.'

Dunning's eyebrows shot to the top of his head. 'You?'

'Yes. '

Next to me I heard Lucatz let out a gasp.

Dunning frowned. 'Is this some kind of joke?'

'No joke, captain. I'm being perfectly serious. I am the murderer. It's obvious. Nobody else did it so it has to be me. So you can tell the crew. You have your culprit. I killed the nuns. It was me.'

'And when, pray, are you supposed to have done these things?'

I frowned. 'That, I admit, I'm a little vague about. Possibly while I was under the influence of my cousin Bruno's brandy concoction.'

'I see. So lying unconscious on your bunk, you got up, went out, murdered seven nuns and returned to your bed all while still unconscious?'

'Well not all at once, obviously. I must have come round between each murder.'

'And the friar?'

'Yes, I wondered about that. I suppose I must have murdered him as well. I could have done. I was among those who left the ship in Saint Nazaire.'

'But you weren't anywhere near where it happened.'

'The crew doesn't know that.'

Dunning sighed wearily and sat down on the only chair in the cabin. 'Brother, why are you doing this?'

'We all saw the crew just now. They are practically ready to mutiny. They need someone to blame. A real live murderer made of flesh and bone not some phantom spirit. Fine. Let that someone be me. The men will then be satisfied and they can get on with the important task of sailing the ship to Bordeaux as quickly as possible.'

'You do realise you could be hanged?'

'Oh, I don't think it would go that far, would it? Just lock me up until we arrive safely in Bordeaux.

Then I'll recant and you can let me go,' I smiled triumphantly.

Dunning nodded. 'Very clever. But the men may not wait until Bordeaux. They may be a little more impatient – and possibly take matters into their own hands.'

'You wouldn't permit that,' I smiled confidently.

'I may not be able to stop them. As you say, their mood is black. And they certainly want someone to blame. Someone, as you say, made of flesh and bone. Bone that snaps easily inside a noose.'

I grimaced rubbing my neck affectionately. 'It was just an idea.'

'Well I've a better one.' He slapped his hand down on the large tome that was lying on the table in front of him.

'What's this?'

'The ship's Bible. My own actually, but I take it with me on every voyage.'

'Very nice. What do intend doing with it?'

'We can't determine who murdered the nuns – as you pointed out, there are too many possibilities. But the friar's murder is a different matter. Only five people left the ship in Saint Nazaire – you, Brother Lucatz, the prioress, your cousin Bruno and me. You we have already eliminated as you were with the first mate at the time of the murder. The rest must swear an oath.'

'That's a bit excessive isn't it?' I objected. 'From what I've heard it could have been anyone in Saint Nazaire. There's no proof anyone from the ship was involved.'

'The mayor of Saint Nazaire disagrees. And if I am to be chased the length of the French seaboard I want a chance to clear my name. This way we may solve that murder and reinstate my ship's reputation. Three of those who went ashore in Saint Nazaire are here now. I've asked Mister Benit to fetch the other two. I will ask each in turn to swear on the Holy Book as to their innocence.'

'This is never going to work,' objected Lucatz. 'The murderer will simply lie.'

'And imperil their immortal soul? We shall see. I will begin.' Dunning placed his right hand on the Bible and the left on his heart. 'I do solemnly and sincerely swear before God and the true living Christ that I did nothing to hurt any man or woman since boarding the *Gretchen*. Neither did I commit murder.'

He then turned the Bible round and invited Lucatz to do the same. My heart was in my mouth wondering what he would do. But before he could do anything there was a commotion at the door as the prioress barged in looking extremely angry followed by First Mate Benit and Bruno. I was shocked to see Flora. She looked drawn and tired – from all that endless wailing no doubt. But she was as doughty as ever and did not take kindly to Benit's man-handling.

'What's the meaning of this outrage?' she demanded. 'Why have I been brought here?'

'Dame Flora,' said the captain. 'Thank you for coming. I won't keep you long. All I want you to do is swear on the Holy Book that you had nothing to do with the recent deaths.'

Dame Flora looked at the Bible and scoffed. 'You are asking me if I murdered my own ladies?'

'Not just them. The friar in Saint Nazaire as well.'

'I will do no such thing.' She glared at me. 'Is this your idea?'

'No madam,' said Dunning. 'It is mine. I ought to warn you, if you do not swear you will remain a suspect. Well?'

She stared at the Bible, then looked round each of us in turn. A grin slowly spread across her face. Finally she clapped her hand on the cover. 'I so swear, and may God forgive you all.'

She then turned to go, but just before she finally disappeared she turned back and gave me a look that would have turned Lot's wife not to a pillar of salt but to one of granite.

'Right Bruno,' I said when she'd gone. 'Your turn next.'

'Do I have to?' he whined.

'Just do it.'

He shuffled forward, held his hand out over the book, but instead of placing it on the embossed crucifix on the cover he waggled his fingers over the top of it.

'When you say *anything* to do with the murders, do you mean anything at all?'

The captain was looking at him suspiciously. If he wasn't careful he'd end up getting himself arrested.

'Bruno,' I said emphatically. 'It's a simple question. Did you murder the friar or the nuns?'

'No.'

'Then put your hand on the blessèd book and say so.'

I clapped his hand smartly onto the cover and held it there. He mumbled his affirmation, and then withdrew it again quickly as though the cover were on fire.

'There. All done.' I pushed the Bible back towards Dunning.

'That just leaves Brother Lucatz,' said the captain.

Lucatz frowned and kept his hands inside his scapular. 'Walter hasn't sworn yet,' he mumbled.

'We've already established Brother Walter doesn't need to,' said the captain.

Still Lucatz hesitated. It was a very awkward moment.

'I don't think Lucatz needs to swear either,' I said at last.

'I think he does,' said Dunning.

Still Lucatz did not move. Finally he shook his head. 'I'm sorry, I can't do this,' he said and stomped out of the cabin.

We both stared after him, dumbfounded.

Dunning raised his eyebrows. 'Well now. What do we make of that?'

I ran after Lucatz and grabbed his arm. 'What the devil's the matter with you? There was your opportunity to clear yourself. Now you've convinced the captain of the opposite.'

He pulled his arm away from me roughly. 'I'll not be party to blackmail.'

'You won't be party to anything swinging from the yard arm. Don't you realise by refusing to swear you've as good as admitted your guilt?'

'I admit nothing. I'm telling you that I had nothing to do with any murders. If that's not good enough then there's nothing more I can do.'

I shook my head sadly. 'You pig-headed old fool. You've just signed your own death warrant.'

And that indeed is what may well have happened had not Fate intervened.

Chapter Twenty
MUTINY ON THE GRETCHEN

I rose with the sun next morning having had a sleepless night going over the events of the previous day and fearful that Lucatz might be arrested at any moment. He, by contrast, slept the sleep of the innocent and is still asleep as I write this. Let him. This may be his last day of freedom. Clearly I was more worried about his predicament than he was. Why he wouldn't take the oath yesterday was beyond me. Everyone else who had gone ashore in Saint Nazaire had, even Bruno and Dame Flora. It would have cleared up matters once and for all. I put it down to his Lengadocian blood, stubborn to the last. It could mean the death of him this time – literally.

Emerging bleary-eyed from the hutch I ventured out onto the deck to wash my face in rainwater and gaze out onto the horizon. This was day twenty of our journey, we were much further south and the weather was sunny and warm which was some small comfort. On days like this I could understand the romance of the sea as eulogized by the poets and with the ancient Greeks cry, *Thálatta! Thálatta!* - The Sea! The Sea! While I wouldn't be sorry to see the back of the *Gretchen* I had to admit I had grown fond of the old girl.

What was I talking about? Permanently wet and nauseous, never still, no possibility of a decent wash down, rancid food, brackish water and the ever-present danger of sinking or being eaten by sea-monsters. I couldn't wait to be off this invention of the Devil and vowed never to venture on another like it for as long as I lived!

I shielded my eyes from the sun and gazed up at sail still furled against the yard arm. There was a stillness in the air this morning, nothing stirring, the only sound the rhythmic creaking of *Gretchen's* timbers as we rocked gently to and fro in the water. The sea shimmered turquoise in the morning sunshine. It appeared unusually calm more like a lake than an ocean and seemed to go on for ever. It looked so solid in fact that I had the oddest urge to simply stroll away and leave the ship and its problems behind me. Fortunately I managed to resist.

But wait a moment. The sail still furled? That shouldn't be. If I'd learned anything over the past three weeks it was that during the day the sail was never left furled. Lowering it was the first duty of the crew every morning as soon as it was light. And come to think of it, where was the crew? There were always men to be seen doing things with ropes or nets even on still days. But there seemed to be nobody about. Even the crow's nest looked empty. Where was everybody?

A noise behind me made me start. It was Captain Dunning emerging from his cabin with First Mate Benit. Hogtie was also with them, unusually. I watched with mild curiosity as Benit ran from one side of the ship to the other leaning over the bulwarks and returning to Dunning shaking his head.

Voices raised. Hogtie and Benit rushing off in different directions. What were they up to?

I intercepted Benit as he descended the stairs. 'What's going on? Mister Benit, is everything all right?'

'No brother. Everything is not all right. Far from it.'

Before I could quiz him further he started furiously ringing the ship's bell ending any further discussion.

Now Hogtie reappeared dragging along behind him what looked like a huge log.

'Brother, can you help me with this?'

'What? Oh - yes of course. What do you want me to do?'

'Help me get it over the side. It's the kedge,' he said in answer to my unspoken query.

The kedge. This was a machine I'd not yet come across. Apparently it's a sort of sea anchor used to stall the ship in water that is too deep for a regular anchor. It provides enough drag to prevent the ship from drifting when the sail is furled. After dropping it over the starboard bow we went over to the larboard bow and did the same with a second log. Between us we managed to get both over the side, but it was heavy work for two.

'Why am I doing this?' I panted. 'I mean, I don't mind, but where are the rest of the crew?'

'Gone,' he panted back.

'What do you mean "gone"? You mean they've vanished now too like the nuns?'

'Not vanished, brother. Deserted.'

'What? When?'

'During the night. They took the dinghies.'

He nodded towards the stern of the ship where the ship's two row-boats were usually stowed. We'd been told about these on day one of the voyage. In event of a shipwreck they were our only means of getting off the ship. And now they were missing – both of them.

'Why have they done this?'

'You know why. They think the ship be jinxed.'

'But they could have left at La Rochelle. Captain Dunning explained all that.'

'Seems they didn't want to wait.'

I looked at him suspiciously. 'You're a member of the crew. Why didn't you go with them?'

'I too old to start runnin', brother.'

'But you knew what they were planning?'

'Aye. Last night.'

'Then why didn't you warn the captain?'

'I couldn't. I wor tied up – see?' He showed me what looked to be rope marks on his wrists. 'I only managed to get free this morning.'

'Leaving just enough time for the others to make good their escape. How convenient.'

Hogtie looked sheepish and lowered his voice. 'They be good boys, brother. Just afeared, that's all. They don't deserve to hang.'

'Well, let's hope Captain Dunning agrees with you.'

By now all the passengers had emerged on deck looking confused and bewildered.

'What's happened?' asked Lucatz rubbing sleep from his eyes. 'Why the alarm?'

'It seems we've been abandoned.'

'Abandoned?' said the contessa still in her fur-trimmed night-wear. 'What nonsense is this?'

217

'No nonsense, countess. The crew have deserted. Every last man of them.'

'Oh God!' said Bruno. 'That means there's no-one to sail the ship.'

'You have a genius for stating the obvious, cousin.'

He scowled at me.

'It's God's judgement,' nodded Dame Flora sourly. 'I could have predicted this would happen.'

She may well think it was God's idea but it was me she blamed - for reasons best known to herself. I'd given up trying to work it out.

Dunning now appeared. We all crowded round him.

'Well captain?' asked the contessa.

'Hogtie and I have been all over the ship. There's no doubt. The men have gone. And they've taken the two dugouts.'

'So there's just the nine of us?' said Lucatz.

'It looks that way.'

Benit came back. 'I've run out the red flag. It's the recognized distress signal,' he explained.

Eight pairs of eyes stared at the captain in fear and bewilderment: Lucatz, the contessa, Dame Flora, Bruno, Carmela, Benit, Hogtie and me. We were all that was left.

'Are we enough to sail her do you think?' asked the contessa.

'With just six men? Three of whom never sailed so much as a dinghy before? I hardly think so.'

'There are the women as well, captain. Don't forget us women.'

'How can I forget?'

'Can't we just simply land?' I asked squinting over the bulwark. 'I can see the shore from here. It can't be more than a mile away.'

'And how do you propose to get us there?'

'We simply raise the kedge anchors and allow the *Gretchen* to drift in. It's a calm sea. A nice gentle ride in.' It seemed the obvious solution to me.

Dunning shook his head. 'We'd be dashed to firewood on the rocks in no time. Or we may drift the other way, out to sea. No. We are best sitting tight and await rescue.'

'Assuming anyone comes,' said Benit.

'What do you mean?' said Bruno. 'They will won't they?'

'Haven't you noticed? We haven't seen another vessel since we left Saint Nazaire.'

'Is that because the mayor is still chasing us?' I asked.

'I doubt if even the mayor of Saint Nazaire can reach this far,' said Dunning. 'Besides, if he really was after us I'd expect more ships not fewer. It's more likely the calm weather - or sheer bad luck.'

'Well I for one am not prepared to do nothing,' said the contessa. 'I've seen the crew raise the sail. I'm sure we can do it.'

'There is more to sailing a ship than simply raising the sail, my lady,' said Dunning.

'So we give in? Let those cowards win?'

'I'm not giving in, just being practical. However, we will need to keep watch for any sails. Someone should go up to the crow's nest.'

'Bruno can do that,' I said.

'Oh no,' he objected. 'I've no head for heights. You do it, cousin. You've been up there already.'

'Neither of you will go,' said Dunning. 'I want all available men down here.'

'Then Carmela will go,' said the contessa.

'Mama!'

'Oh, stop whimpering, girl. Where's your backbone? We are Montefiores. Your grandfather fought at Acre.'

Carmela's eyes filled with tears though whether of anger or frustration I wasn't sure.

'Someone on this vessel is trying to destroy my mission,' muttered Dame Flora glaring at me again.

'Is that what you think this is all about?' I said. 'Your precious mission?'

'You tell me.'

'That's not why it's happened,' said Bruno. 'The crew are right. It's the women. There are just too many on this ship.'

The countess rounded on him: 'Monsieur Henri take notice! Your services are longer required!'

Bruno shrugged. 'Suits me.'

'Please,' said Dunning wearily. 'There are too few of us left. We need to stick together, that's the only way we are gong to survive this. With God's good grace, if this weather continues we may yet have a chance. But we must all remain calm or we are doomed.'

As the meeting broke up I caught Lucatz up.

'Looks as if you've been let off the hook,' I said nodding after the captain. 'For now at least. He can't afford to be locking up one of the few remaining men he has available.'

'God moves in mysterious ways, brother.'

Didn't he just.

Chapter Twenty-one
HERE BE MONSTERS

For the next three days we drifted, hardly moving at all, within a stone's throw of land but frustratingly unable to reach it. Benit assured me that the hidden rocks were too dangerous to risk letting the ship get any closer. Even with a full crew we could not have navigated our way through. If we'd had just one of the dinghies we could easily have rowed across, but the crew had been too canny for that. By taking both they'd ensured we were confined to the ship giving them plenty of time time to get away.

Nor did any vessel pass us by while we languished. First Mate Benit had been right about that too. There hadn't been a single sail, not for days. Even Hogtie was mystified. Normally there should have been at least one or two winers passing by, or a fishing vessel or something. But there was none. It was as though the spirits of the sea had conspired against us. I was beginning to think the *Gretchen* might be cursed after all.

At least the weather had held although I wasn't sure that was entirely a good thing either. True, we weren't being battered by gales but with no wind at all we had no means of propulsion either. God himself seemed to have run out of puff. But this was a busy seaway. Something must turn up eventually. All we could do was sit tight and wait.

In the meantime we tried to make the best of things. Food was a priority. With the ship's cook among the deserters a galley roster had to be drawn up. Who would have guessed the contessa could cook? No-one I hope because she couldn't. The meat she prepared was raw and she burned the pottage. I mean, how does anyone manage to burn pottage? It's practically liquid. I'd had some experience in the abbey kitchens and did my share. Bruno was useless of course and Dame Flora remained ensconced in her cabin. Well, she had her biscuits, and plenty of them now her ladies were gone. Lucatz volunteered to take charge of the lower deck which suited me. The thought of going down there again filled me horror. He claimed supplies were running low which surprised me since we had stocked up well in Saint Nazaire. Apparently rats had got in and spoiled some of the food. We couldn't afford to lose any more.

And so time passed as we watched and waited. Carmela was in the crow's nets but whenever anyone had a few minutes spare they would look out to the horizon to see if there was any sign of a sail. But there was nothing. Then late in the afternoon of the third day I saw Hogtie and Benit peering out across the starboard bow out and looking agitated.

'What is it?' I asked them. 'Have you seen a sail?'

'Aye,' Benit replied.

I crossed myself. 'God be thanked! We're saved!'

But he shook his head. 'Not quite,' and took himself off to inform the captain.

'What does he mean, not quite?' I asked Hogtie. 'Who are they?' Then a dreadful thought struck me. 'Not Nazairey men?'

Hogtie shook his head. 'Worse. Pirates.'

'What? I thought you said Eustace the monk had been executed.'

'There be more pirates in these waters than ol' Eustace, brother.'

I frowned. 'How can you tell they're pirates at this distance?' I said squinting at the indistinct speck on the horizon. 'It could be anybody.'

'You was wondering why there wor no other ships, brother. There be your answer.'

I squinted again at the horizon. 'Maybe they won't see us.'

'They already have.'

He was right. Even I could see the pirate ship had altered course and was heading in our direction.

'How long before they reach us?'

'Two, mebbe three hours.'

'But there's no wind. Even a pirate ship needs wind.'

'They can row. Slower than sail but we en't goin' nowhere. Yep, reckon they be with us afore nightfall.'

'Can't we bluff them? Pretend we are better manned than we are? Or better still, a plague ship. Isn't there some warning flag to put out? I've heard that sometimes works.'

Hogtie shook his head sadly. 'They not fools. Most o' them lads was ordinary crewmen once. Any tricks we can come up with you can be sure they already knows.'

'Is there nothing we can do?'

'Pray brother. I recommend you pray.'

And pray I did, to every saint I could think of who might darken the skies, mask the moon, conjure fog, turn off the stars - anything to make us invisible.

By now everybody on board had got the message and were frantically watching the little dot on the horizon that was growing bigger even as dusk deepened. Captain Dunning appeared on the quarterdeck with First Mate Benit. He looked out to sea and then did something I'd never seen him do before. He climbed the mast himself half way to the crow's nest. A minute later he was back down again followed by Carmela.

'Women to their cabins!'

'No!' said the contessa resolutely standing her ground like some latter-day Boadicea. 'I will not cower.'

'My lady, this is not a game,' said Dunning. 'Do you know what those men will do to any female they find aboard the *Gretchen*?'

'Certainly. Which is why I intend to go down fighting. I'll take a few of them with me.'

'Me too,' said Carmela and stood alongside her mother.

'That's my girl,' the contessa smiled and stroked her cheek.

'The contessa's right,' said Benit. 'We can't just wait for the end.'

Dunning hesitated a moment longer then set his jaw. He nodded. 'Hoist the sail Mister Benit.'

'What?' I said. 'What's the point if there's no wind?'

'We can at least look as though we mean business. And who knows? We may yet outrun them.'

'Aye-aye captain,' said Benit pleased to be doing something positive at last, and went off to untie the stay lines.

'Isn't this dangerous, captain?' I said. 'There's still the shallows.'

'Which would you prefer, brother? Your brains dashed out on the rocks or your throat cut? Well?'

'I'm thinking about it.'

Benit was soon back having loosed the lines. Bruno, Lucatz and I lent a hand. Between us we managed to get the sail down but with no wind it hung empty as a eunuch's scrotum and about as potent. I then helped Hogtie haul the two kedge anchors back up out of the water. This was even heavier work that dropping them overboard since now they were waterlogged.

'By the way,' I gasped collapsing onto the deck once we'd finished. 'I've been meaning to ask – and in case I never get another chance. Why do they call you Hogtie?'

'My father sold me to a sea-captain when I wor a scrap,' he panted back. 'But I worsn't happy about it. They had to bind my arms and legs – hog-tied see?'

'So you never really wanted to go to sea?'

He shook his head. 'I gets sea-sick just thinking about it.'

'Now you tell me.'

Darkness closes in quickly at these low latitudes but not quickly enough for my liking. For the time being the pirate vessel had vanished from sight so there was a chance they couldn't see us either. By morning we might even have drifted into some haven and vanished from view. Meanwhile we crept along excruciatingly slowly as the distant lights of shore fires twinkled by. Watching them, Hogtie's words came back to me unsummoned:

'They take any of the crew they can persuade to join them. Any that don't have their throats cut. As for the women, the young ones they use for their pleasure, the rest they throw overboard.'

Was that to be the final fate of the *Gretchen*? Pretty soon we'd know.

Chapter Twenty-two
NEMESIS

For hours we drifted in silence, every eye skimming the horizon for any sign of the pirate vessel. We were spaced at intervals along the starboard side of the ship facing out to sea but it was impossible to see anything in the dark. All lights were extinguished. There was no moon. No sound either other than the wash of water against the side of the ship - and Dame Flora's desultory moaning in her cabin.

'Can't you shut her up?' I whispered to Lucatz. 'She sounds like one of those ancient sirens luring sailors to their deaths.'

'I've tried,' he whispered back. 'There's no getting through to her. With luck the pirates will think she's a madwoman and avoid us.'

'Do you think they're still out there?'

'I should think if they were coming they'd have found us by now,' he said confidently.

'Quiet you two!' barked Benit in a half-whisper from somewhere behind.

I cringed. In the distance sheets of lightning lit up the sky: one of Biscay's famous summer squalls was beginning. It was a long way off but the wind was beginning to pick up a little and we were moving albeit tortuously slowly. Maybe my prayers were being answered. I found myself willing us along.

The lightest puff of wind, dear Lord, that's all it would take.

'Did you hear that?' whispered Lucatz.

I strained my ears. 'Distant thunder.'

'Can you see anything?'

'No. I think they've missed us.'

'I hope you're right.'

But then a flash of lightning lit up the sky and the full horror of our situation was revealed. Far from missing us the pirate ship had crept up silently alongside us and was now just feet away.

'Oh dear God!' I gasped as the vessel loomed into view. Ranged along the length of the pirate ship men armed with knives and swords were making ready to leap the short divide separating us as soon as it was close enough. If it hadn't been for the lightning they'd have silently boarded us before we knew they were there. Their presence thus revealed, however, there was no longer any need for stealth. They let out a terrifying war-cry that made my blood freeze in my veins.

'Make ready to repel boarders!' bellowed Dunning.

A pointless order if ever there was one. Ropes and bill-hooks were already being hurled across the gap between us like the web of a giant spider dragging us together. One pirate had already leapt across the gap and was balancing just a couple of yards away from me on the bulwark.

Now, I'm not the bravest of men and given a moment to think about it I'd have dived for cover. But I can tell you at moments like this you don't think, you act. And so it was I found myself rushing towards the man, my own knife drawn which he easily kicked from my hand. So I grabbed the nearest object I could find, a length of timber, and went at him again. My chief thought was that I must keep him from setting foot on the deck of the *Gretchen* for once he did all would be lost. Seeing my predicament Lucatz rushed to join me and together we did manage to keep him pinned on top of the bulwark but he was proving too strong even for the two of us and I knew at any moment he would leap down and be upon us.

It was then, just as all seemed lost, that the miracle occurred. For several minutes before I'd been vaguely aware of a rustling behind me like the shuffling of mice in a roof-space only I'd been a little too preoccupied to take much notice. Now another flash of sheet lightning momentarily lit up the entire ship what I saw made the hairs on the back of my neck stand up. Lined up behind us were the ghosts of the seven dead nuns. They were all bare-headed and dressed entirely in white with a wide yellow cross emblazoned across their breasts. With their arms outstretched before them and their long hair flaring out behind they looked like the seven angels of doom.

I stopped for a moment to stare in wonder. My pirate attacker also saw them and he too hesitated. It was only for a moment but it was enough. First to recover his senses was Lucatz who struck at the man's shin with all his strength. The pirate cried out in pain but managed to recover. Following Lucatz's lead I too struck at the man's other shin. This time he buckled and before he could recover a second time Lucatz gave him an almighty shove in the chest. The man lost his footing and disappeared between the two vessels just as they came together with a sickening crunch. A moment later the two vessels parted again and the man had gone. Lucatz and I looked at each other in disbelief. Then something flew up and landed on the deck between us. I looked. It was one of the pirate's ears.

By now the squall had arrived in force and was lashing wind and rain on us. The two vessels writhed against each other like two fighting bull seals. Somehow we had to separate them.

Dunning was up on the quarterdeck yelling orders against the storm through cupped hands: 'Drop sail! Hard a larboard!'

Behind him I could see the contessa and Carmela leaning with all their weight on the tiller and the contessa screaming like some demented banshee into the wind: '*Bastardi! Bastardi!*'

Now Benit and Bruno heaved on a rope. The great sail struck and flapped uselessly in the wind. They tried again and again it failed. We were faltering. At any moment the two ships would collide again and this time the pirates would leap aboard.

'Axeman!' yelled the captain. 'Do your work!'

At this order I saw Hogtie take the axe from his belt and run to the foot of the mast. I remembered his warning that when all else failed the last resort was to fell the mast and guessed what was coming.

'No!' I screamed. 'Hogtie you can't!'

But I was too late. He brought his axe down on the mast with a bone-shattering crunch. I feared the worst but I was wrong. Instead of the mast he had cleaved the guy-rope holding one corner of the sail that was now flapping in the squall. Realising this I quickly ran across to the others, grabbed the same rope and together we managed to secure it to the prow of the boat. The sail was now cast lengthwise and straining unnaturally against the wind. Surely it must snap. I looked imploringly at Hogtie who grinned back at me. 'Axeman!'

By now Dunning was leaning far out over the starboard side. 'Drop kedge!'

'Come on!' Hogtie yelled and pulled me after him.

The kedge anchoring the starboard beam dropped into the swell with a mighty crash and instantly the ship dragged to that side. The *Gretchen* slewed a quarter turn left so that the deck was now almost vertical. Hogtie and I were flung off our feet and sent sliding towards the larboard bulwark. I was convinced we would both go over the side, but somehow the great ship managed to right itself again just in time and I could see then what Dunning had done. No longer parallel to the pirate ship our prow now faced directly onto their beam and was heading directly for their midships.

Hogtie was back on his feet again and dragging me after him. Together we pulled with all our strength on the back-stay of the sail. The sail miraculously filled and the *Gretchen* at last gathered speed as we raced towards the pirate ship. Their tiller-man saw the danger and tried frantically to steer out of our path, but he was too late. The *Gretchen* rammed into the side of the pirate vessel tearing into its timbers with our mighty oak keel. The pirate ship, though lighter and faster, was no match for our great weight and was sliced completely in two. I could hear the shattering of wood and the screams of the men as we slid over them. The *Gretchen* ploughed unstoppably onwards as the two halves of the pirate vessel parted behind us.

But now we had another problem. We were speeding towards the shore heading straight for the rocks with no hope of stopping. It was what the captain had always feared. The coast here was as treacherous as any we had encountered so far. I could hear the rocks grinding and the ship splintering under us as the shore rose up beneath us.

'Captain!' I yelled against the wind. 'What can we do?

But Dunning was finished. He shook his head. He had saved his people but he could not save his ship.

'We can't sink!' I yelled at him. 'Not now!'

But there was nothing to be done. The shore hurtled towards us. When the inevitable moment came there was an almighty crunch beneath us as we juddered to a sudden halt flinging everyone and everything forward. We had stopped and were rocking gently in the swell. But I knew it could not last. The sail was still set and billowing. In a moment the wave that had carried us forward would return and we would be sucked back out to sea again. There was only one thing we could do. We had to get off the ship.

I ran to the prow. 'Jump!' I screamed.

No-one moved. The *Gretchen* rocked and swayed again.

'Jump!' I yelled again. 'Or we will die!'

Still no-one moved. There was another heart-stopping splintering of wood as I could feel the great ship rise up on the swell. Before I could think I found myself clambering up onto the prow and there, balancing halfway between life and death, I looked back at my companions staring wide-eyed up at me. Taking one last look at the foaming surf beneath us I crossed myself, closed my eyes - and leapt into the abyss.

I hit the water hard. But instead of sinking as I had expected I found the water was just two feet deep. Miraculously I had landed on some kind of rock-shelf. I'd fallen awkwardly and cried out in pain as my left ankle cracked. But I was upright and that was all that mattered. The beach sloped gently upwards ahead of me.

Laughing hysterically, I looked back hoping to see the others follow but all I could see was the *Gretchen* looming above me in the darkness. It was rocking violently now in the swell wet and black and eerily immobile. Then like a giant beached whale the old girl heaved and rolled again. I screamed once more but it was no good. A moment later the great ship slid back and disappeared into the blackness of the night. The *Gretchen* and all on board had gone.

PART THREE

Chapter Twenty-three
ESCAPING DEATH

I'd come ashore on what I later discovered to be the *Ile de Ré* - a small island off the French coast near the port of La Rochelle. As luck would have it the *Gretchen* had beached on the western-most shore of this island known as the *Côte Sauvage*. And savage coast it certainly was for here were the rocks and submerged reefs so feared by Captain Dunning. However, what was lethal for a ship had been my salvation. Had I landed on the island's northern shore I might well have drowned in the deeper water. In the event all I did was twist my ankle which was painful but not life-threatening. Despite this I managed to drag myself up onto the beach where I must have passed out.

When I opened my eyes again, instead of cold wet sand I found myself lying on a soft bed between starched sheets with the scent of lavender in my nostrils and an army of small creatures busily fussing about me. Clearly I had died and gone to Heaven and these were my ministering angels. My injured foot, less painful now as it should be in Heaven, had been bound to within an inch of its life. From a purely professional point of view I have to admit I was impressed. Heaven had surely mastered the art of bandaging. I eased it onto the floor but when I tried to put pressure on it I winced.

'*Non, non,* do not do that. You will undo all our good work – tut-tut-tut!'

This was one of my angels speaking - and in English, too, thus proving once and for all that God really is an Englishman, albeit with a French accent.

'How did you know I was English?' I asked the creature as she pushed me back into bed.

'That was easy,' she said. 'You stank of fish, you were covered in seaweed and your robe was ripped to shreds. No self-respecting Frenchman would be so ill-mannered as to present himself to strangers in such a state. *Alors*, you must be English. Besides,' she sniffed, 'you had English coin in your purse.'

I looked about me. 'Where am I? How did I get here?'

'You are in the convent of Sainte Catherine des Vagues at La Rochelle. I am its abbess, Mother Ophélie. As to how you got here, a fisherman found you lying on the beach of *Ile de Ré*. He thought you were dead and took you to the priory of Saint Clément for burial. Fortunately the brothers there noticed you were still breathing and brought you to us. We have better facilities here to cope with the sick and dying.'

'Am I dying?'

'Not yet. But it was touch and go for a while.'

'How long a while?'

'A week.'

'A *week?* But I can't stay here. I must go.' I started to climb out of bed again and again winced with the pain.

'You are not going anywhere,' she said firmly pushing me back into bed again. 'Apart from anything else you have nothing to wear. As I said your robe was in tatters.' She looked at me. 'I assume it and the tonsure are genuine? You really are a monk?'

'Brother Walter de Ixworth from the abbey of Saint Edmund in Suffolk, England.'

She nodded. 'I have heard of this Bury Saint Edmund's - a name, incidentally, I have always thought absurd. Of course you must *bury* Saint Edmund. He is dead!'

She chuckled at her joke and repeated it to the other angels in French. They all giggled appreciatively but I think it got lost in translation.

Ophélie quickly became serious again. 'However, robe or no robe, you will not be going there just yet. Not until you are well enough. I have not invested days of care only to have you die on us as soon as you leave. It is bad for our reputation. So, back into bed with you.'

She clapped her hands and one of the other angels brought over a bowl of steaming broth. Ophélie stirred it, filled a spoon and proffered it to my lips. 'And now, eat.'

'I'm not hungry.'

'It was not a request.' She pushed the spoon up to my mouth and held it there. The last person to do that was my nurse when I was a child and I was ill with the fever. Just as I did then I obeyed and found I was hungry after all. Chicken and barley broth. It was good. I took the bowl from her and devoured the contents while Ophélie looked on nodding with satisfaction.

'What about the others?' I said after the third mouthful.

'Others?'

'My companions. My ship, the *Gretchen*, it went down in the storm. I managed to get off but I'm not sure they did.'

She shook her head. 'There were others – alive that is. You were the only one.'

'But they can't all have drowned, can they?'

'How many?'

'Eight – or possibly fifteen.'

'Don't you know?'

'No.'

I tried again to work out if the seven ghostly figures on the deck of the *Gretchen* were real or not. Had I really seen them or had I been dreaming? No, that pirate saw them too, I was sure of it. I could see it in his face. It was because of them that he stumbled. If they hadn't appeared when they did I wouldn't be here now nursing a twisted ankle but lying at the bottom of the sea, food for fishes. Lucatz saw them too I was certain. But what had happened to them? And to the others?

'Try not to think about it now,' said Ophélie. 'Let us concentrate on getting you well first. We can talk again later. In the meantime, rest and sleep.' She clapped her hands together. '*Alors mes sœurs, allons-y. Vite, vite!*'

She took my empty bowl, gathered up the other angels and ushered them out of the room, giggling as they went.

Just before she closed the door I called out: 'Oh mother?'

'*Oui?*'

'Thank you.'

She smiled the briefest of smiles then raised an admonishing finger. 'Rest and sleep.'

A whole week since the shipwreck with no news of survivors. Could anyone have survived? If so what had happened to them? Maybe the monks at the priory where I'd been originally taken might know more. But that was on the Ile de Ré and I was on the mainland.

It took a few more days of bed-rest and more chicken broth to rebuild my strength but as soon as I was able to put some weight on my injured foot I hobbled down to the cliff edge to look out at the island. It was barely a stone's throw away yet I had no way of getting to it. And even if I did, the priory of Saint Clément was on the far western side of the island according to Mother Ophélie, a good fifteen miles further on. It was very frustrating. I stood for some time staring across the watery divide wondering how I could get there. When I turned back I saw a figure watching me from a distance. It was Mother Ophélie. She didn't say anything but the following day she brought me a visitor.

'Brother Onefre,' explained Ophélie helping me along to the parlour.

'From Saint Clément?'

'He was the one who brought you to us. He understands a little English - enough at any rate to answer your questions. I will leave you two alone together.'

Brother Onefre was a kindly old monk, weather-beaten from his time in a wind-swept monastery on the edge of the Atlantic. I took his hands in mine and thanked him for my life. He gave a modest shrug of his shoulders as though rescuing half-drowned corpses from the sea was an everyday chore for him. Considering where his priory was located at the edge of the Atlantic, maybe it was.

'Is there no hope of survivors?'

'*Hélas,* you were the only one.'

'No bodies either?'

At this he looked a little coy. 'There were other bodies, yes, which was why you were nearly missed. You have to understand there are many shipwrecks along this stretch of coast. Bodies are frequently washed up on our beach. The local people bring them to us for burial.'

'What did you do with them? Can I see them? I may be able to identify them.'

He grimaced painfully. '*Mon frère,* it was over a week ago and in this heat...'

I nodded. 'You buried them. Of course you did. I'm sorry.'

He gave a regretful shrug of his shoulders.

'So there's no way of knowing who they were?' I asked hoping against hope. 'Maybe they survived. Maybe the ship sailed on.'

The old man's face was sad. 'The fisherman who found you also found this.'

He produced a small piece of timber with writing on it. It had complete letters "TC" and part of the letter "H". I recognized it instantly as a piece of the *Gretchen* nameplate. I grasped the thing tightly as though it were the Holy Rood itself.

'Was this all? Nothing else?'

He shook his head. 'It was a severe storm, *mon frère*. But there are many beaches and inlets along this coast. They could have easily put in there. I dare say in time...'

He tried to sound optimistic but I could tell he thought it was a hopeless quest. If any had survived the storm his abbey would surely have heard by now. Yet I didn't want to give up hope. Not until I was certain. I desperately wanted to find out what had happened to my companions. Short of going to the island and digging up the remains I could see no way of knowing whose they were.

At least I was properly dressed again - Brother Onefre had brought me a fresh robe from his monastery. But what should I do next? Should I carry on to Gascony and explain what I knew to Lucatz's abbot? Or should I return to Bury and try to discover more from there? I didn't know what to do for the best.

As it turned out the decision was not mine to make. The next time Mother Ophélie came into my room she was looking distraught.

'Is something wrong mother? Have I outstayed my welcome? I promise to be out of your hair soon.'

'No brother, it's not that.'

'Well then what?'

She couldn't look me in the eye. 'I am so sorry.'

She stepped aside and two French guards came in accompanied by a smaller man.

'What's this?' I grinned nervously. 'My escort back to England?'

'An escort, yes brother,' said the smaller man. 'But not to England.'

Chapter Twenty-four
ESCAPING DEATH (AGAIN)

They put me in chains, tied me on a donkey and led me into town. Once there I was transferred to a wicker cart and trundled through the streets along with a whole lot of robbers and felons all of us shackled together. My protestations of innocence fell on deaf ears. I didn't know why I had been arrested or what I was supposed to have done. For now there was nothing I could do but go along with them.

We eventually came to a halt outside a large stone building which turned out to be the town hall. Here we were herded from the tumbril and into some sort of ante-chamber that was dark and stuffy and filled with the great unwashed of La Rochelle. On the way we had to pass through what was evidently the execution yard. This was a large open-air arena arranged more as a *théâtre de spectacle* than as a place for the meting out of justice. It consisted of a row of upright posts, ten in all, set on a platform high enough so that spectators could enjoy a clear and uninterrupted view of proceedings. As we shuffled along I had a good chance to gauge the mechanics of death.

To each post was attached a small coil of hempen rope which could be looped around the neck of the malefactor. Some were already *occupé* waiting for the rest to be filled. Once all ten positions were filled the executioner would pass along the line inserting his *baton* into each coil of rope in turn and twisting it until he – or she for there were women and children among the victims – choked to death. If they were lucky their necks would snap thus ending their suffering quickly. If not then the process might take a little longer. The victims or their families could speed matters along by bribing the executioner to end the process quickly. Against that were the spectators who might pay for the opposite: to slow things down thereby prolonging the agony and increasing the entertainment value. There was often a tussle between the two to see who could bribe the executioner the most, to his considerable profit. All this I had gleefully explained to me by one of my fellow prisoners, a grinning dwarf with watery eyes and bad teeth.

'Why are you here?' I asked him in French. 'What was your crime?'

He shrugged fatalistically. '*J'ai donné un coup de pied au chien du maire.*' He'd kicked the mayor's dog.

No-one remained in the ante-chamber for long. Over a door at the far end hung a small statuette of the Holy Mother looking particularly sad and bereft of promise. This door, I imagined, led to the courtroom and I looked forward to going through it and putting an end to this outrage. One by one prisoners were marched through the door which would remain closed for barely a minute or two before opening again, the first prisoner marched out and the next marched in. In this way a dozen could be processed in the space of half an hour while from the execution yard came the periodic sound of cheers and applause as Madame Garotte consumed her latest batch of victims.

At last it was my turn. The door to the Madonna Room opened and I was ushered inside. To my astonishment what I found there was not a courtroom at all but a small office filled with a desk the size of which even Prior Herbert would have envied. Behind it sat the presumed instigator of this legal charade, a short, stocky man with the bored expression of someone waiting for the end of the day so he could get home and have his supper. In fact he hadn't bothered waiting for supper but was nibbling something from a side-dish that looked to me suspiciously like garlic cloves.

By now I was angry, filthy, tired and in pain from my injured foot. I was in no mood for pleasantries.

'*Monsieur le maire* -' I began.

'*Op!*' He stopped me with a raised finger. '*Pas de maire, monsieur. Je suis le Sénéchal.*'

'Seneschal, mayor - whatever you choose to call yourself - why have I been arrested? You have no right. I have done nothing wrong. I am a senior member of a very important English abbey – the abbey of Saint Edmund. My master, the abbot of Saint Edmund's - *l'abbé de Saint Edmund*,' I translated carefully in case he didn't get the message, 'will be very displeased to find one of his flock has been treated like a common criminal. Very displeased indeed.'

I would have folded my arms defiantly if they hadn't still been chained together.

The man smiled. 'And my master, *le roi de France* - the king of France,' he translated equally carefully, 'would be displeased to know that a *monque* was a murderer.'

My jaw fell open. 'Murderer? I'm no murderer. What are you talking about?'

He glanced down at a piece of parchment on the desk in front of him. 'You were a passenger aboard a Hinglish sheep, *le Chréchien - oui?*'

'The *Gretchen*, yes,' I nodded impatiently. 'So?'

'What 'appened to this Hinglish sheep?'

Did I really have to go through all the details - the nuns, the mutiny, the pirates? I decided to keep my answers as brief as possible:

'There was a storm, a violent storm. We were driven onto the rocks. The sheep – I mean ship – was damaged and disappeared beneath the waves.'

He nodded thoughtfully. 'And, er, 'ow is it you did not disappear with it?'

'I escaped.'

'Hescaped 'ow - exactly?'

'As a matter of fact I jumped.'

'You jumped? From a moving sheep? In the middle of a storm?' He raised incredulous eyebrows to his guards who shook their heads and laughed at the suggestion.

'I know it sounds fantastical,' I said glancing at them. 'But that's what happened.'

'You must be a very good swimmer, *monsieur.*'

'No, I can't swim. I didn't need to. I landed on my feet incidentally twisting my ankle in the process,' I added as definitive proof. 'Ask the sisters of Sainte Catherine des Vagues if you don't believe me.'

The mayor nodded sagely. 'And the others? What 'appened to them?'

'I'm ... not sure.'

'They remained haboard?'

'Yes – possibly. I don't know.'

'So, to sum up: you hescaped but your colleagues you habandoned to their fate.'

'I didn't *abandon* them. They could have jumped too if they'd wanted. They chose not to. Look, the truth is I don't know what happened to the others. That's what I've been trying to find out.'

'All of which is good news for you.'

'How is that good news?' I asked indignantly.

He shrugged. 'If there are no survivors, then there can be no witnesses to the murder.'

'There you go again. I've already told you, there was no murder.'

'Not on the sheep, perhaps. But I am talking about the murder of a certain friar in Saint Nazaire.'

I was shocked by the sudden change of subject. Amazed he even knew about it.

'That wasn't me.'

'You were in Saint Nazaire when the murder took place?'

'Yes, along with three of my companions.'

'All of whom are now conveniently dead.'

'You make it sound as though I planned the whole thing.'

He gave a condescending smile.

I was growing sick of this. 'I told you I had nothing to do with it.'

'So you say. In any case it does not matter. My colleagues *en Bretagne* wish to 'ave this matter resolved. They know it was someone from your Hinglish sheep who murdered this friar. *Hélas*, you are the only one available.'

'So I'm to pay the penalty? Even though I'm completely innocent?'

This was ridiculous. French law? French lynching more like. Time to wheel out the heavy artillery:

'*Monsieur le Sénéchal*,' I said as condescendingly as I could. 'We are here in the fine city of La Rochelle, are we not? And if memory serves, La Rochelle lies within the county of Poitou – *oui?*'

He gave a bored shrug. '*Et donc?*'

'*Et donc* – so - your overlord and mine is not, as you said, the king of France but the king of England - *le roi d'Angleterre*. Poitou is part of the Duchy of Aquitaine and King Henry, *my* king, is still its duke. As an Englishman I demand to be judged by other Englishmen under English law.'

There, I thought triumphantly. Let him chew on that - along with his garlic.

The seneschal's lip curled. 'And for 'ow long do you think a twelve-year-old boy will be able to 'old on to 'is *duché?*' he asked wryly.

'Long enough for there to be at least one more trial,' by which I meant his if he didn't release me.

The seneschal glowered. I could see his puny brain working it out. He might not bother about the abbot of Bury but he wouldn't dare risk upsetting the king of England. He was weakening, I could tell. Oh yes, I had him now. A conciliatory smile spread slowly across his face.

'*Cas prouvé. A l'échafaud.*'

Échafaud? That's French for scaffold isn't it?

'No, wait!' I protested. 'You can't!' But already the guards were pulling me towards the door.

Outside in the yard the executioner was leaning casually against the scaffold steps while above him nine of his clients, already with ropes around their necks, waited patiently for his tenth - me. The crowd was growing impatient. It seemed I had taken longer than usual to pass through the Madonna Room. Seeing me being led up the steps they began to jeer loudly. Doubtless I was something of a novelty. They can't have too many monk necks to stretch never mind an English one.

I would have continued to protest my innocence but I could see there was no point. Instead I resolved to die with dignity, to show these French peasants how an Englishman went to his Maker. I was first in line. The rope went around my neck and I felt the executioner insert his baton and slowly begin to tighten it. My windpipe rapidly became restricted so that I couldn't breathe and my tongue was pushed out. The jeers from the crowd grew fainter as they and the sky and everything else started to fade. Panic made me judder as I fought uselessly for breath. Slowly my life began to ebb away. The voices faded. The day was turning dark. Down some long tunnel a strange light appeared and someone at the end was beckoning me... come... come...

But before I finally lost consciousness there was a commotion at the bottom of the steps. I couldn't turn my head to see but I was sure it was the little man who had arrested me at Saint Catherine's. There then ensued some agitated exchanges with the executioner. Finally the garotte was slackened and I could breathe again. I gulped in a lungful of air that tasted like sweet nectar as the garotte was removed to groans of disappointment from the crowd.

'What's happening?' I gasped as the little man removed the shackles from my ankles.

'This appears to be your lucky day, *mon frère*. The wreck of a ship has been found.'

My heart leapt. 'The wreck of a ship? You mean the *Gretchen*?'

'No, another.'

I shook my head. 'I don't understand.'

'We are plagued with pirates along this stretch of coast, my friend. You seem to have done the seneschal a service.'

The pirate ship. I'd almost forgotten about it.

'Is that all?' I asked. 'Just the pirate ship? No other?'

'No other ship, but many more bodies.'

'How many more?'

'I am sorry, *mon frère*. They are the only details I have.'

'In that case I want to see for myself. Where are these bodies? I must see them.'

The man shook his head. 'Not a good idea. In the light of what has happened the seneschal is prepared to overlook the unfortunate business in Saint Nazaire – for now. But that could change.'

'I already told him, I had nothing to do with that.'

'Nevertheless, if I were you I would return to England by the quickest possible route. And,' he added with a wry smile, 'avoid passing through *la Bretagne*.'

There's not much more to say of my sojourn in France. Even if I'd wanted to stay there was no point. I had no idea where the wreck of the pirate ship had been found let alone where the bodies ended up or whether my friends were among them. My only option was to take the advice of my little friend and return to England with all possible haste.

My journey back was relatively uneventful – certainly compared with the journey down. Mother Ophélie loaned me a little money for necessities along the way. It took me a week to get to Cherbourg staying at various Benedictine houses. A further week before I could find a cog to ferry me across the Channel to Portsmouth and three days by road to Bury, the final few miles on the back of a hay cart. I cannot tell you what joy it was to see the familiar turreted gates of the town and Samson's tower looming benevolently over the abbey church. I fell down on my knees to give thanks to Almighty God for my deliverance. I was home. I had made it. The nightmare of the past two months was over.

Or so I thought.

PART FOUR

Chapter Twenty-five
REUNITED AT LAST

'Ah, the prodigal returns! Come in thou lost and wasteful child! We have the fatted calf already prepared have we not, dutiful clerk?'

Prior Herbert beckoned me from the far end of his cavernous study. His secretary, Jephthet, sniggered as he closed the door behind me cutting off my escape. As I think I've mentioned before, Herbert looking pleased with himself is always a worrying sign, and never more so than when his clerk is also looking chirpy. I therefore approached his desk with some trepidation.

'Well now brother let's see. How long has been? Two months?'

'Nearer three,' I said warily.

Herbert nodded. 'Three months. We've missed you, haven't we Jephthet?'

Jephthet sniggered again.

'And in that time have you achieved all that you set out to achieve? All that was commissioned of you?'

I squirmed uneasily. 'Not quite, Brother Prior.'

'No? How so?'

'There were … difficulties.'

'Difficulties? Please - elucidate.'

'Well for a start I hurt my foot.' I wiggled my left ankle for him to see.

He looked and tutted. 'Oh dear. Better now?'

'Yes - thank you.'

'Good. Anything else?'

'Well…'

'Come along, speak up. Don't keep us in suspense. Tell all.'

'I hardly know where to start.'

'Start at the beginning. How is Father Ambrose? In robust health I trust?'

'Father Ambrose?'

'*Abbot* Ambrose. Of Saint Gilles. The abbot you were meant to meet there.'

'I … didn't meet Father Ambrose.'

Herbert nodded. 'Too busy making the sisters welcome I expect.'

I grimaced. 'They didn't meet him either.'

'Oh? Why might that be?'

'The sisters … never arrived in Saint Gilles.'

Herbert's eyebrows knitted severely. 'Never arrived? But Brother Walter, that was the whole point of the exercise. The purpose for which you went. The *raison d'être* of your journey. How, pray, did the sisters not arrive in Saint Gilles?'

'I … lost them.'

'You *lost* them?' He looked with incredulity at Jephthet who by now was positively squealing with glee.

'Well, not *lost* exactly,' I squirmed. 'Temporarily mislaid would be more accurate. And not all of them. One died of natural causes. Agatha. The rest … disappeared.'

Herbert was shaking his head with disbelief. 'Brother, you are not making much sense. You say nine nuns disappeared? From a ship? In the middle of the ocean? How is this possible?'

I sighed. He obviously knew. But how? The answer came with a nod to his clerk. Still giggling, Jephthet skipped to the prior's private chapel and pushed open the door. In they all filed one after another: Rebecca, Theresa, Ursula, Prudence, Magdalene, Mairi and Federica.

My heart leapt when I saw them.

'God be praised!' I cried clapping my hands together. 'You're alive! All of you. It's a miracle!'

'Dear Brother Walter,' smiled Rebecca coming quickly up to me and taking my hands in hers. 'We are indeed all here. And no miracle.'

The sisters now crowded round me like a gaggle of excited geese.

'So it wasn't an illusion? I really did see you on the deck?'

Rebecca frowned. 'Yes, I'm sorry about that. We didn't mean to frighten you. It was the pirates we were trying to scare.'

'And you did! Oh, you were magnificent! But where did you come from? Where had you been?'

'In the tuns of course.'

'In the where?'

'The wine tuns, brother.'

The wine tuns! The giant barrels in the *Gretchen's* hold where wine was stored. Except there wasn't any wine in them, or anything else on our trip as Captain Dunning kept reminding us. They were completely empty.

I shook my head in amazement. 'What about the others? Brother Lucatz, the contessa, Dame Flora?'

'They are all alive and well,' she reassured me. 'At least they were when we last saw them.'

'Which was where?'

'In Rochefort where we came ashore. After that I don't know. We all went our separate ways. The sisters and I decided to come back here.'

'You didn't wish to continue south?'

'As you see.'

I nodded. 'Then tell me what happened after I jumped ship. Why didn't you follow me?'

'We wanted to. We were about to. But then you cried out.'

'I'd twisted my ankle.'

'We didn't know that. We hesitated and by then it was too late. A wave caught us and we were swept back out to sea.'

'So how did you escape? The *Gretchen* went down, I saw the wreckage.'

'No the ship did not sink. There was a lot of damage and we were taking on water, but we managed to stay afloat. The next day a French trawler saw us and towed us into port.'

'Then whose were the bodies?'

'Bodies brother?'

'The bodies on the beach.'

She shrugged. 'Pirates?'

Pirates. Of course! It was the dead pirates and not our people Brother Onefre had buried. He wouldn't have known the difference.

'Then it's real?' I giggled stupidly. 'Everyone on board the *Gretchen* survived? I can't believe it!'

'Believe it brother for it is true. Here,' she smiled taking my hands in hers again. 'Feel life!'

'This is all very heart-warming,' said Herbert watching us with distaste. 'But it does not alter the fact that you, Brother Physician, are guilty of a gross dereliction of duty. You were given a simple task, to accompany these vulnerable young women to their

255

new home in the south of France, and quite clearly you failed.'

'No,' said Rebecca turning on him sharply. 'Forgive me Brother Prior, but Brother Walter is not to blame for what happened. That is why we are here today. To exonerate him – and to thank him.'

'To *thank* him?' Herbert practically choked on the word.

'Yes indeed. If it wasn't for Brother Walter we would not be here.'

'I should have thought the opposite were true. And you, sister, haven't yet explained why you went into hiding. From what I've been hearing your actions caused the crew of the *Gretchen* to abandon ship, the ship to be cast adrift on the high seas and be left vulnerable to attack by pirates.'

She shook her head fiercely. 'Not so. The *Gretchen* was adrift because of bad weather. The crew abandoned ship because of their own superstitions. And the pirates would have attacked whether or not we had a crew. You could even argue that if it wasn't for our actions the pirates might have won. And much as I respect your office, Brother Prior, we do not have to answer to you.'

Herbert glowered at her impotently. 'Others may think differently.'

'Like who?'

'Your own bishop for one.'

'Ely has no bishop at the moment. Bishop Robert was dethroned last May – as I'm sure you are aware.'

'The pope then.'

She gave a wry smile. 'I should have thought His Holiness had enough to concern himself with just at the moment without bothering about a few wayward English nuns.'

'Got it all worked out, haven't you, sister?' I chuckled with grudging admiration. The girl had definitely grown into a woman since I last saw her. 'But wait a moment. You said you hid in the wine tuns. We looked in them, I'm sure of it. We looked everywhere on the ship.'

'We?'

'Brother Lucatz and I.'

At the mention of Lucatz's name Rebecca smiled a little. It was then that I knew. Someone had to have helped them, they couldn't have done all that alone. It was Lucatz. It had to be. Hogtie had been right about him if for the wrong reasons. Lucatz hadn't been *murdering* the nuns, he'd been *protecting* them. He'd secretly arranged everything from hiding the nuns to persuading me that Bruno had followed me into the hold in order to throw me off the scent. I remembered also how after the mutiny he'd taken charge of food rationing - which inexplicably always seemed less than it should have been. Small wonder with seven extra mouths to feed.

And when I thought about it other things began to make sense too. The argument with Rebecca just before her disappearance. They hadn't been arguing. They'd been finalizing their plans. And all that tosh about Ghost ships and flying nuns. Flying nuns indeed! Flying robes more like. He'd arranged that too. The question was why?

Before I could ask Rebecca cut short the meeting:

'We did not come here for argument but to thank Brother Walter for what he did for us and to put his mind at rest. That we have done. Now, with your permission Brother Prior.'

Without waiting for his reply the sisters abruptly filed out with Jephthet practically tripping over his own feet in his haste to open the door for them.

'*They* may wish to thank you,' growled Herbert once they'd gone, 'but I do not. You were charged with the simple task of escorting nine nuns to Saint Gilles in France but instead they are back here and I am in the invidious position of having to explain to the Bishop of Ely – when a new one has been appointed - why he may not now dispose of his property in Ipswich.'

'The sisters are reviving the order of Our Lady of Ipswich?'

'It would appear so.'

I frowned. 'I wonder why they didn't wish to continue on to Saint Gilles.'

'You can ask that? Because of your incompetence of course. Despite what Sister Rebecca said I hold you responsible.'

'Nine nuns.'

'What?'

'You said nine nuns. There were eight here just now.'

'Yes eight. Nine less the nun who died – Agatha wasn't it?'

'But the ninth nun was the prioress. Dame Flora and Agatha. That's two less. There should only be seven sisters now, but there were eight.'

Herbert scowled. 'Eight nuns, nine. What does it matter? The point is they are here and not in Saint Gilles.'

'Yes, quite,' I nodded. 'Brother Prior, will you excuse me?' I started for the door.

'No I will not excuse you. I haven't finished with you yet. Brother Walter come back here. Brother *Walter!*'

But I wasn't listening. I dashed down the stairs as fast as my injured ankle would allow and caught up with the nuns as they were crossing the yard. Dressed in identical robes, all nuns look alike. Except one nun was different. She didn't have the black veil of a fully professed nun but the white veil of a novice.

'Lady Carmela? Is that you?'

She stopped and turned to face me. '*Sister* Carmela now,' she smiled.

'You've joined the Order of Saint Mary Grace? When was this?'

'Sister Carmela approached us before we left the ship,' said Rebecca coming over.

'What did your mother, the contessa have to say about it?'

Carmela shook her head. 'Do not worry about my mother. She will not miss me. It was sons she really wanted in any case. Besides, I have a new mother now.' She inclined her head towards Rebecca.

I looked at her in surprise. 'You have assumed the mantle of prioress, Rebecca? I hadn't realised.'

'I was elected by my sisters.'

'What about your old prioress?'

'Dame Flora did not wish to return with us to England.'

'Did not wish to or was not allowed to?'

'Let's just say we thought it best we had a change.'

'That's not the only change. Your habits?' I noticed they were wearing the regular black veil of the Benedictines not those extraordinary white ones.

259

'If you remember we lost our old ones,' Rebecca replied wryly. 'Besides, they were impractical. These suit us better. And now brother, if you've no more questions.'

'Just one. The yellow crosses I saw sewn on your undergarments. What was the purpose of those?'

Her lip curled into an enigmatic smile. 'A symbol of our repentance, brother.'

Repentance. Now there was an interesting word.

Chapter Twenty-six
ANSWERS

'It's good to have you back, master.'

'It's good to be back, Nahum. Have you managed to blow anything up in my absence?'

I peered purposefully around my laboratorium giving my assistant a searching look as I did so.

'The roof, four retorts, three ferrets and your entire stock of burdock leaves, master.'

My jaw fell open. 'God in Heaven, boy!'

He gave a cheeky grin.

'Oh yes, very good Nahum. One day you'll cut yourself on that sharp tongue of yours. What's really been happening in my absence?'

'Prior Herbert's been in practically every day – keeping an eye on things, he said. But so has Brother Jocelin m-making s-sure the p-p-prior didn't interf-f-f-fere t-too m-much.'

I wagged an admonishing finger. 'I'll tell him, my saucy little man. Jocelin doesn't like his impediment mocked.'

Nahum inclined his head. 'I mean no disrespect, master. I'm very fond of Dom Jocelin. He lets me read to him.'

That I could believe. Now well into his seventh decade of life, Jocelin was practically blind and needed a novice to lead him about. He could no longer decipher even the largest letters without the aid of a reading stone. This for a man who lived his entire life for the written word was a cruel punishment. And Herbert was too mean to give him an amanuensis.

I looked at Nahum's guileless face. 'Tell me,' I said as casually as I could. 'When Prior Herbert was here, did he say anything to you?'

'About what, master?'

'Oh, I don't know. Anything at all. Your future here at the abbey perhaps?'

'He did indeed. He told me that in return for spying on you he would recommend me to your position as abbey physician when you finally vacate it.'

'He did what?'

'Oh, not in so many words, but that's what he meant. Prior Herbert is not the most subtle of persuaders.'

'And were you persuaded?'

'Of course not master.'

'Your loyalty commends you.'

'Not yet anyway. Maybe in a year or two when you've taught me all you know. By the way, I have another mime for you.'

I sighed. 'Go on.'

He started gesticulating wildly, flailing his arms about like a demented monkey.

'Onethumb's been in,' I nodded. 'And if I'm reading your signing correctly my brother Joseph wants to see me.'

'As soon as you can, master.'

It is often said that old age and wisdom go hand in hand, that with white hair and sagging jowls comes knowledge and sagacity. Don't be fooled. That sapient sneer is probably painful corns and a furrowed brow comes from trying to remember where we last saw our slippers. Not that longevity is not a desirable commodity especially in those set in authority over us. Princes, you may note, do not live long. Few have ever made it to their fiftieth birthday. King John died two months short of his forty-ninth while his brother Richard was a mere forty-one when a lucky shot from a crossbow hit its mark. (Not so lucky for the bowman, however, who was flayed alive for his trouble.) Their father, the second King Henry and our present king's grandfather, did manage to make it past his half-century. However, by then he was so bow-legged that he walked like a gibbon and was suffering from an anal fistula so painful that it would have made Samson's protuberances feel like gentle balsam by comparison. That's what comes of having an empire that stretched from the Scottish borders to the Pyrenees. Keeping all that together meant spending most of his reign in the saddle with predictable results. No, if a long life is what you crave then it's better to be a churchman. Abbot Samson was seventy-six when he died while Gilbert of Sempringham reached the unconscionable age of 107. Not that he would have known it. By then his mind was so addled he was barely able to keep track of his own saliva. I am a little over half Gilbert's age - fifty-five next Lammas Day, God permitting. Having lived so long and seen so much I didn't think it was possible to be surprised any more. But I was wrong...

The first thing I noticed as I approached Joseph's shop was that the mezuzah, the piece of parchment inscribed with a Hebrew verse from the Torah only lately affixed to the doorway, had been removed: the holes where the nails that held the casing were clearly visible. The wand Caduceus – or was it Asclepius? - was also absent from across the doorway so I knew Joseph was on the premises. The door was open on this late July morning and I looked in. Onethumb was the only person I could see working there with a pestle and mortar.

We went back years Onethumb and I, twenty years to be precise to a time when he was a raggedy street urchin living from day to day by his wits and what he could thieve. Since then he had grown up, married, become a father and for the last half dozen years he'd been, on my recommendation, Joseph's personal assistant. Not bad for a nameless orphan with one deformed hand and a mute into the bargain.

Stepping across the threshold I made the sign of the Cross: 'God bless all in this house.'

As soon as he saw me Onethumb's face lit up. That cheered my heart. At least someone was pleased to see me.

'How are you, old friend?' I said to him taking his one good hand in both of mine.

He nodded that he was fine.

'And Rosabel and the little ones, Hal and little Rosa?'

He signed that his wife and children were also doing well. But he was more concerned about me. He had heard disturbing tales of shipwrecks and murder.

'Who's been speaking out of turn?'

He nodded to the back room from where came low voices and signed that my cousin was here.

'Bruno? Here?'

I marched in through the curtain that separated the shop from the living area. Sure enough, Bruno and Joseph were there lounging on the preposterous cushions that pass for furniture in Joseph's house and chatting as though nothing was amiss. I stood in the entrance glowering at the pair of them.

'Ah, there you are Walter,' Joseph beamed when he saw me. 'You got my message. Good. Come in, come in my brother. Don't stand on ceremony.'

'Never mind all that.' I dismissed and turned angrily to Bruno. 'What happened to you? Where have you been? And why didn't you tell me you were back?'

'Walter, Walter,' laughed Joseph flapping a negligent wrist. 'Give the man a chance to answer.'

'Well I'm sorry,' I said. 'It's just that after all that's happened I'd have thought he could at least have the decency to let me know he was alive before paying social calls.'

'I didn't know you were back,' said Bruno. 'I thought you were dead.'

'Sorry to disappoint.'

'No, that's not what I meant -'

'Howsoever,' Joseph interrupted. 'You both are here now so no harm done. Sit you down my brother. Relax.'

'I don't want to sit.'

'Then don't. But I'll thank you to remember this is my house. If you are going to behave like a boor then you can leave and come back when you are in a better mood.'

He was right of course, it was extremely ill-mannered of me. My excuse is my continued state of nervous exhaustion which is hardly surprising given all that had happened. So I sat, but I was still seething inside. I was so distracted in fact that I'd hardly noticed until then that Joseph had reverted to his former attire of pilos and gown once again. Gone was the kippah and the long Jewish robe he had worn the last time I was here. Gone too was the pedestal holding the Tanakh, or Jewish Bible, that had been on prominent display.

'I see you've given up on your religion again,' I smirked. 'Back to your old heathen ways are you?'

'It was the clothes. My customers expect to see me in my magician's cloak. It adds to the mystique - not to mention profit,' he chuckled.

'The Tanakh too I see.' I nodded to where the pedestal had stood in the middle of the room.

'Yes. Too showy. I wouldn't want to be accused of being a peacock.'

At this Bruno snorted, no doubt remembering my guff the last time we were here together.

I shot him an admonishing glare. 'Are you going to sit there and snigger or are you going to tell me what happened?'

Bruno sighed. 'Not much to tell really. You know most of it. The pirate boat sank – that was the end of them. Next day a French ship saw us and gave us a tow into port. That's about it.'

'Did you not think to try to find out what happened to me?'

'We thought you'd drowned.'

'Your concern is underwhelming. What happened after you'd landed in Rochefort?'

'How did you know it was Rochefort?'

'Never mind. Well?'

He shrugged. 'We split up. The captain went off to talk to some French officials. Everyone else went their own way. I came back here. And it wasn't easy, either. I got robbed twice.'

'My heart bleeds. Did you not wish to continue to Italy with your patroness, the contessa?'

He squirmed. 'We decided to part company.'

'Job not match up to your expectations? Or you to hers?'

He frowned. 'You got it all wrong about me and the contessa, Walter. I was only ever her manservant.'

'I've heard it called worse,' I sniffed. 'What about the others? No need to tell me about the sisters. I've already spoken to them.'

'You've seen them?' interrupted Joseph. 'The nuns?'

I nodded. 'They were at the abbey yesterday.'

Bruno chortled. 'That was quite a show they put on, wasn't it? Coming back from the dead like that.'

'Hardly from the dead. They'd been on the *Gretchen* all the while, in hiding.'

Bruno's eyebrows went up. 'No! You mean all that about them being murdered...?'

'Was false,' I confirmed.

'Well I never! Why?'

'I was hoping you'd be able to tell me.'

'Huh! Don't ask me. I gave up trying to work it out after those two jumped off the mast. I'm surprised they came back here though. I thought they'd carry on with Lucatz and the prioress.'

I looked up. 'Wait a moment. You're saying Lucatz and Dame Flora left together?'

'Looked that way to me.'

'Which way did they go?'

'Same as they were always going. South.'

'Towards Languedoc. You're sure about that?'

267

He nodded.

'And they left together? You're sure about that too?'

'Why wouldn't they?'

Why not indeed. Except if my suspicions were right and Lucatz had been helping the nuns hide then I would have expected him and Dame Flora to be less friendly than they were. I certainly wouldn't have expected them to continue as travelling companions.

I looked across at Joseph who had been sitting quietly listening to us. 'You don't seem very surprised by any of this.'

He smiled. 'Let's just say it fits.'

'With what? You've got your enigmatic face on. Is there something you know? Something you're not telling us?'

He stroked his long beard thoughtfully, got up slowly and poured three cups of wine.

'What do you know about Lucatz?' he asked handing me my cup.

'What sort of question is that? He's my oldest friend. We were students together.'

'Yes, but do you know why he was here?'

'We all know why he was here. What, are you asking me to go over it again?'

'Indulge me.'

I sighed. 'The nuns of Saint Mary Elms wanted to go to Languedoc to bolster the presence of the Church in a region racked by a deviant religious sect called the Cathari Brethren. Lucatz came to escort them. I suppose you're now going to tell me that isn't the case?'

'Oh no, that is why he was here all right. But perhaps what you didn't know is that he came not as a Benedictine monk but as a Perfectus.'

I frowned. 'As a what?'

'A Perfectus. It's the highest rank in the hierarchy of the Cathari Brethren.'

If the sky had fallen on my head just then I don't think I could have been more shocked. For a moment I couldn't speak.

'Rubbish!' I exploded at last.

'Yes, I thought that would be your response which is why I didn't mention it before. I'm sorry Walter, but it's the truth. Lucatz was - *is* - a senior member of the Cathar confederacy. A very senior member as a matter of fact.'

I snorted. 'You don't know what you're talking about. I know Lucatz. We studied together. We professed together as novices, for Christ's sake.'

'That was forty years ago. People change. He might have been a monk then but not any more. Believe me. He's a true convert to the Cathar faith.'

'I always thought there was something funny about him,' sneered Bruno.

I glared angrily at him. 'Bruno, you don't know what you're talking about, so please keep your mouth shut.'

'Sorry I spoke.'

I returned to Joseph. 'How do you know this?'

'I didn't. Not for certain. Not until he came here. But I do not say these things lightly. I have made extensive enquiries. There can be no doubt.'

I shook my head vigorously. 'No, it's not possible. I just spent a month sharing a cabin with the man. Don't you think I would have noticed if he'd become a heretic?'

'You are a very trusting person, Walter. But in this case you are allowing yourself to be blinded by your commendable loyalty to your friend. Religious dissenters are good at hiding their allegiances. As a Jew I should know,' he added wryly. 'But deception can only go so far if a man is to remain true to his real faith.'

'He was true to his faith,' I insisted. 'His Christian faith.'

'And so far as that goes he was.'

I frowned. 'What does that mean? Was he a Christian or wasn't he?'

'Both.' Joseph smiled indulgently. 'What do you know of the Cathari?'

'Not much.'

'Then permit me. The Cathari are indeed Christians insofar as they follow the teachings of Jesus Christ. But there are differences. They regard the material world as the product of an evil god while the spiritual world is the realm of a good god.'

'There is only one God,' I insisted.

'The Cathari believe in two: a good god of the New Testament and an evil god which they associate with the Old Testament – or the *Tanakh* to give it it's proper name. That is why I displayed my copy of it so prominently when he was here. I wanted to test his reaction to it. As I suspected, he avoided it.'

'And that's it? That's your proof?'

'Not only that. You may also remember that he also declined to eat my food.'

'So did I.'

'Yes, but that's because you were sulking.'

'I wasn't sulking. I wasn't hungry. And Lucatz refused because he was still recovering from his journey.'

'No. He refused because my food consisted of nothing but meat – deliberately so.'

'Yes, I remember that,' said Bruno. 'Never seen to so much meat – lamb, beef, even pork. Didn't you notice?'

'I noticed you stuffing your face with it.'

'But not Lucatz,' said Joseph. 'If, as I suspected, he really is a Perfectus of the Cathar faith then I knew he wouldn't touch it.'

'Why? Is meat supposed to be evil too?' I scoffed.

'Yes, as a matter of fact. Meat is animal and animals reproduce. The Cathari believe that any form of reproduction preserves the material world and thereby perpetuates evil. Therefore meat is to be avoided. They don't like marriage for the same reason.'

I shook my head. 'I don't believe a word of this. I know Lucatz. He's far too sensible to believe in this sort of nonsense.'

'Did you see him eat meat? Not just here but anywhere?'

'Yes of course he did.'

'When?'

I tried to think back but all I could remember was those damned beans he bought in Jersey. And then there was the dinner Captain Dunning provided. The contessa's pheasant. He didn't eat that either – still complaining of a bad stomach. But he didn't have a bad stomach. I was the one who kept throwing up over the side of the ship, not him.

Bruno was frowning. 'Did I hear you say these Cathari don't like the Old Testament?'

Joseph nodded.

'Ah, well that explains it.'

'Explains what?' I said irritably. 'What are you talking about now?'

'Why he refused to take the oath. You remember, in the captain's cabin? Dunning wanted us to swear we didn't murder that friar.'

'Yes. And I remember you were reluctant to do so.'

'But I did in the end. So did you. So did the Captain and so did the prioress. Everybody who went ashore in Saint Nazaire swore. The only one who didn't was Lucatz.' He grinned triumphantly. 'Well don't you get it? The Bible contains the Old Testament – the ... what did you call it Joseph?'

'The *Tanakh*.'

Bruno nodded triumphantly. 'There you are then.'

I glowered at him although I was also slightly relieved. I'd thought the reason Lucatz hadn't taken the oath had been because he was indeed the friar's murderer. But if he really was a Perfectus then that might explain it. Murderer or heretic. I wasn't sure which was worse.

'How do you know all this?' I said to Joseph. 'You're a Jew. This has nothing to do with you. Why are you even interested?'

'As I've told you many times in the past, Walter, wherever there is religious conflict Jews always somehow manage to suffer. So we have learned to keep abreast of all such matters. That way we are never surprised.'

I still wasn't convinced. 'You're saying those ridiculous clothes you wore, the Tanakh, the food and the mezuzah were all a ruse to expose Lucatz?'

'I had to be certain of my facts before I acted.'

'Acted? How?'

'Me,' smiled Bruno modestly.

'*You?*'

'I asked Bruno to tag along to look out for you,' said Joseph.

'You thought I came to kill you and all the time I was protecting you,' Bruno said proudly.

'Then a fat lot of use you were. Where were you when I was being garotted?'

'When you were what?'

I turned to Joseph. 'Why didn't you tell me all this before?'

'Would you have believed me?'

'No. And I don't believe you now.'

He looked at me kindly. 'I can understand your reluctance. You're very fond of your friend Lucatz, aren't you?'

'Of course I am. He's been like a brother to me. None closer,' I added spitefully.

'That was a very long time ago.'

'Time does not diminish friendship.'

'But it can alter allegiances. If Lucatz truly is a convert to Catharism then he is a dangerous man. There is no-one more zealous than a religious convert.'

'Lucatz would never harm me.'

'He might if he thought it would save your soul. Zealots have been known to weep genuine tears of regret as they prod their victims into the martyr's flames.'

'Lucatz isn't like that. And if what you say about him is true then why did he come all this way to escort nine nuns – nine *Catholic* nuns - back to his homeland? How do you explain that?'

'I couldn't if the nuns were truly Catholic.'

'Oh, I see. So now you're saying the sisters are Cathari too?'

He shrugged. 'It's a reasonable assumption. You say they were going to bolster the presence of the Catholic Church in Languedoc. But what if the opposite were true? What if they were going in support of their Cathar sisters?'

I shook my head. 'Not possible. I saw them yesterday. They are all true Catholics.'

'Now perhaps. But when they boarded the *Gretchen* they were under the influence of their prioress.'

My jaw dropped open. 'You think Dame Flora was a Cathar?'

'Without doubt the most committed of them all. I gather from Bruno you and she didn't exactly see eye to eye? She wouldn't if she saw you as the enemy.'

That I certainly couldn't deny. Her antipathy towards me personally had puzzled and saddened me from the very beginning. But if she was a committed Cathar then it would explain her behaviour. It must have been quite a shock when I turned up with Lucatz that first day in Ipswich.

'All right,' I said. 'Assume for the moment that you're right and the nuns were all Cathari adherents. What changed their minds?'

'That I admit is a puzzle. But for whatever reason at some point they must have begun to have doubts. Their prioress would never have accepted their apostasy – by all accounts she was a formidable woman. It would have taken a brave nun to stand up to her. I'm guessing that's what led to their extraordinary deception on board the ship. On a ship there is nowhere to run to. Hiding was the only way they could escape from her.'

'No, wait a moment,' I said shaking my head. 'Rebecca summoned me to Agatha's bedside to hear her last confession - her *Catholic* confession according to the customs of Holy Mother Church. Is that the action of a heretic? She practically dragged me from my bed to administer the last rite to Agatha as she lay dying. She was weak and emaciated – pitifully so.'

Joseph merely nodded. 'That sounds about right. Towards the end of their lives the most dedicated Cathari stop eating altogether. It's part of their desire to enter the afterlife in as pure a state as they can untainted by material things like food. But it sounds as though this Sister Rebecca of yours thought otherwise. If true she would have wanted a priest – you - to administer to a dying sister. Did you manage it?'

'No. Someone spiked my wine before I had a chance.' I glared accusingly at Bruno.

'I know you thought it was me. But it wasn't. I never touched your wine. Why would I?'

'Why would anyone?' agreed Joseph. 'Unless they wanted to stop you conducting a ritual that they believed would damn another's soul for ever.'

'You mean it was Lucatz who spiked my drink?'

I was finding all this hard to take in. I refused to accept the picture Joseph was painting of my friend. I knew him. Joseph didn't. There was a bond between us which had been forged so long ago and which I was convinced still held true. Yet doubts still lingered in my mind. I couldn't dismiss the fact that the strange feelings I'd had since the beginning of the trip were in part due to Lucatz. He never quite behaved as I expected, as a proper monk should. For one thing he never once joined me in singing the daily office. Nor did he know the words of the Te Deum. And then there was his reluctance to take the mass or recite the grace. I had excused him that as I'd excused him so many things. Was I so gratified to see him that I was blind to everything else?

'There are still things you haven't answered,' I said. 'That friar in Saint Nazaire. Who was he? Why did he die and at whose hand? Five of us went ashore that day: Bruno, Lucatz, Dame Flora, Captain Dunning and me. It wasn't me who killed that friar so it must have been one of the other four.' I shot an accusing glare at Bruno.

'I swore on Captain Dunning's Bible, didn't I?'

'Eventually.'

'Well it wasn't me. At least, not directly.'

'What does that mean? Bruno, if you know anything about this you must speak.'

He squirmed but eventually he came out with it:

'All right. I did meet up with the friar – or rather, he met up with me. He asked me if I knew where Lucatz and the others were. He said he was a friend of theirs. I didn't know who he was. He seemed all right, so I told him. But that's all I did. I swear he was still alive when I left him.'

Reluctantly I believed him. Whatever else Bruno was he was no murderer – he'd bungle that like he bungled everything else. But if not Bruno then who? I turned back to Joseph:

'I don't like what you did, tricking Lucatz in that underhand way and sending me off ignorant of the facts. If you had any doubts about him or Dame Flora or the nuns you should have told me. Your actions placed us all in mortal danger. Lucatz was my friend and I still count him as innocent until proven otherwise. He's not here so he can't answer for himself. Whatever his beliefs, whatever he has done he will remain dear to me. And I will remain loyal to him.'

With that I stomped out of the shop without even saying goodbye to Onethumb and with tears in my eyes, though I wasn't sure what hurt the most, my still-painful foot or my wounded pride.

Epilogue
Autumn 1220

What is truth? It is a question I have pondered for much of my life. Samson once told me truth is what is decided by those put in a position to interpret it and that there can only be one version or everyone will have their own ideas and the result would be anarchy. At the time I did not question his judgement. Now I'm not so sure.

It is always a shock when something we take to be immutable turns out not to be so, or when someone else's interpretation appears to be radically different from our own. And when that someone is a person we respect then we have to take their opinion seriously even though we may fundamentally disagree with it. In other words there is no single truth merely opinion and another's opinion is equally as valid as our own. The church fathers would not agree with me and I wouldn't expect them too. But they are as entitled to their opinion as everyone else.

A few months after my return from France I received a letter. It was unsigned and said very little other than to convey the sad news that my good friend Lucatz de Saint Gilles was dead. Bearing in mind what I've written about him in these pages you can imagine this was a great shock to me and filled me with deep sorrow. The details are stark and simple: Since the death of both Pope Innocent and of his champion in the war against the Cathari, Simon de Montfort, there had been a temporary lull in the fighting. But by the end of 1219 it had begun again this time under the leadership of Montfort's son, Amaury. It seems Lucatz was caught up in the fighting and was struck by a crossbow bolt during the second siege of Castelnaudary which continues to rage even as I write these words.

With the letter came another which was in Lucatz's own hand and addressed to me personally. This letter, with a great many revisions and corrections, was clearly still a work in progress since it was dated October 1219 and never sent. It is also written in the *Oc* dialect which I have here translated. It is worth reading in full for it explains much of what happened aboard the ill-fated *Gretchen*, what led up to it and what has occurred since. It begins:

My dearest beloved friend and brother in Christ, greetings.

By now you will know all but I wanted you to hear it from me. No doubt you despise me and think that I used our friendship for my own ends which if true pains me more deeply than I can say and has prompted me to write these words.

Let me say straight off that it was never my intention to deceive you. It is true our past association was the reason our Council of Elders chose me to come to England, but my only desire was to see my old friend again while there was still time, for once the true purpose of my mission was known I knew it would not have been possible for us to meet again. And so it has turned out to be. Beyond that I never meant you to be involved at all. That really was the fault of your prior. Indeed, I tried to dissuade him from letting you accompany me. I also tried to dissuade you. If you recall on that first day I tested your faith and was pleased to see you had lost none of your tolerance for others. For that reason I was content to take you along in preference to any other. Still, just coming with us was a risk for if you were ever to discover our true purpose your life would have been be in grave danger.

As you will have guessed by now I am an adherent of the Cathar faith. This I am sure came as a shock to you and you may wonder how and when I converted. It was not always the case. When we were novitiates together I was a true Catholic. It was only after we graduated and you returned to England that I changed although I had been interested in Gnostic teachings for a long time before that. You have to understand that I have lived among these people for most of my life and have known them to be decent, honest folk who wish nothing more than to live in peace with their neighbours and to be allowed to practise their faith. You met many yourself when you were studying in Montpellier so you know what I say to be true. No doubt you will hear many claims about us but most are either exaggerations or plain falsehoods put about by our enemies. Despite what you may think we remain true Christians and believe in the saving grace of our lord Jesus Christ. Our argument is with the fathers of the church of Rome which we believe has become corrupt and worldly. But my purpose here is not to proselytize much less try to convert you. It is to answer the questions regarding our voyage which I am sure must continue to rankle with you.

As you know by now the sisters of Ipswich were never what they claimed to be. Not Benedictine nuns sent to bolster the church in the south but as new converts to the Cathar Faith sent to swell our numbers here. They were recruited by their prioress, Dame Flora, herself a recent convert. You may wonder how a woman from the far north of your island should have come to adopt a faith of a people so far away. The answer lies in the Cathar attitude towards women which is very different to that of the Church. We believe the spirit to be sexless and can inhabit a male or a female body equally and indeed has done so at different times and in different incarnations. We therefore accord equal status to women as to men. Naturally this idea has great appeal to women and particularly to strong women like Dame Flora. But therein lay her weakness for she dominated the other sisters to the extent that they could no longer think for themselves. In the end that is what led to her downfall.

I said just now that had you not joined us on our trip then things might have turned out differently. What nobody knew, except possibly Dame Flora, was that the sisters were already beginning to have doubts even before leaving Suffolk. In response Dame Flora increased her control over them even more. Every aspect of their lives was dictated by her and they were deliberately isolated from any other possible influence. But this simply had the effect of suffocating them and driving them farther away. What finally tipped the balance, however, was something quite unexpected. Can you guess at it? It was you my friend, or rather the sermon you preached on board the Gretchen. *I can see you shaking your head in disbelief as you read this but it is true. I don't think you realised just how powerful your words were. Do not misunderstand me, you are no Paul preaching to the Romans, but what you said that day was enough to sway the waverers among the sisters. Dame Flora saw this. She may even have anticipated something of the sort. You see, the sisters had been exposed to little else other than her own philosophy. Your sermon opened their eyes to other possibilities. Flora saw you as a threat long before I did – why do you think she disliked you so much?*

You see now what I mean when I say I regretted your joining us on the ship? You were a danger to our entire enterprise without ever realising it. I had to try to limit your influence and here I make a shameful confession. It was I who spiked your brandy-wine. I know you blamed your cousin Bruno and it was wrong of me to let you do so, and I hereby exonerate him of blame entirely. You were about to administer the last rite of the Catholic Church to the dying Agatha and I couldn't allow that. She alone of all the sisters remained a true adherent of the Cathar faith and wished to enter the next world pure in body and spirit. Your ministering would have jeopardised that. I had to neutralize you at least until her body had been committed to the deep. I can only apologize to you and to your cousin for the deception. But the worst you suffered was a thick head and the loss of a day or two until you recovered. Incidentally, I was not surprised it was Rebecca who came to fetch you. She was the most ready to revert and the first to do so.

Then came your sermon after which the remaining sisters also wished to recant and return to the Catholic faith. When I knew of their decision I naturally tried to dissuade them from it. You even saw me trying one last time to dissuade Rebecca, but to no avail, she was determined. So be it. If I have learned anything it is that there is no purpose in forcing belief on unwilling minds. It must be from the heart or not at all. Once I realised their re-conversion was sincere the only honourable course was, if not actually to assist them, at least not obstruct them.

You may wonder why they did not simply declare their belief to the world. The answer to that too is Dame Flora. She would never have accepted their apostasy. I'm not sure quite how far she would have gone to frustrate them but they didn't want to take the risk. At the very least she would have made their lives intolerable.

So a plan was hatched. The sisters would disappear and only reappear once we made landfall in Bordeaux. But how do you do that on board a ship? The answer was to hide them in the empty wine barrels in the hold of the ship as I suspect by now you know. It was only meant to be for a few days. In the meantime I would supply them with what they needed to survive until we reached Bordeaux. Unfortunately events conspired against us. The crew took the notion of a cursed ship far more seriously than we had anticipated and mutinied. That and the weather delayed matters further and the sisters had to remain hidden for far longer than we wanted. Only when the pirate attack began did they finally abandon their hideout and made their dramatic reappearance, with devastating effect.

Here there was a break. The letter continued on a different page:

There is one other matter which I feel I should explain: the subject of the nuns' suicide. In truth I panicked. Our plan was going badly wrong. You were searching the ship again and I was fearful you would soon discover the truth. I had to come up with a plausible explanation of what had happened to the sisters and suicide was the best I could manage. I'd remembered what had happened in Béziers all of which was true. Twenty-three burghers did indeed follow each other into the chasm below the city wall. I saw their gesture and was profoundly affected by it. In fact it was that that finally converted me to the Cathar cause. I was so appalled at the actions of Abbot Amalric's forces and impressed by the strength of the burghers' faith that I had a Pauline conversion - not on the road to Damascus but at the gates of Béziers. Those twenty-three burghers went to their deaths with true conviction in their hearts wanting their lives to have meant something. I do not expect you to understand much less agree but you deserve to know.

I come now to the most painful episode in the entire affair: the death of the friar in Saint Nazaire. I'd been aware of him for some days tracking us along the shore as I believe you had also. Dressed in that distinctive robe of black and white he could hardly have been missed. I knew exactly who he was of course. He was a follower of Fra Dominic Guzman, the man I mentioned to you. Fra Dominic was the founder of a new order of preachers whose self-appointed mission it has become to win over adherents of the Cathar faith to Catholicism, by persuasion if possible, by other means if not. Incidentally, Fra Dominic would, I am sure, have been impressed with your sermon aboard the Gretchen. *Would that he had been so successful in persuasion.*

But to return to the man in Saint Nazaire. He was, I have no doubt, sent by his superiors in Toulouse to follow us and arrange our arrest once we were back on dry land. That's what he was about to do when Dame Flora stopped him. Yes, I'm afraid it was she who killed him. It happened so quickly I was unable to prevent it although I did my best for him. But his injuries were too severe and we were being chased by the citizens of Saint Nazaire so I had to abandon him. No doubt you will think me derelict of my duty for not going to the Saint Nazaire authorities and denouncing Dame Flora. What you have to realise is that we are fighting a war, and in war, regrettably, there are casualties.

I hope I have been able to make things a little clearer and that some day you will be able to forgive your old friend who never meant you harm and that we may meet again one day either in Heaven or here on earth in a new life.

There the letter ended. It confirmed much of what Joseph had guessed and I am grateful to my anonymous correspondent for sending it to me. I never believed Lucatz was capable of murdering that friar or anyone else. For all we were on opposite sides of the argument – opposite sides of the *war* – I never felt I was in any danger. He did his best to accommodate the nuns even to the extent of opposing his most loyal acolyte, Dame Flora. So you will forgive me if I shed a tear for the loss of a man I hold to have been among the most honourable and decent I have ever been privileged to know.

I wasn't entirely surprised at the news of his death. The Church is determined to eradicate the Cathar heresy and there seems to be only one way of achieving that: the total annihilation of its adherents. Argument couldn't do it. Torture, bullying, even rape have proved powerless. Only eradication will do. I wonder if the church fathers will ever manage to achieve it. A small part of me hopes they do not.

Lucatz seemed to think it was my influence that caused the nuns to revert and set in motion the subsequent events that took place aboard the *Gretchen*. I am not convinced and not merely from modesty. Sister Rebecca had far more influence over the other sisters than even Lucatz realised and she was well on the way to revision long before I came on the scene. But whoever caused it I can't help wondering what would have happened if they hadn't converted. Lucatz, Dame Flora and the sisters might have sailed on together to the Occitan and disappeared among the throng of heretics already there. The crew of the *Gretchen* would not have deserted but remained aboard and still be plying the wine route between England and Gascony. On the other hand the nuns might have gone the way of so many others in that bedevilled region and died for their cause along with Lucatz. So maybe I can take comfort in the thought that I may have had a hand in saving the lives of those eight young women. But "what if" is a game for children. We have to live with what is.

I have kept Lucatz's letter partly because it is the last tangible connection with my old friend but also because it places the blame for my inclusion on the doomed journey firmly at the door of Prior Herbert. Not that I would use this fact to do him mischief but given our, shall we say, less than amicable relationship in the past the letter might be useful leverage should the need ever arise. Prior Herbert did in fact come up to me after chapter the day after my visit to Joseph's shop. He berated me for leaving the matter of the nuns unresolved and threatened me with exile to Castle Acre – or worse, Wales:

'I thought we'd settled the matter with the nuns,' I told him.

He smiled his syrupy smile. 'Well you thought wrong. However, one does not wish to be too harsh in these matters, especially when there may be extenuating circumstances.'

'Extenuating circumstances, Brother Prior?' I asked suspiciously.

'You haven't forgotten our agreement? Your cousin, Bruno.'

Ah, he was talking about my inheritance again.

'What about him?'

'Well, he's not really your cousin, is he? Married to your father's cousin, I believe. That makes him a very distant relative indeed.'

'He's still a member of my family.'

'*We* are your family now, brother. You gave up your earthly family when you entered the cloister – a fact you should remember when deciding what to do with any property you may, or may not, come into. Remember also your vows – in particular the one about poverty.'

So saying, he bounced off confident that he had won his case. Well, that settled it. He'd convinced me. I knew now who was going to inherit my mother's estate. It was going to my cousin Rowena – and, God forgive me, her husband Bruno. And my mother can spin in her grave.

Whether or not Dame Flora actually murdered that friar as Lucatz asserted we shall never know. She never admitted it and by his own account Lucatz was the only other witness and he himself was dead. When she returned to the *Gretchen* that day no-one yet knew of the murder and so I suppose she had time to destroy any incriminating evidence. You might think that there should have been evidence aplenty in the form of the friar's blood but I know from experience that contrary to popular belief a slashed throat produces very little blood since death is almost immediate, enough to stain the hem of Lucatz's robe but no more. I wasn't even sure then that for all her faults Dame Flora was capable of committing such a heinous act.

However, a few weeks ago I happened to be called out to visit a patient in Bury town. This in itself is not unusual. A great many Buryites call for my services as a physician. What was unusual on this occasion, however, was the part of town to which I was summoned: a very poor one. The services of a qualified physician do not come cheap, even one in holy orders. Most people will try a local wise woman first who will ply them with all sorts of fake potions and incantations and only when these fail do they send for someone such as me. The request on this occasion was to me personally, and it was well-timed. Being late afternoon I had an hour before the next office of vespers was to be sung, so I grabbed my satchel of medicines and herbs and set off up the hill. I was passing through one of the dark alleys in this warren of rat-infested lanes and walkways when the attack came. A heavy blow on the back of the head knocking me down. Dazed, I was only half aware of the scuffle which followed before passing out. I awoke back in the abbey with a vaguely familiar hairy face staring down at me. It was Hogtie. For a moment I thought he'd been the one who'd attacked me and I started up in fear. But he pushed me down and told me what happened. My attacker had been Dame Flora.

'I followed her back to England, see?'

'Why?'

'Love, brother,' he sighed. 'It makes a fool of every man. Before you say it, I know she had a face like a Turk's codpiece and a spleen to match, but there be no accounting for the ways o' the heart, do there? Anyways, after we finished in France I decided to give up the sea. I been a-sailorin' long enough. So I come back home, followed Dame Flora all the way. Not that she noticed me acourse, which was just as well. When she wor lurkin' in that alley wi' a club I knew summit bad was afoot and soon as I saw you comin' along I guessed what it was. But I couldn't let her kill my old friend Brother Walter. Much as it pained me I had to stop her – for her sake as well as your'n. So when she whacked you with that club I did the same to her. Not hard, just enough to knock her out. Then I tied her up and brought the pair o' ye down here to the abbey,' he grinned.

I'm very relieved that he did. Once in the abbey gaol I visited the lady and eventually got the truth. I gathered she continued to blame me for everything – the failure of her mission, Lucatz's betrayal and most of all the loss of her precious "ladies". My sermon was the final straw. It seems she saw me as her nemesis sent by Lucifer to thwart her. Sorry to disappoint her yet again. I'm no devil. I'm just not that interesting.

'It wor a bad thing she did,' frowned Hogtie sadly. 'A very bad thing.' Then he brightened. 'But you has to admit it took some spunk.'

Apart from a nasty gash on the head I quickly recovered my senses, such as they are. As she was still a prioress, ostensibly at least, Dame Flora was able to claim benefit of clergy and so avoided the death penalty. In any case, it could never be proved she killed the friar. She could still have been publicly flogged for attacking me and cast into the wilderness. But I had a better idea. At my suggestion, and with Abbot Hugh's agreement, she was banished to the convent at Prouille in Languedoc known as the "cradle of the Dominicans". It was here that the first nunnery of that sect to which the murdered friar belonged was located. It was also on the road to Castelnaudary, the town where Lucatz died. I should imagine, given Dame Flora's inclinations, death would have been more preferable. Instead she would have to remain among women whose beliefs she did not share to lament her crimes. It seemed a suitable punishment to me.

There is one other thing before I finally sign off. The letter from Toulouse wasn't my only correspondence that month of August. Along with his usual monthly delivery of supplies from the apothecary, Onethumb brought me a parcel. Not entirely unexpected - it was my birthday after all. It was a book, a beautiful bound copy of the Tanakh written on the most exquisite vellum by a Jewish scribe, or *sofer*. It must have cost a fortune and taken a year at least to copy out. Being written entirely in the Hebrew script I could understand not a word, but I knew what it contained. As Joseph was at pains to point out, the Tanakh is the Old Testament in all but name. The cover, too, was of the finest quality leather, velvety soft and tooled in gold. But on the cover was added something that wasn't part of the Tanakh and certainly shouldn't have been there. I recognized it immediately. It was a cross, but not just any cross: the twelve-pointed cross of the Occitan, symbol of the Cathari. The message was clear: Reconciliation. It was simultaneously a cry for tolerance between all religions of whatever hue, Joseph's way of making amends for what he had done to Lucatz and for our parting on bad terms. I admit I was touched. And it was a good excuse to go and see him. I will do so in a few days and thank him for my gift – once I've finally swallowed my pride.

So there you have it, the case of the disappearing nuns. One died of natural causes with her beliefs intact and another was incarcerated having to hide hers. But there are still eight remaining if you include Carmela. As far as I know they are all still at Saint Mary Elms in Ipswich which lies within the orbit of the Bishop of Ely. The see remained vacant until the following March when Abbot John of Fountains was enthroned by which time I had lost touch with Rebecca, Carmela, Ursula, Magdalene and the rest. One day when time has worked its magic and the hurt has dulled sufficiently I may find cause to visit them. It would be painful to relive those terrible times out on the Atlantic swell but pleasurable to see the ladies again. I wonder if perhaps they have reverted again to those absurdly outlandish head-dresses? It would be amusing to find out.

HISTORICAL NOTE

CATHARISM
The Cathar heresy emerged out of the various Adoptionist, Gnostic and Manichaean sects that had been flourishing in the eastern Mediterranean since the 4th Century. From there it gradually spread west taking root particularly in the south of France around the city of Toulouse. Although ostensibly a Christian sect, the Cathari believed in the existence of two Gods which was contrary to the doctrine of the Catholic Church and therefore anathema to it. From the beginning of his election in 1198 Pope Innocent III had tried to suppress the heresy using missionaries but with little effect. On 15th January 1208 the papal legate, Pierre de Castelnau, was murdered after an acrimonious argument with Count Raymond of Toulouse who was a known sympathizer of Catharism. As a result Innocent abandoned all further attempts at peaceful persuasion, declared Pierre de Castelnau a martyr and launched the Albigensian Crusade so-called because it centred on the southern French town of Albi. Despite the best efforts of successive popes and the Inquisition Catharism continued in southern France for another century. The last known Cathar Perfectus in Languedoc, Guillaume Bélibaste, was executed in 1321.

THE SIEGE OF BÉZIERS
The siege occurred more or less as described in Chapter 16. However there is no record of any burghers committing mass suicide by throwing themselves from the battlements.

DOMINICANS

The Order of Preachers, also known as the Dominicans, is a mendicant Catholic religious order founded by the Spanish priest Saint Dominic de Guzman (1170 – 1221) and approved by Pope Honorius III in December 1216. In England they are known as Blackfriars because of the black cloaks they wear over their white habits which distinguishes them from Greyfriars (Franciscans) and Whitefriars (Carmelites). The purpose of these orders was to leave the walls of the cloister behind them and go out into the community to preach and live by begging for alms (mendicancy). From its earliest foundation the Dominican Order had as its goal the conversion of the Cathar heretics of southern Europe to Catholicism. In later centuries they became associated with the Spanish Inquisition, the first Grand Inquisitor of Spain, Tomás de Torquemada (1420 - 1498), having been drawn from the order.

SWW September 2017

UNHOLY INNOCENCE

May 1199. Richard the Lionheart is dead and his brother John has just been crowned King of England.

John travels to St Edmund's abbey in Suffolk to give thanks for his accession. His visit coincides with the murder of a twelve-year-old boy whose mutilated body bears the marks of ritual sacrifice and martyrdom. This isn't the first time such a thing has happened. Eighteen years earlier another child was murdered in the town in similar circumstances.

Abbot Samson needs to find out if this is indeed another martyrdom or just an ordinary murder and appoints the abbey's physician, Master Walter, to investigate. Walter discovers a web of intrigue and corruption involving some of the highest in the land but unbeknown to him his own past holds a secret which will put his life in danger before the final terrible solution is revealed.

ABBOT'S PASSION

Easter 1201. Following a treaty between King John and King Philip of France, England is at last at peace. Alas the same cannot be said for Saint Edmund's Abbey. The pope's new legate has arrived determined to stir up controversy. For Abbot Samson this brings the possibility of a new ally against an old enemy. But his intrigues lead to disaster with Brother Walter being placed in mortal danger and a full-scale battle in the nearby village of Lakenheath.

In the middle of all this the legate's clerk is murdered and a London merchant is wrongly accused. In desperation the man is granted sanctuary at the abbey's shrine, but it is only a brief respite. The whole weight of the judiciary and the church are against him.

Amid rape, religious bigotry and trial by combat Walter has to find the real murderer before a terrible injustice is done and the wrong man is hanged.

WALTER'S GHOST

Summer 1206. Before it was renamed, Bury St Edmunds was known as Bedricksworth after the ancient family who lived there. Now the last surviving member of the Bedrick clan, Arnulf Bedrick, wants an heir to carry on the family name. Marrying for a fifth time, this is his last chance to achieve it. But Arnulf has a secret.

Now jump forward seven hundred years to New Year's Day 1903. The antiquarian and celebrated writer of ghost stories, M. R. James, is excavating the graves of five medieval abbots of Bury. But in one of the graves he discovers something that shouldn't be there.

How are the two events connected? What is the secret found buried in the abbot's grave? Over it all hovers the ghost of Brother Walter who drives the investigation on to solve not only a seven hundred year old murder mystery but also another in the twentieth century in the way only Walter can.

MONK'S CURSE

December 1211. After thirty years as abbot of Saint Edmund's, Samson is dying. Before he takes his last breath, however, he calls Brother Walter to his bedside in order to recite the tale of the Green Children of Woolpit. This is a well-known local legend about two children who were found wandering in a Suffolk field half a century earlier.

Samson also reveals he has recently been visited by a mysterious woman who claims a murder is about to take place. But Walter cannot find out who the woman is or anyone else who has seen her. Did she really exist or was she, like the green children, just another product of a dying man's imagination?

Walter is reluctant to get involved but as he starts to investigate he realises there is more to both tales than first appears and eventually unmasks a tale of abuse and corruption going to the very heart of government.

Can Walter finally solve the mystery of the Green Children of Woolpit and prevent a murder being committed, or is he already too late?

BLOOD MOON

November 1214. King John has returned to England having lost his empire to King Philip of France. Humiliated and desperate for support, he again travels to Bury St Edmunds where Abbot Samson has died and a battle is raging among the monks over who will be his successor.

In the midst of this there arrives in the town a seemingly inconsequential young couple and their maid. The wife is heavily pregnant and gives birth in the night to a baby daughter.

But then the maid is mysteriously murdered and it is soon apparent that the family is not all that it appears. With rebellion looming, abbey physician Walter of Ixworth is drawn once again into investigating a murder and a conspiracy that threatens to engulf the country in civil war and ultimately leads to the final nemesis that is Runnymede and Magna Carta.

DEVIL'S ACRE

January 1242. Brother Walter is dying. He is an old man but the prospect of death does not disturb him - indeed, he welcomes it to meet with old friends and see God in the face. But before he finally joins the Heavenly host he is determined to solve one last mystery that has been plaguing him for decades.

But there are dark forces afoot that want to frustrate his efforts and are prepared to go to any lengths to keep secret events that even now could disturb the government of England - even murder.

In his mind Walter returns to those far off times when Abbot Samson took him on a bizarre journey away from the comforting familiarity of Bury Abbey and into the wilds of barbaric Norfolk where the abbot's power is limited and be met by a far greater one in the guise of the Warenne family of Castle Acre - or as some still choose to call it, the *Devil's Acre*.

THE SILENT AND THE DEAD

Winifred Jonah seemed like an ordinary Norfolk housewife, jolly, plump and harmless. Yet her bland exterior concealed a sinister secret. At fourteen she had already murdered her aunt and uncle and forty years later it was her husband's turn to die. Even so she might have made it to her own grave without further incident if she hadn't met Colin Brearney. He thought she was going to be a pushover, but he had no idea who he was taking on. The day Colin knocked at her door was the beginning of a nightmare that could only end in blood, silence and death...

Made in the USA
Lexington, KY
09 November 2017